ROAD'S END

D0888033

Rebecca Campbell Barrett

ROAD'S END

Published December, 2016

All rights reserved.
Copyright © by Rebecca Campbell Barrett
Cover art copyright © 2017 Rebecca Campbell Barrett
Cover design by BeauteBooks

No part of this book may be reproduced or transmitted in any form or by any means, electronic or mechanical, including photo-copying, recording, or any form of reproduction, or by any information storage and retrieval system, without permission in writing from the publisher.

ISBN 9780692347645
ISBN: 069234764X
Library of Congress Control Number: 2016914110
Witch Creek Publishing, Mobile, AL

for Ginger Davis McSween

Hey, you.

TABLE OF CONTENTS

PART ONE

Helen

CHAPTER 1

MARCH, 1917

I T CAME TO her in the small, unguarded moments, moments when memory slips through the veil of time. The sound of his voice echoed in her mind from across the years. She thought of Ireland in those moments, of the lush green of the rolling hills, of the glens and forests, of the wide blue ocean. She remembered these things as if she had known them. It occurred to her that she never saw his face in these dreams, either waking or sleeping. It was always Ireland, the Ireland of his making with his words and his voice.

A cow lowed and roused Helen from her reverie. She felt the heat of the sun through the fabric of her blouse and turned her face toward it. Spring had arrived and she was glad to see the end of the bitter cold of winter. The cow lowed again and she turned her gaze toward the holding pen.

The calf had been born blind and had wandered into a sinkhole caused by the heavy spring rains, breaking its neck. Helen looked around for someone to deal with the animal's discomfort. Nothing and no one stirred about the farm. She sighed, dropped the knife into the basket of cut dogwood branches, and crossed the back yard. The cow met her at the gate to the pen.

She tugged gently at the heifer's ear. "Come along, mama."

Bessie followed after Helen. Her udder heavy with milk, she crowded into the stall in anticipation of relief.

Helen leaned her head into Bessie's side as she milked. The sweet scent of feed overlaid that of hay and earth and warm milk. She let her thoughts drift to the supper to be gotten and the blouse she was embroidering.

When she finished milking she released some hay into the feed trough. A scurrying sound came from the hayloft and she thought of rats. A deep thud followed by a low giggle and the scrambling of feet caused her to pause in her chore. She edged around the feeding cow and looked through the slats of the hay rack just in time to catch a glimpse of red disappear around the door at the far end of the barn. Helen stared down the length of the building and out into the afternoon, listening. All was silent. She retrieved the milk and the basket of flowering branches.

The kitchen still retained the heat of the midday meal preparations. Helen placed the milk and the flowers on the table. As she turned to the cupboard she saw Anna sitting on the floor in the corner, her back resting against a sack of flour as she read.

"Were you in the barn just now?"

"No, ma'am." Anna looked up from the book and sat up straight.

"Did you gather the eggs?"

"Yes, ma'am. Only eight today."

Helen drew the churn into the center of the room. "Bessie had to be milked. Can you make the butter?"

Anna marked her place with a slip of blue ribbon. "Where's Addie Mae?"

"Gone home. Her mother's sick." Helen caught the look of misgiving in Anna's expression. "I think I can manage a little supper. Warmed over peas, some cold ham." She glanced around the kitchen. "Maybe even a pan of biscuits."

Anna blushed and stood to do her mother's bidding.

Helen watched as Anna pulled a linen cloth over the mouth of the churn and strained the milk into it. Her deftness at the task revealed she had done this often for Addie Mae.

Helen knew the kitchen was one of Anna's sanctuaries. She felt like an intruder, that she was infringing on the hallowed ground of Addie Mae. Well, she was she supposed. Helen had long since given up any claim on the kitchen.

Anna dragged the stool across the floor, dropped down onto it, positioned the churn between her knees, and fell into the lift, drop, lift, drop rhythm with the dasher.

Helen turned to the stove and opened the lid, clattering it against the iron cooktop. She stuffed wood into the firebox and jabbed at it with the poker.

In the early days of her marriage Addie Mae had taught Helen the fundamentals of the kitchen but the cook stove was not something easily mastered. She had finally learned the art of making biscuits when the desire to do so abandoned her.

She stared out the window at the distant fields and sighed for the young woman she had been, for the eagerness with which she had attempted to slay the huge black dragon of a stove, to subvert it to her will. That desire had died along with so many others as those early years burned away the tenderness that was her heart.

At times she wondered how she continued to live, to draw breath each day. But then Reuben would walk into the room or she would hear his voice or something would remind her of him and she knew that as long as she had her son, she could endure.

DUST MOTES DANCED in the slanting sun. Helen lifted the pan of hot biscuits from the oven and smiled at the result. The men would be in from the fields soon. "Set the table, Anna."

Anna finished scouring the churn and wrapped the butter in a clean piece of white cloth. She eased the churn into the corner of the room and skipped down the steps from the kitchen, crossed the alley to the house.

Helen wiped her hands on her apron as she looked out across the farm from the window. She saw the mule team plodding in from the field trailed by Reuben, the reins looped carelessly around his neck. She smiled again and began to spoon peas into a bowl.

HELEN PUT ON a fresh blouse, brushed her hair, and swept it into a chignon at the nape of her neck. Her husband entered their bedroom just as she finished. "Supper's ready."

He dipped his chin in acknowledgement.

She crossed the dog-trot to the dinning room as Anna brought in the dish of cold ham from the kitchen and placed it on the sideboard next to the bouquet of fresh cut dogwood. They stood at their chairs, Anna, Helen, and Reuben, until Luther entered the room.

He carried the Bible and opened it to a passage in Proverbs and read. "*I passed by the field of a sluggard, by the vineyard of a man lacking sense, and behold, it was overgrown with thorns; the ground was covered with nettles, and its stone wall was broken down. Then I saw and considered it; I looked and received instruction. A little sleep, a little slumber...*"

Helen raised her bowed head and looked from her son to her husband and back again. Reuben didn't bow his head, nor did he appear to hear his father's words.

Luther continued to read. "*...a little folding of the hands to rest, and poverty will come upon you like a robber, and want like an armed man.*"

The message was clear. Luther was unhappy with something Reuben had done, or not done.

Luther followed the reading with a brief prayer. Only after he sat did the rest of them settle into their chairs.

They ate in silence for most of the meal. Finally, Luther spoke. "Did you and Moses mend the fence in the foot field?"

Reuben paused in the act of buttering a biscuit. "No. I didn't get to it."

Helen felt her shoulders tense. She glanced from Reuben to her husband.

Luther paused with the glass of buttermilk halfway to his lips. "You didn't get to it?"

"No."

He set the glass on the table and wiped his mouth with a napkin. "You think you'll get to it anytime soon?"

Helen watched her son, steeling herself for the conflict to come. But the belligerence wasn't there. The expected bowing up for a fight failed to materialize. Instead the shadow of a smile skittered across his face and he flushed. He was relaxed, unconcerned. It was then that she noticed a piece of hay caught in the dark curls of his hair and she understood.

Reuben looked sated, indolent. This was a look Helen knew. This was the look of spent passion. Suddenly she realized something that hadn't registered with her earlier when she was in the barn, an image engraved on the retina of her eye but unnoticed in the overall picture. Along with the flash of red disappearing through the barn door had been a glimpse of a bare, slender ankle.

LUTHER PAUSED IN the dog-trot just outside the door to the sitting room. Helen played the piano below the charming portrait of her grandmother, her back to him, lost in her music. He knew her moods by her music. Through the troubled years of their marriage he had learned to listen for the subtle changes. They were like a road-map to her soul, the highs and lows of their life together, and the sorrow. So much sorrow. It had become the sole means for him to know what was in her mind, and perhaps her heart. He frowned at the darkness of the piece she played. Something had unsettled her.

CHAPTER 2
OCTOBER, 1900

SADIE BELLE'S YOUNGEST son, Abraham, came up the drive on a mule belonging to Wallace Tucker. Both mule and boy were orange from head to toe with red clay. The rains of late summer had lingered well into the fall and made the two miles from Road's End almost impassable.

Abraham rode around the house to the back door and stopped well back from the side porch that ran along the south side, out near the old black cauldrons used for boiling clothes on wash-day. He halloed the house.

Luther heard him as he crossed the holding pen from the barn. "Abraham," he wiped his forehead with a handkerchief, "you look like you've been rooting with pigs."

"Road all a mess, Mistah Carroll. That how come I be up here. You wanted up to the landin'."

Luther shoved the handkerchief into his back pocket. "Why's that?"

"Big ole box come acrost the river on the ferry. Heavy too. No way as I know to get it up the road, all muddy like it is."

Luther's brow creased in a frown. "What's in it?"

"Don't know, suh."

"Well, I reckon I'll have to come into town and see." He headed for the back steps. "Tell Addie Mae to get you something to eat. I'll head to town in a while."

THERE WAS A letter with the large wooden crate and two smaller crates besides. They had come down from Charleston by way of a pair of freight wagons. Luther soon determined by the sounds coming from the largest crate whenever it was moved that it contained a piano. There was no way to tell about the other two crates.

He turned the letter over in his hands a couple of times, examining the florid script that bore Helen's name. There was no return address. He put the envelope in his coat pocket and stared long and hard at the cargo as he wondered how he was going to move it two miles, uphill most of the way, over a road slick and rutted from the rains. And where the contents would fit once he did.

He had followed Abraham into town with the wagon but it had been difficult enough for the mules to pull it empty. Wallace Tucker stood at his side, leaning heavily on his crutch.

"Can't see no way to get it up to the house 'til the road dries out."

Luther shared his opinion but he felt a burning desire to present these crates to his wife immediately. He sensed that the contents would somehow ease the tension between them. He knew whatever it was would give her pleasure and perhaps alleviate the boredom of their isolation. And maybe it would even distract her from doting on the baby.

The child had been born in the heat of a June the likes of which Road's End hadn't experienced in Luther's memory. Even the hilltop where the farm sat hadn't offered any respite from that hellish heat. The dry spell from early May to mid-June had baked the earth and threatened the tender emerging crops. Reuben had come screaming into the world as if he resented leaving his mother's womb. Since that moment she had kept him close, so very close, as if she too felt the separation as acutely.

Luther tried to conceal his jealousy, for he was jealous. He was jealous of the life Helen had before their marriage, the life he could never give her, jealous of the self-possession that kept her always polite and amiable but always distant. He wanted desperately to break through that cool reserve, to see her lost to pleasure, excitement, to see her look upon him with something more than benign courtesy. He would deliver these crates to her whatever it took and he set his mind to that task.

Behind Toxey's General Store, he found what he needed. It was a skidder left there several years before when a logging crew had worked the area. Its purpose was to haul logs out of difficult and remote places, a type not commonly used in the deep South because of the sleigh-like runners more suitable to snow and ice. That was probably why it had been abandoned in Road's End. Luther thought the runners would glide over the slick, muddy clay road much like they were designed to do on ice and snow.

In the end it had taken ten mules and the improvised sleigh. Six mules had pulled the skidder and four had been hitched to the farm wagon for the smaller crates. By the time the cargo and four men arrived at the house, everything, men, animals, wagons and cargo, was covered in red clay.

Luther saw Helen standing on the front porch as the procession neared the house. Their approach hadn't been a quiet one, the creaking of leather harnesses, the cracking of the whip, and the tinkle of the piano keys having preceded the struggling men and animals.

Everything ground to a halt at the top of the drive. Helen came down the steps to stand at the end of the pea gravel walkway to the house and looked over the assembled crew, the men indistinguishable from one another in their cloaks of red clay.

Luther released the harness of the lead mule and took two exhausted steps toward his wife. He hadn't the strength left to even wipe the mud from his face.

"For you, Helen."

She looked from Luther to the skidder and back again. A small cry of joy rose from her throat as she dashed across the small distance between them and threw her arms around his neck.

His arms came around her and he closed his eyes and rested his chin on her head as he held her in a long embrace. He felt on the verge of tears.

All the effort, the mud, and the expense of this exhausting day had been worth it. They had been married almost a year and this was the first time she had ever touched him of her own volition. And she clung to him, recklessly disregarding the damage the red clay would do to her blouse and skirt.

"Thank you, Luther. Oh, thank you." Helen lifted her head from his shoulder. "It's Grandmother's piano, isn't it?" She smiled with genuine happiness and tears rolled down her cheeks, tracking through the mud from his shirtfront. "How did you manage it?"

Luther's smile faded a little. "I wish I had managed it. I'm afraid I only dragged it from Road's End."

Her joy was undiminished by his confession. She hugged him more tightly then turned to the skidder and climbed over the makeshift rail and placed her hands on the large crate. "We must open it. We need a hammer."

Luther laughed. "Not yet. We need to unload it first. The mud will need to dry. We don't want to ruin anything."

His wife was happy. She was happy because of him. Luther swallowed against the lump in his throat. She had called him by his Christian name for the first time.

Luther watched as she clung to the crate while the mules pulled the skidder and its load to the saddle house. The precious cargo would be safe from the elements there until a space could be prepared in the house for it. Her happiness caused a tightness in his chest, almost a pain. And she had forgotten all about the child watching from the porch, lying on a blanket dangerously close to the edge.

HELEN PLAYED WITH her whole heart. Luther had only heard her one other time during his stay in Charleston. It had been lovely then, drawing all eyes in her direction during an evening gathering of notables at her home, the Senator's home. But the music she produced since the arrival of her grandmother's piano transported the entire household. She would sit beneath the portrait of her grandmother, the content of one of the other crates, and play soaring pieces that mystified Luther with their complexity.

At times he would hear snatches of her music drifting on the breeze across the fields where he labored and it made his heart swell with joy that he had been able to give her this. Even when she wasn't playing she now went about her activities humming. With time Luther began to forget that it hadn't been all his doing that had made this possible.

The demands of the farm became less pressing as winter shortened the days. An early supper preceded an evening by the fire, he in his chair and Helen at the piano or reading one of her books, yet another gift from Charleston. The only thing to mar his happiness was the constant demands of the baby. But the boy had begun to sleep through the night and it became Helen's practice to put him to bed before their evening meal. They had found a harmony of sorts.

He would come upon her at odd times during the day as she sat reading or doing needle work and she would smile at him and occasionally reach out her hand to him. The idea that she might come to love him began to grow and he burnished that thought as if it were a rare gold coin.

CHAPTER 3
MARCH, 1917

REUBEN STOOD BEFORE the mirror over the washstand and gave his hair a critical look. He ran the brush through his dark curls again and frowned as they immediately sprang back. It occurred to him that he could use some of Luther's pomade, but he immediately dismissed the thought. He would rather look like the country bumpkin he was than ask his father.

His father. Things were more strained than usual between them lately. Reuben knew this was, in large part, his fault. In recent months he had come to resent everything his father asked of him. If only he would buy a car. There was money enough and Reuben had worked for it just as hard as his father.

They were as unalike as it was possible to be, in looks, in temperament, in ambition. But there was one trait he and his father shared. Like Luther, Reuben could flare with towering rage. Unlike him, his rages were quick, hot, and soon over. Luther contained his wrath but for all that, it was no less felt in the household.

Today he didn't have time or thought to spare for his father. Mara would be at the roadhouse tonight, she had promised to be there, waiting for him. He felt the heat in his face and closed his eyes as he remembered the curve of her breast, the feel of her skin as soft and smooth as a puppy's belly. He took a deep breath, opened his eyes and set about buttoning the collar onto his shirt.

ANNA LOOKED DOWN from the rafters of the saddle house as Reuben backed the horse into the traces of the buggy. She grabbed one of the support beams with both hands and swung down, dropping onto the hard packed dirt floor of the low ceilinged building.

"Where you going?"

Reuben settled the horse and began threading the leads through the harness. "Out and about." He looked up from his chore and smiled at her. "Hiding out?"

"No. Just reading."

Reuben's smile faded. "You've been doing that a lot lately."

"I'm always reading."

"I mean hiding out."

"I'm not hiding."

For a second she thought he would challenge her but instead he said, "Addie Mae was looking for you. She made teacakes."

Anna shrugged. "Where you going?"

Reuben watched her for a moment. "Finley."

"What for?"

"To have a little fun."

Anna considered this briefly. "What's there for fun in Finley?"

Reuben chuckled. "Nothing for you, missy."

She frowned. "Papa won't like it."

Reuben gave the horse a slap on the rump. "So?"

She worried her lower lip between her teeth. "He doesn't mean it, Reuben." Her forehead creased with a frown. "He can't help it."

His hands stilled on the heavy harness. "I know." He stared off toward the distant fields briefly, cleared his throat, then lifted her onto the seat of the buggy. "You sure know a lot for such a little girl."

"I'm not little. I'm eleven next month."

"So you are." He stepped up into the buggy beside her and made a clicking noise with his tongue against the roof of his mouth. The horse moved forward. When the buggy reached the front of the house he drew up. "You shouldn't worry about things you can't change, Anna. They are what they are and there's no knowing why. There's no changing them, either."

She scrambled down from the seat. Her voice broke when she spoke. "You're wrong."

"Poor, Anna."

It was the tenderness in his voice that made the tears spring to her eyes and she turned and ran before Reuben could see them. He did too know what was wrong. They all knew. She ran full out, as if she could outrun his words. But even as she fled she knew; you can't outrun the truth.

The only mothering she had ever received was a benign neglect. She knew this wasn't normal. Her mother loved Reuben. Anna had been aware of this since before she was four, an early age for such an epiphany.

It had been one of those hot summer days when the wind was so dry it sucked the moisture from your throat and nose and dust settled on your skin like a fine powder. Reuben was ten. Their noon-day meal was over, and the household was quietly escaping the heat of the day in whatever pastime suited their individual needs.

Anna lay under the bed, her cheek pressed against the cool linoleum, lethargic with the heat. Across the dog-trot, Reuben sat at the dining table bent over a book, his head resting in one hand as he read. The delicate clink of china against china as their mother placed dishes in the sideboard was the only sound to be heard.

Her mother came into view framed by the two open doorways. She paused by Reuben's chair then tenderly threaded her fingers through the dark curls of his hair. He smiled and turned a page, never looking up to acknowledge the endowment of something so rare and precious.

Tears roll down Anna's cheeks and she experienced a longing so profound that she would always remember this moment. It was the casualness of it, the absolute ordinariness of it that made it so desirable and so unattainable. Anna wished that she had dark curls. Maybe then her mother would touch her like that, would hold her in her lap and love her.

CHAPTER 4

AUGUST 1903

REUBEN LIKED THE morning best. His mother let him sit on her lap at her dressing table and she brushed his hair. It was their special time together, a time when she hugged him and smiled at their reflection in the mirror. She was the most beautiful creature in the world. He liked that they both had the same dark hair. He wished he had eyes like hers. They made him think of the blue of the sky just before his bedtime.

He placed the palm of his small hand against her cheek and she smiled as she took it in hers and kissed each of his fingers.

Footsteps sounded in the dog-trot followed by a light tap on the door. Reuben slipped from his mother's lap into the kneehole of her dressing table, hidden by the volume of the skirt of her dressing gown, and peered between the folds at the closed door.

"Yes," his mother said.

The door opened and his father entered the room.

Reuben didn't hide beneath the dressing table because of fear. Reuben wasn't afraid of his father. It never occurred to him to be afraid because his mother was unafraid. Reuben took his cue in all things from his mother.

At some level he was aware that other people feared his father. It had to do with the papers he kept in the big desk in the dog-trot. When his father made entries into the ledger Reuben saw how it upset the people who came before him. They worried their hats in their hands, or caught at the collar of their shirts as they stood there in the open breezeway, their eyes downcast.

Even though he wasn't afraid, Reuben didn't much like his father. This was because of his mother as well. Reuben was jealous of the softness in her voice when she spoke to his father, of the way she did little things that pleased him, like bring him whiskey with honey every evening. There were always flowers in the house and music for him. It made Reuben angry when she cried over burned biscuits and fallen cakes and he grew to hate the old, black, iron stove as much as she did.

But there was a new thing that Reuben hated more than all the others. It was something he couldn't name but it brought tears to his mother's eyes for no reason and it made her more pale than normal. Today was the first day she had held him in her lap for many weeks. It was the first day she had seemed like herself in all that time and this frightened Reuben.

His father stood behind her and ran his hand down the length of her hair. "How do you feel this morning?"

"I'm fine. Really." She turned to face him. "You shouldn't worry."

"Should you be out of bed?"

She took his hand between hers. "Stop worrying, Luther. I'm well again. I promise."

He hesitated, gave a slight nod. "I'm going into town. Is there anything you need?"

"No."

He nodded again and turned to leave the room. "Where is he?"

His mother sat very straight and still. "Who?"

"The boy."

"Reuben. His name is Reuben."

His father lifted his hand and let it fall back to his side. "Where is he?"

She turned to face the mirror and didn't answer.

His father paused, his hand on the doorknob. "I'm sorry, Helen. I don't mean to upset you." He stared at her but she didn't look around at him. "You shouldn't have been lifting him. Everything would have been fine if you hadn't--"

"Stop it." She twisted around on the stool and glared at him. "It happened. It's over. There's nothing we can do to change it. You can't blame him."

"You coddle him too much. He's over three years old for god's sake." His father's face turned red. "And we both know it wouldn't have happened if you hadn't felt the need to always be carrying him around. He's too heavy. He's too heavy and now--" He pressed his lips together until they went white then he took a deep breath. "I'll be back by noon."

The door closed quietly behind his father, and his mother burst into tears. Reuben crawled out of his hiding place and patted her hand. He hated his father. He hated him as much as he hated the hot, black stove.

CHAPTER 5
APRIL, 1917

REUBEN READ THE headline in the *Geiger Times* again and a slow smile spread across his face. This was it, his chance. He folded the paper carefully, put it in the bib pocket of his overalls and returned to loading feed onto the wagon. As soon as he got back to the farm and unloaded he planned to head to Finley. It was Saturday and Mara would be at Blue Betty's. He smiled more broadly. They would celebrate.

He had debated using a full team for the trip and wished now that he had. Still he made good time with the pair of mules over the ten miles from Smithfield.

Eubie was in the process of untying the ferry when he pulled up at the landing. The Watkins man and his Brush Roadster were already on board. All the arguing in the world wouldn't convince Eubie to take Reuben and his team as well.

It took forever for Eubie to return to the landing and Reuben was in a foul mood by the time he loaded his team and wagon onto the barge. If he was honest with himself he would acknowledge the wisdom of Eubie's caution for even though the river was low from the recent dry spell, and the current was slower than usual, the ferry rode low in the water on the crossing.

Reuben led the mules and wagon off the ferry and climbed onto the seat. Wallace Tucker gimped his way down the steps of Toxey's General Store with his one good leg and crutch as Reuben whipped up the mules for the last two miles home. Reuben saw Wallace trying to flag him down out of the corner of his eye but he pretended he didn't. If he stopped to jaw with Wallace it would be dark before he got to the farm.

By the time he unloaded the wagon, pumped water into the trough for the mules, and threw some hay into their stalls, dusk had fallen. He lowered the suspenders of his overalls and stripped to the waist. The water in the trough was good and cold. It left him shivering when all the dust and sweat of the day was washed away. With his shirt clinging to his damp body and his hair dripping wet, he made for his room, an enclosed portion on the far back corner of the wrap-around porch.

"Reuben." His mother's voice stopped him at the foot of the steps leading onto the back porch.

"Mother." He waited as she approached from the front corner of the porch.

"You missed supper. I'll fix you a plate."

"Don't bother. I'll eat something later." He was antsy to get going. It was a good fifteen miles to Finley. He thought of the Watkins man with his shiny red Roadster and felt the sting of envy. If they had a car the drive would be nothing. But there was no hope of that. His father was too cautious, too concerned about the prospect of war. He preferred to hoard his money in the bank. Reuben would have to take the buggy.

Helen stopped several feet from him. "You're going out."

Something about her voice was different. Reuben couldn't see her features in the gloom. He hesitated. "Yes. For a while."

"You should eat something first."

"I'm not hungry."

She laced her arms together at her waist. The air felt heavy with unspoken words. Then she turned and walked back toward the front of the house.

REUBEN OPENED THE door to Blue Betty's and stepped into a room filled with a thick layer of smoke. The low clapboard building stank of sweat, booze, cigarettes, and an overabundance of toilet water. Blue Betty sat at a small table near the door, a cigarette between the fingers of her right hand, and a glass of gin in her left. She looked him over then gave a faint nod.

The gap-toothed man with a pistol holstered over his left shoulder returned to monitoring the other occupants of the room.

A bar ran along one wall of the establishment. An unlit pot-bellied stove stood in the far right corner. The back door lined up with the front and was open to the night air. Half a dozen tables were scattered around the room. Most of them were occupied by men and an occasional woman, all of whom had a head start on a Sunday morning hangover. On the wall opposite the bar a grizzled old black man banged on a piano. Mara sat on the piano bench beside him, facing the room. Her head was thrown back in laughter at something the tall, rawboned, blonde man standing beside her was saying.

Reuben stopped at the bar and bought a beer, then made his way around the tables toward the piano. Mara watched him the whole way. The tall, lanky guy beside her turned to see what had captured her attention. He frowned and took a sip of his beer.

"Reuben." Mara uncrossed her shapely legs and stood. "Meet Henry."

She spoke with a heavy accent. To Reuben it was exotic, sexy, and it did strange things to him. "I already know Henry." Reuben extended his hand and after a second's pause, Henry shook it.

"How you been, Reuben?"

Reuben grinned, his gaze settling on Mara. "Better now."

Henry looked down into his beer, gave a little shake of his head, and drained his glass. "You heard the news?"

"Germany?"

"Yeah."

Reuben nodded. "Got a copy of the *Geiger Times* in Smithfield today. Big headlines." He ran his gaze down Mara's curves then finally gave Henry his full attention. "You signing up?"

Henry's eyebrows shot up in a look of surprise. "You crazy? I'm not going to get my ass shot off for some moneybags Yank."

"Bullshit," Reuben said. "You've been listening to the hicks around here."

"Well, better to stick where your bread is buttered. I've got the boll weevil going at my cotton faster than I can hoe it. If he outruns me, there's no food on the table."

Reuben didn't want to hear about the plight of cotton farmers all over the south. His heart was set on leaving the hard labor and sweat of the fields behind him. "What about the ships they've sunk?" He could feel his temper rising and he tried to contain it. He didn't want to listen to reason. The war was his chance to escape. In his mind it was just and noble simply by being. "American ships. Seven, last I heard. Not Limeys or Frogs, our ships."

"Well, if that's true, it's all because of Wilson. He can't keep his hands out of it. All this talk about what's happening in Belgium, the Zimmerman telegram. All to stir everybody up."

Reuben ground his teeth and shook his head. "So we're just supposed to forget our allies?"

"Allies?" Henry grinned and shook his head. "You think the English wouldn't have done the same thing if they'd had an excuse? Or the French? The Archduke getting shot, that's all smoke up everyone's ass. You want to go rot in a stinking trench in France because the Kaiser's out to improve his land holdings?"

"So, you think the Huns will stop with Europe? What about Mexico? You plan on learning Spanish?"

"More like German. If it came to that, the Krauts wouldn't let the Mexicans have their territory back." Henry shook his head. "Wake up, son."

Mara placed her hand on Reuben's arm. "Stop this talk of war. Is nothing to do with us."

"Nothing to do with us?" Reuben's voice rose along with his temper. "Mara, we can't just sit on our hands."

"Why?" She flicked the back of her fingers up her throat, under her chin, and out in a quick gesture Reuben had seen her make many times when she was angry or upset with him. "*Nu fii bulangiu!* Listen to Henry."

"I'm no chicken. If Henry's too scared to fight it's nothing to me. I'm joining up."

Henry shoved his shoulder, his lips rigid with anger. "You saying I'm a coward?"

Reuben's glass of beer crashed to the floor, and his fists came up as Mara stepped between the two of them, facing Reuben.

"Fool! Idiot! What? You want to die?" She spat on the rough worn floor. "You think I wear the veil of black for dead boy?" Her dark eyes blazed with fury. "I need a living man, not a dead boy."

She turned on her heel and crossed the room toward the front door.

Reuben and Henry watched her go. Henry eyed Reuben for a second. "*Curva.*" He raised his empty beer glass. "How about another?"

Reuben continued to stare at the door. She had called him a boy, had ridiculed his dreams of escape, of the glory to be had in the war.

"Don't worry, son. There are gypsies all over Europe. You'll find plenty just like her when you get to France."

In the blink of an eye Reuben round-housed Henry with a right that contained all the fury and frustration of a seventeen-year-old work hardened young man. It laid Henry out cold on the floor.

Before his thoughts could catch up with his actions, Reuben felt the strong hands of two men as they collared him and barreled him toward the door of Blue Betty's.

REUBEN WENT IN search of Mara. No one at the gypsy campsite would tell him anything. The men of the family—brothers, cousins, uncles—ringed around him and spoke in harsh tones in the language of the Romani, a language he couldn't begin to understand. But the message was clear.

From there he made his way to Apple Orchard and the hoped for relief to be found in illicit, potent alcohol. Loud music came from a leaning shack on the edge of the community. People lounged across the sagging front porch and out into the yard. When he pulled up they all fell silent. The music and voices from inside filled the void.

At the door he was met by a giant of a black man, arms crossed, outrage barely contained in his stance and in his eyes.

"You lost?" His voice was like the echoing boom of a deep explosion.

"No. I'm thirsty."

The man shook his head. "Can't help you."

Reuben stood his ground. "Who can?"

"Nobody 'round here."

Reuben looked up into the hostility on his face. "What's your name?"

"Ain't got one."

Reuben nodded and made his way back through the crowd gathered in the yard of the house. He knew it was his father that made them look at him with blank expressions and shake their heads. The son of the Justice of the Peace would find no friend among them.

He climbed onto the seat of the buggy. Abraham suddenly appeared out of the shadows of the dark lane and handed a quart fruit jar of the clear, liquid fire up to him. "Folks don't want you here."

Gray threaded the hair at Abraham's temples and the scar slashing down his left cheek looked more pronounced with time. Or perhaps it was simply a trick of the meager light.

"Don't be coming back, Mistah Reuben."

Reuben dug a silver dollar from his pocket but Abraham shook his head. "You ain't been here and you ain't coming back."

REUBEN WOKE ON the hard seat of the buggy. The morning dew had soaked through his clothing and he was chilled to the bone. He lay there getting his bearings as the sound of the ferry banking at the landing stirred him into action. As he sat up, his gut gave one giant heave and he leaned forward and puked a watery mess onto the buggy's traces. The sun edging over the horizon glinted off the river and pierced his eyes like a bolt of lightning. He dug a handkerchief out of his pocket and wiped his face then sat with his head in his hands until Eubie came up beside the buggy.

"The hell happened to you?"

Reuben raised his head and swallowed, unsure for a moment that he wouldn't be sick again. "Got back too late to catch you last night."

"Umm huh." Eubie eyed him for a moment and shook his head. "Won't be crossing for a little bit. Got to wait for the good reverend."

Reuben mentally cursed his luck. He looked into Eubie's knowing regard and saw a slight yielding.

"Come on into the hut." Eubie started walking toward a small lean-to he used to wait out the hours of the day when crossings were few and far between. "I'll brew up some coffee." He turned back to eye Reuben again. "But wash up at the pump first." He grunted and continued on toward the hut. "I don't imagine the reverend will take too kindly to riding the river with the stink of rot-gut moonshine."

After he had cleaned up as best he could, Reuben presented himself at the hut for the offered cup of coffee but found the aroma of it had him quickly seeking the open air.

Eubie gave him a little time to collect himself and came out to join him on a long bench under the canopy of an oak tree. "Burnt biscuits. That's the trick." He looked out from under the brim of his battered hat at Reuben, one eye permanently squinted. "Least ways, that's what I've always heard." He grinned, revealing tobacco-stained, yellow teeth gaped and crooked.

Reuben nodded, not certain he could attempt speech without being sick.

Together the two of them sat in silent companionship until they heard the wheezing rattle of the preacher's old Ransom Olds as he came down the embankment toward the landing.

REUBEN PULLED THE buggy into the stock-yard and sat for a moment thinking what to do. In the end he decided it would be best to leave the horse in harness. His father and mother would need it to travel to church with Anna squeezed be-tween them. Again his anger that his father was too cheap to buy an automobile brought blood to his face. They lived like tenant farmers when there was money enough. The war had been a boon for American farmers and Reuben didn't see why some of that good fortune couldn't be enjoyed by the family.

He watered the horse and put a bucket of feed for him to eat. He dipped his hands in the water trough and ran them through his hair, brushed his hands over his coat and shirt and went to the house.

Addie Mae carried a stack of dirty breakfast dishes along the alleyway between the house and kitchen as he came around the corner. She gave nothing away with her expression.

Reuben took a deep breath and climbed the back steps. He paused at the doorway to the sit-ting room. His mother sat in her chair facing the opening, her eyes downcast and her hands in her lap. His father stood with his back to the door, his hands clasped behind him, his shoulders rigid with anger. Reuben cleared his throat.

His father swung around, his brow drawn like a thunderhead, and glared at him. But it wasn't his father's reaction that stilled Reuben's heart. It was the expression on his mother's face when she saw him standing there.

It was pain he saw. Raw, unguarded pain that quickly changed to sorrow before she lowered her gaze.

"Well?" His father's voice was tight with the struggle for control. "What have you to say for yourself?"

Reuben couldn't look away from his mother's downcast face. It never occurred to him that his actions, so careless and self-centered, could cause her such sorrow. He wanted to weep with shame.

Instead he faced his father. "I missed the ferry."

"Look at you. You stink of liquor and God knows what." Luther's face blazed with anger, his fists clenched at his sides. "Have you no regard for your family? For your mother?"

Reuben looked down at the floor. "I'm sorry, Mother. I didn't think." He raised his head with pleading in his voice. "I was celebrating."

Helen's head jerked up and she stared at him.
All the color drained from her face. "What--" Her
hand went to her throat. "What have you done?"

Reuben shook his head. "Nothing." He couldn't
understand the depth of her dismay. "I drank too
much." He felt the heat rising in his face. "And I'm
sorry for it. But there's going to be war. We're joining the fight with the Allies."

Helen half rose from her chair, her hand outstretched toward him, then fainted.

FOR THREE WEEKS Reuben stayed close to the
house, never venturing further than the near
fields. His mother's fainting had scared him more
than he wanted to admit. Even so, he had difficulty
understanding why she had been so upset that he
had stayed away from home overnight. It wasn't the
first time he had done so, but then he hadn't been
away with the buggy and had to come in stinking
of vomit and alcohol and face the disapproval of
his father.

He justified her reaction with these thoughts
because he couldn't let the cause be anything but
his drunkenness and his father's displeasure. He
couldn't let go of his hope of going to war so he
dismissed all thought of that as the cause of her
dismay. Life on the farm was suffocating him and

his longing for Mara was a constant ache that only gave way in the aftermath of total, backbreaking exhaustion. He was desperate to escape his life.

Once a week his father rode into Road's End and brought home the newspaper. Reuben read and re-read the debates about the motives and costs of what lay ahead for the nation. He discovered there was a recruiting station in Montgomery and one in Birmingham. Until more recruiting offices could be manned, it was possible to register at the post offices of smaller towns throughout the state. He was in a fever to join up but he dared not broach the subject in his mother's hearing.

As Justice of the Peace, Luther was summoned to a meeting of local officials in Demopolis to work on war plans. He would be gone overnight, possibly two nights. Reuben could hardly wait for his return to learn what was happening.

On Thursday the plow shaft splintered. Reuben spent the afternoon in a half-hearted attempt to repair it. In the back of his mind was the thought that here was an excuse to leave the farm. He wanted desperately to experience the atmosphere of the nearby towns in the face of war. And he wanted to be with Mara. The two desires tore at him until finally he gave in.

On Friday he rose earlier than usual and took care of the livestock, set Moses to the tasks he could manage on his own, and informed his mother that he had to go in search of a new plow shaft.

She studied his face, placed the palm of her hand against his cheek briefly, then forced a faint smile. "Be careful."

He knew she saw through his ruse and he blushed with shame. "Don't worry about me, Mother. I'm just going into Smithfield." He hesitated then placed a shy kiss on her cheek. "I'll be back before you know it."

Helen stood on the porch and watched as Reuben rode down the long winding driveway. Just before the first curve, he turned in the saddle and waved.

As soon as he was out of sight of the house he put his heels to the horse and tore down the road. He would have to hurry to accomplish all he had to do this day.

Thoughts of Smithfield and a new plow shaft were gone as soon as he set out. The first order of business was Finley and the gypsy camp.

Eubie eyed him curiously when he walked the horse onto the ferry but made no comment. Reuben tried to contain his euphoria and told him about the broken plow shaft. Eubie nodded and spit tobacco juice over the edge of the barge into the swirling brown water of the river.

A small group of men waited for the ferry on the far side of the river so Reuben was able to escape Eubie's knowing eye and head up stream.

He came upon the campsite from the South. A lazy thread of smoke rose from the fire pit, a buggy and horse stood in the deep shade of a nearby river oak. He glanced around the wagons of the campsite. All was silent. Reuben's gaze returned to the horse and buggy and realization hit him like the kick of a mule. He reigned in Jubilee and stared just as his father stepped out of one of the wagons, settling his hat on his head as he came down the steps.

Reuben's blood boiled as he slid from the saddle and came face to face with his father. "What are you doing here?"

His father straightened his shoulders, his features set in grim lines. "I could ask you the same thing." He tugged at the lapels of his coat, settling it more comfortably. "You're supposed to be at home working."

"And you're supposed to be in Demopolis." Reuben ground his teeth. "Working."

The flap of the covered wagon lifted and Mara stepped out, her hair a tangle of dark curls, her peasant blouse falling off one shoulder. "So, the dead boy comes to Mara." She flipped her hair back over her shoulder with an impatient movement of her hand. "Too late."

Reuben thought his head would explode. Before he knew what he was doing he swung at his father.

Luther had been watching him and caught his arm. As he did so, he stuck out his foot and clipped Reuben's leg. Off balance, Reuben crashed to the ground.

Reuben rolled to his feet and crouched before his father, blinded by rage and humiliation. "I'll kill you." He spat dirt from his mouth. "How could you?" The anger and hurt thickened his voice. "Does Mother known?"

His words ignited an answering rage in Luther. "You insulting little bastard. Do you really think I'd touch a gypsy whore? That I'd expose my wife to gossip and innuendo like your worthless piece of shit father?" Luther tore at his coat as he shouted, trying to wrestle free of the sleeves. "Hasn't she suffered enough because of you? I should have whipped your sorry ass long before you had the chance to cause her more pain."

As soon as the words were out of Luther's mouth, Reuben saw his rage evaporate. The stricken look that replaced it was more telling than his words. Luther shook his head as if he could erase what had been said but Reuben knew the truth of it. Deep in the core of him he had always known. His fists dropped to his sides and he sank to his knees. All the fight left him.

It had always been there, that feeling that he was separate from everyone but his mother, the feeling that she didn't belong in the world of his father. Of Luther. He drew a ragged breath. His mother, the anchor of his world, she was lost to him now. He could never go home again. If she saw him she would know and that would destroy her. She must never hear of this slip of the tongue. He would not allow her to suffer this shame.

The gypsy king came out of the wagon and looked first at Luther then at Reuben. He raised his fist in the horned sign to ward off the evil eye and took Mara by the arm. With a jerk of his head he sent her crawling back into the wagon.

Reuben watched her go with no feeling of loss. He couldn't think beyond his mother's pain. His leaving would hurt her but it was the only thing he could do to save her.

The gypsy king addressed his words to Luther. "We go today. No more gypsy camp."

Luther didn't appear to hear. He staggered toward his buggy like someone lost. He tried to climb onto the seat but didn't appear to have the strength to lift himself upward. He leaned his back against the wheel of the buggy and covered his face with his hands. "What have I done?" He drew a ragged breath. "Dear God, what have I done? She'll never forgive me. She's truly lost to me now."

Reuben rose from the dust and gathered the reins of the horse and walked to where Luther stood. "Don't tell her." He swallowed hard against the lump in his throat. "I won't be coming home. I'm joining up."

"That will destroy her." Luther stared at the ground.

"Not as much as the truth and if I came home she'd know." He stood there trying to find the right words. "Maybe now things will be better for everyone."

He swung up into the saddle. "I'll leave the horse in Demopolis." With that he turned north and rode out of the camp. He had seven dollars in his pocket and the clothes on his back.

SHE KNEW WHEN Luther entered the room.

He removed his hat and threw it onto the piano. "I'm so sorry, Helen."

Without being told she knew Reuben was gone, that even if he returned to her he would never again be hers. At that moment the last flicker of light in her heart died.

CHAPTER 6
JULY, 1899

T HE LILTING IRISH brogue wasn't uncommon in this part of Charleston. It could be heard on any street corner or in any shop. In fact, there were streets where Gaelic was just as often spoken as not. No, it wasn't the accent, but rather the timbre of his voice that captured Helen's attention. She turned toward the sound, her eyes searching the smoky, dim room for the speaker. He held court at the far end of the pub, a lamp to his right illuminating a sharp, angular face. Black hair curled over the collar of a jacket sagging with age and wear. There was nothing handsome or remarkable about him except that he was tall for an Irishman. Helen wondered at the awe with which her companion held this oracle of County Sligo.

"That's him, Helen," Padraic pressed a glass of lager into her hand. "That's Declan O'Rourke."

Helen took a sip of her drink and grimaced. "You're telling me we left the theater early for this?" She sidestepped a drunken patron as he made his way toward the bar. "I don't see anything extraordinary about him at all. He's just another broken down Irishman tilting at windmills, looking for a handout for the cause." She turned to her companion. "Say you haven't given him money, Padraic."

"Helen." Padraic's voice held a gentle chiding note but he wouldn't meet her gaze.

"So, you have."

He took a large drink of his beer. "Where's your Irish pride, Helen? They've finally gotten the attention of Parliament. They just need to hold things together until they can force the Prime Minister to address the issue."

"The British army will address the issue, not Parliament, you simpleton."

"You have no faith."

Helen smiled. "Why should I? I'm an American. My father is a United States senator. Ireland isn't my country no more than it's yours." She shook her head at the foolishness.

"There's no one more Irish than Monty. And you're half Irish."

"Father was born right here in Charleston. There's nothing Irish about him except his parents and his brogue which gets more pronounced in every election year."

Padraic leaned in close. "Truer words were never spoken. Now be a good girl and give me a kiss."

"Not on you life." She took a step back. "I've already been scandalized by simply being in this place. Tongues will be wagging in every parlor in Charleston before you can finish your vile tasting drink." A movement near the door caught her eye. "Oh, dear. Here comes that bumpkin from wherever. I wish Father would either give him what he wants or tell him his case is hopeless. He's been hanging on the fringes of society all summer."

Padraic watched Luther Carroll as he stood near the door adjusting to the dim lighting and cloud of tobacco smoke. "I thought he'd left town weeks ago." He took a sip of his beer and frowned at the taste. "He's never going to get funding for a bridge in nowhere Alabama from Monty and his committee. Alabama's Senator has nothing Monty wants. He'd have been better off to wait until next year. Elections always make politicians more amenable."

Helen turned her back on the new arrival and let her gaze return to Ireland's latest warrior chieftain. The distance between them and the deep brogue made his voice a song without words. She heard it in the bones of her body and turned away. "Let's go. The smell of this place is unbearable."

THEY WENT TO Madame LaFont's for coffee and cake before taking the carriage along the bulkhead to catch the ocean breeze. Charleston sweltered in the July heat and the boredom of summer.

"When do you leave?" Helen turned her face to the breeze, lifted her chin and closed her eyes.

"Sunday. Noon." Padraic felt for her hand and took it in his. "You should marry me and save me this blasted waste of time and money."

Helen opened her eyes but didn't turn to look at him. "You don't love me. What kind of marriage would that be?"

"The best kind. You're my best friend in the world, Helen." He pulled the carriage to the side of the roadway and looped the reins around the brake. "And I do love you. I always have."

Helen wanted to believe him. She yearned to be settled and free from her father's rule. And there was a restlessness she felt that she couldn't define. It left her out of sorts and distracted. But she and Padraic had known each other since they were infants and the love he felt for her was not what he should feel for a wife. She sighed. "I know you love me, dearest, but not as you should." She turned to him and smiled. "I won't be one of those wives who is the pity of polite company because her husband is off making a fool of himself by fawning over every debutante in Charleston."

"I'd never do such a thing."

"No, I'm sure you wouldn't but you'd be unhappy with time. The right girl will come along and there you'd be, tied to me. Better to go enjoy the season in Europe. Flirt with all the pretty girls."

"I won't find one as pretty as you. And do you think I'll really find love in Europe? This is all Mother's folly and Father's pride."

"Then don't go."

"I won't if you'll just marry me."

"Well, there you have it. An impossible situation." She resisted the urge to rest her head against his shoulder. "Enjoy yourself, Padraic. I'd give anything for a year in Europe. I haven't been to Paris since Grandmother became ill."

"Then come with me. At least to Paris. You can stay for a while with your cousin and we'll see the city and countryside together."

"I can't."

"Why?"

"You know Father and Uncle Paddy control my inheritance and Paddy is hopeless against Father's will. I won't come into it until I'm twenty-five—if there's anything left of it by then."

Padraic sat silently beside her. "He isn't a bad man, Helen."

"No. Just a very foolish one, foolish in his misplaced Irish pride."

"Does he know of O'Rourke?"

"There isn't a Fenian who steps foot on the docks of Charleston that he doesn't know about."

MAMIE MET HER in the foyer when she got home and took Helen's wrap. Voices came from the direction of the library.

"Who's here?"

"Master Simmons and his son and a mans I don't know."

The door to the library was ajar and Helen pushed it open. Four men looked up from the library table as she entered the room. She recognized the Irishman immediately. He looked across the room at her with a quicksilver glance of awareness, appraisal, and dismissal before returning his full attention to the map spread across the table.

Helen felt the blush travel up her throat to her face.

Her father removed a cigar from his mouth. "Helen, darlin', come meet our guest."

He meant the Irishman, of course, because the other two men were known to her. Her godfather kissed her cheek as she drew near. "How lovely you look tonight, Helen. Been out for the evening?"

"A late supper after the theater."

Paddy Simmons had been her grandmother's lawyer and now shared the trusteeship of Helen's estate with her father. His son, Henry, was studying law and planned to join him in practice when he finished his formal training. He took Helen's hand, kissed it, then grinned widely. "Haven't seen you all summer, Helen."

She patted Henry's cheek. "All that studying has made you a recluse. When did you get home?"

"Yesterday."

Her father cleared his throat. "Helen, I'd like you to meet Declan O'Rourke. He's just arrived from Queenstown."

Helen inclined her head ever so slightly. "Mr. O'Rourke."

O'Rourke gave a half bow. "Miss Fitzgerald. A pleasure." He held her gaze a moment then returned his attention to the map.

Helen straightened her shoulders. "Well, gentlemen, I won't keep you from whatever it is you find so interesting. I just stopped in to say good night." She was halfway to the door when she turned back and said, "Just don't squander all my inheritance on the lost cause of home rule."

Her father gave her a scalding look. Paddy looked at the floor as if wishing it would swallow him, and Declan O'Rourke's head came up from his scrutiny of the map and for the first time there was a spark of interest in his eyes.

Helen left the room, her head high and a hint of a smile on her lips.

CHAPTER 7

JULY, 1917

REUBEN WATCHED THE city unfold as the train traveled through the outskirts of Hoboken. The squeeze of soldiers clamored for a spot at the windows as their final destination drew near. It had been a hot ride across country through the summer heat and the crowded conditions of the rail cars had not been conducive to sleep.

He had adapted to the Texas heat easily and the hard training had not been particularly arduous to a work hardened farmhand. His marksmanship won him distinction with his sergeant and he still felt the elation of adventure.

As the train traveled from San Antonio, Texas through the heartland of the country, Reuben experienced a growing sense of duty. He had never before traveled more than thirty miles from the farm and to see the changing landscape filled him with awe at how big and diverse this great land was.

All along the way people would lift their hats and wave at the trainload of soldiers as they passed through little hamlets and working fields. This celebration of the cause buoyed Reuben's belief in the war.

The soldiers poured out of the rail cars and stretched their legs and lit cigarettes as they milled around the depot. The sergeants quickly began to form the troops into parade formation by units. In short order the corps marched down First Street, preceded by a brass band, toward the docks.

Most of the men in Reuben's regiment were as young and as green as he was. The citizens of Hoboken lined the twelve or so blocks as the soldiers paraded down the street, cheering and wishing them God speed and happy hunting. The men puffed out their chests and grinned, knowing in their heart of hearts that they would quickly fell the enemy and return home in glory.

Young boys darted from soldier to soldier along the formation, offering to carry their kits, procure cigarettes or a beer, hawking the many establishments along the docks for a meal or hot bath.

Reuben had never seen a city of this size. The celebrity of the soldiers was also a new experience.

The heavy accents of many in the crowd made their words unclear but the obvious desire to please the troops was there in the body language and exuberance of their welcome.

The soldiers quickly arrived at the docks. The long open space along the river had at one time been green with grass but was now a trodden, bare expanse of hard packed earth in the wake of the men who had come and gone before them.

Word spread through the corps that their ship would be in port in a day's time, that the rationing, delousing and fueling would take another two days at least, so they set about pitching camp.

In the evening Reuben and Slim walked around the area looking for a place to eat. They walked up Hudson Street and down River Street with locals bidding them to dine at their establishments. Reuben had never seen anything like it.

"Don't any of the people in this town eat at home?"

Slim grinned. "Boy, you're a real hayseed. Ain't you never ete in a restaurant afore?"

Reuben felt the color rise to his face. "Well, sure, but I've never seen so many. I stayed at a boarding house once. Couldn't afford the restaurant."

"A boarding house, huh?" Slim slapped him on the back. "Well, son, you didn't get anything like you're fixin' to eat tonight." He stopped in the street and gave the establishment in front of them the once over. "Let's try this Kraut house. Get a taste of the enemy."

Reuben stood his ground for a moment then the smile of the pretty blonde standing in the doorway in a frilly apron swayed him to enter the eatery.

The small place was almost full. Men in uniform occupied all but two of the tables. The blonde ushered them to an empty table, smiled and asked in a heavily accented voice if they wanted beer.

Slim slapped her playfully on the backside and said, "Sure as hell do, sweetie."

Her smile vanished and she moved out of Slim's reach. Reuben felt himself color up again and he caught Slim's arm. "Enough of that."

Slim jerked his arm free. "What? She likes it," he winked at the girl, "don't you, honey?"

"Beer." She gave a small curtsey and slipped between the tables to the bar.

Slim eyed Reuben. "What's ailin' you? Don't you know this place is run by Huns?"

"That doesn't mean you can act so familiar with the help."

"Oh, ho. It don't do it?" Slim leaned back in his chair, his legs stretched out beneath the table. "Don't you know any one of these birds would stab you in the back just like that?" He snapped his fingers.

"I doubt it."

"You doubt it, do you?" Slim took a large gulp of the beer that was placed firmly on the table before him by a man with a heavy mustache and hard blue eyes. "Don't you know half this town is German? The other half Irish. None of 'em would piss on you if you was on fire."

Reuben grunted and looked around the room at the men eating and drinking, talking and laughing loudly. The general attitude was one of entitlement and disrespect toward the two women and man who served them food and drink.

The food was a new experience for Reuben. They ate a spicy sausage with a type of cabbage that had a bite to it. The boiled potatoes swam in a creamy sauce with little green specks in it that gave it a tang as well. Neither of the men had any trouble cleaning their plates.

They strolled around the area of the port after their meal, looking in shop windows, smoking, exchanging greetings with fellow soldiers in varying states of intoxication. There were women lingering in doorways, smiling invitingly, cheering the 'handsome, brave' men about to sail away to war.

A particularly buxom brunette captured Slim's attention. "You want home cooking, soldier?"

Slim pushed his cap onto the back of his head and grinned. Other women had suggested that Reuben and Slim might want to buy them beer or cigarettes. This was a new approach. "Well, now, that's exactly what I need."

"We just ate not an hour ago." Reuben dropped his cigarette to the paving stones and ground it with his boot. "I'm not hungry."

Slim shook his head. "Man, you are some kinda thick." He raked his fingers through his hair and winked at the woman. "Lead me to the kitchen, honey, and let's get cooking."

She giggled and linked her arm with Slim's.

He looked over his shoulder at Reuben and laughed. "See you back in camp, son."

Reuben felt the heat rise up his neck to his face. The reality of the situation hit him. All these nice friendly women weren't impressed with their uniforms or their bravery. They were looking to make money off the hordes of men passing through on their way to war.

He wandered on his own for a bit, not taking much notice of where he went. The sights and sounds of the dock area mingled with the odors of cabbage, rancid cooking oil, diesel and the scent of the sea. Suddenly he felt very lonely. The image of Mara came to mind and for the first time he thought of the possibility that he might never return from France. He stopped, staring but not seeing, until he realized he was across the street from the German restaurant where they had eaten their supper.

The light in the restaurant went out as he stood there and the young blonde who had waited on them came through the door, turning to lock it behind her.

She looked up and down the street and the thinning pedestrian traffic then drew a long coat close around her. As she turned to head away from the river, she caught sight of Reuben. After an instant's hesitation, she smiled. It was a shy, fleeting smile. She gave a small bob of her head and started walking up the street.

Reuben hurried across the street and fell into step with her. He saw her brow furrow with apprehension. "Don't be frightened. I just wanted to apologize for Slim."

She pulled the lightweight coat closer, as if she were hiding in it, and shook her head. "Is no problem. He is soldier. I am German."

"But you're an American now."

She shrugged. "My family come to this place when I am ten. We work hard and it is good place until war comes." She glanced up at him. "Maybe will be good again when war is over. The soldiers say they will finish it in quick time."

They walked in silence for a few minutes.

"Where're you going at this hour?"

"I must pay the grocer. He demands money before he will deliver now that there is war." Her voice quavered and she was quiet for a block. "Never before does he demand the money. We are good customer. Always pay, but after. Now he must have money first and then he cheats us. Says there is tax on foreigners." Her voice hardened. "But he tax only the Germans."

"I'm sorry." Reuben didn't know what else to say.

They were nearing the train station. She stopped and turned to him. "You go now. Is not good to be seen with a soldier. People tell Papa. They talk, say I am like women of the street."

Reuben was glad of the darkness in this section of town. For the fourth time in one evening he blushed like a school boy. "I'm sorry. I didn't mean to cause you any trouble."

"Is okay. You are nice boy. I hope you come home from war." With that she turned her back to him and crossed the street to the market stalls that lined this section of the railway.

FOUR DAYS LATER the USS Chesterton set out from Hoboken with nineteen hundred soldiers and crew on board. They were sandwiched in like sardines with hammocks hanging side by side and so closely spaced that the men elbowed each other whenever they moved in their sleep. Most of the division was housed below deck and the heat, crowding, and body odor vied with odor from the makeshift latrines for wretchedness. The sergeants drew names out of a hat for each unit for a precious few minutes on deck each day.

Two days out Reuben was playing cards in a tight corner with three other men. The alarm sounded and the gunners sprinted to their stations. The ship did a hard turn to starboard and the men below deck felt the slow response as the ship turned. Word spread like wildfire. A U-boat had been spotted off the port bow.

Men jostled one another for the few portholes on their deck and an electric tension spread throughout the close quarters as the first vibrations of the depth charges hit the ship. The two destroyers escorting the Chesterton maneuvered in the area where the sub had been spotted.

The men in the hole of the ship grew quiet as the muffled sound of the explosions of the depth charges echoed along the hull of the ship. The destroyers kept up the search for a good half hour, circling the Chesterton in an ever widening pattern. Word filtered down from topside of the hide and seek game in the waters around them. Finally, an oil slick appeared on the water off the port bow. One of the two destroyers forming the escort set off in pursuit of the crippled German sub.

Just above where they played cards was a small porthole and the players jockeyed for position to watch the action. They were on the wrong side of the ship and the only view they had was of the ocean.

"I shoulda joined the Navy." The tall skinny guy named Earl said as he craned up to look out the window. "All I've done since joining up is sweat and eat dirt in a hell hole in East Texas. And I ain't been sick a day since we sailed." He slid down the side of the ship making room for someone else to take advantage of the porthole. "But my maw didn't like the idea of me spending the war on the sea in a tin can since I can't swim."

Everyone laughed. It relieved some of the tension in the small group of card players.

Earl squinted one eye against the smoke rising from the cigarette dangling from the corner of his mouth and asked Reuben, "You one of them Dixie National Guard?"

Reuben shook his head. "I made my way to Fort Travis to sign up."

"That's a long way from home. Didn't want to join a unit with your buddies?"

Reuben studied his hand a minute then allowed a slow grin to lift the corner of his mouth. "Wasn't a lot of them offering. Besides, the post master was being real strict about the age requirement."

"That's what I thought," Earl said. "How old are you, anyway?"

"Seventeen."

Earl grunted. "Just barely, I reckon." He stubbed out his cigarette against the side of the ship and placed the butt in his pocket. "You go with a girl before we shipped out?"

Reuben blushed to the roots of his hair and shook his head.

"Too bad." Earl gathered the cards and began shuffling them. "I tell you what my old Da told me. He rode with Teddy and he learned a thing or two. You got to be careful. Don't go with none of the local whores what sets up near the camps. Sure as hell to get the clap or worse." He thought about it a minute. "And stay away from the Catholic girls. That's mostly the Irish in this case, I reckon. They're worried about being struck dead for their sins and it just ain't worth the bother."

Reuben nodded and kept his eyes on his cards.

THOUGH THE SOLDIERS didn't know their port of call, their destination had been St. Nazaire on the coast of France. The ship altered its course when the destroyer had been unable to track the U-boat. The Captain of the Chesterton thought it would be better to make for Ireland in an effort to mislead the Germans and thereby protect the location where the main body of the Expeditionary Force had landed.

Reuben had his allotted time topside the next day just before dusk. He could see the haze of the coast in the distance. He thought of Mara as he stood there in the wind off the ocean, but Earl's words came to mind and tarnished the memory. It was the kind of talk shared among men and that thought led him to his father's last words. Luther's last words. Had men said such things about his mother? He couldn't bear to think it.

He hadn't allowed himself to dwell on that afternoon at the gypsy camp but now he let his mind return to it like a tongue seeking a sore tooth.

Since his earliest memories Luther had been there. It seemed that he had always been there. But the truth was that he hadn't. There had been someone in his mother's life before Luther. Had it been like him and Mara? The thought of such passion from his mother shamed him. He refused to see her in that light.

Reuben could now see the spires of St. Colman's at Queenstown. The cathedral rose above the land and sea like a benediction. It's spires reached heavenward to a dizzying height above the clustered low buildings of the town. Reuben had never seen such a church. The wonder of it struck him with awe as did the green of the nearer islands leading into Cork Harbor. The intensity of the color, like no green he had ever seen, pierced his heart and he felt a sense of coming home.

CHAPTER 8
SEPTEMBER, 1899

HELEN KNEW FROM the beginning that O'Rourke's pursuit of her had little to do with her looks and charm and everything to do with her wealth. If she were honest with herself, his initial dismissal was at the heart of her desire to bring him in line. Since her childhood she had been the object of admiration by the school boys and young men who entered her sphere and his dismissive attitude toward her had been an unspoken insult.

They played the game through the last of the summer heat. Everywhere Helen went O'Rourke would appear. Someone in Charleston society had taken him in hand, outfitted him in proper clothing, and inserted him into the social fabric of the summer doldrums. By the time the breeze off the ocean held the promise of autumn, Helen had begun to anticipate his presence.

He sought her out whenever their paths crossed. The acquaintance with her father initially made his attentions acceptable to the society in which they both found themselves.

His appearance, which at first had seemed so commonplace to her, began to change. If pressed, she would be unable to say what exactly had brought about the improvement; his eyes perhaps, or the velvety smoothness of his voice. It remained with her like an echo in the mind after each encounter.

He sensed his advantage and his tactics became more blatant. On more than one occasion he managed to find himself alone with her in the midst of a party.

Mrs. Mansfield's anniversary dinner and dance had been a much anticipated event. The first week of September brought an early taste of fall and the cooler evenings made for delightful weather for dancing into the night.

Helen fanned herself and watched the dancers as she took a breath and enjoyed a cup of champagne punch. As her gaze drifted over the party, she saw Luther Carroll approaching her. Before she could escape he was at her side, bowing before her.

"Miss Fitzgerald."

Helen inclined her head ever so slightly. "Mr. Carroll."

"Are you enjoying your evening?"

"Yes, thank you, but I fear I've quite overdone it." She brought her fan into play to create a buffer between them and glanced around the room in search of rescue.

Her companion studied her for a moment then leaned his body away from her in subtle acknowledgement of her rebuff. His face flushed. "I think your Fenian has not yet made an appearance."

Helen's breath caught and she raised the fan to cover the lower part of her face as she fanned. Her words were clipped when she spoke. "Whatever do you mean, Mr. Carroll?"

"O'Rourke seems to have given Mrs. Mansfield's dinner a pass."

"Really? I hadn't noticed. Mr. O'Rourke is of no concern to me, I assure you." She felt the color rising in her face. "I hardly know the man. He is but an acquaintance of my father's."

They stood in silence as the dancers came together and parted repeatedly to the tempo of the music. Luther turned his gaze toward the dancing couples but no joy in the picture they formed could be detected in his expression. "I'm glad to hear it. I fear O'Rourke isn't a man to be trusted."

Helen felt the outrage rise in her chest. How dare this country bumpkin assume he could moralize to her. "Indeed." Her fan fluttered rapidly. .

"Yes. But I imagine he'll be gone soon. He's been quite successful in his mission, I hear." He looked into her eyes, bright with anger. "All for the best I think."

"And you, Mr. Carroll? I dare say we will be deprived of your presence before much longer. You've been among us all of the summer." She looked away from him. "Time enough to accomplish your mission, I should think."

Her companion stiffened. "It is as you say. But I've not been so successful I fear." He bowed to her again. "Good evening, Miss Fitzgerald."

Helen watched him walk across the ballroom toward the arched entrance to the foyer of the Mansfield house and wished for something to throw at his stiff back. Loathsome, intolerable, wretch of a man!

She felt eyes upon her and turned to see Sybil Einhorn watching her. Helen closed her fan with a snap and gave a nod of acknowledgement in her direction. She watched as Sybil spread her fan. No doubt to hide her knowing smile, Helen was sure.

Her anger simmered and she was quite curt when Henry Simmons asked her to dance. As soon as he turned away at her sharp words she felt ashamed. But more than shame she felt guilt.

Luther Carroll had been right. She was watching and waiting for O'Rourke. It had been over a week since she had encountered him though the social activities of Charleston were gearing up and her days and nights had been filled with teas, luncheons, theater outings and dinners at the homes of her acquaintances. As she watched Sybil gossiping behind her fan to Maude Loudemire, Helen wanted to stamp her foot.

She slipped through the tall window that stood open behind her and onto the side porch. As she turned toward the courtyard softly lit by flares, she found herself in O'Rourke's arms.

He gave her a moment to pull away and when she did not, he kissed her.

LUTHER CARROLL DISAPPEARED from Charleston society in mid-September. Declan O'Rourke kept his footing in both camps of Charleston's population. His brogue was still heard in the taverns and hovels of the Irish poor while wining and dining with the upper crust in the stately homes of the moneyed.

Helen kept up a fevered pitch of activities so as not to miss an occasion where she might see O'Rourke. She couldn't seem to help herself. As

October drew to an end, he was not so often in polite company. Helen spent sleepless nights in dread that he had gone, then he would suddenly reappear.

On Saturday evening, Helen planned to attend a performance by Madame Thetis at The Academy of Music with Henry Simmons. She hadn't wanted to go but knew that she couldn't decline. After such a hectic schedule of social engagements at the beginning of the season, it would be noted if she failed to attend this most touted happening. She had not seen or heard from O'Rourke in ten days.

The theater on King Street was a mash as they drew near. Henry helped her from the carriage and took her arm, squiring her around the snarl of traffic and the horse excrement. She looked around anxiously, searching out familiar faces and greeting friends and acquaintances as she and Henry made their way to their box.

Helen hardly heard the first performance. The theater was overly warm and she felt the need for fresh air. She was about to suggest they step outside briefly when she saw O'Rourke arrive at the box directly across from where she sat with Henry. He took the hand of Sybil Einhorn and held it to his lips. She smiled up at him and said something as he drew a chair close to her and sat.

It wasn't that he had appeared in Mrs. Einhorn's box that made Helen's breath catch. It was the intimacy of the way he took her hand and kissed it, the way they angled their heads together. She knew that look, that intimacy, all too well.

She forced herself to watch the stage and Madame Thetis' performance. When Henry smiled across at her she managed to smile back though she felt numb and slightly ill.

At the intermission, she excused herself and went to dampen her handkerchief with cold water. This she pressed against her neck and both cheeks, all the time staring at her reflection in the dimly lit mirror of the ladies parlor. The crush in the small, cramped space quickly became unbearable and Helen slipped from the room and along the passage, finding refuge in the folds of the curtains leading to the stairwell to the balcony.

When she thought she had herself under control and was about to return to her box, she heard his voice.

"What took you so long?"

For a moment Helen thought he was speaking to her but Mrs. Einhorn's laughter made her freeze in her tracks.

"Oh, my dear, dark knight. You don't fool me with your sweet words and empty promises."

"Empty promises? Not I."

"Only because I know better than to listen to the words of a Fenian, no matter how charming."

O'Rourke chuckled deep in his throat. "You are a lady of the world, dear Sybil."

"Yes." She sighed. "Not so your little pigeon, eh?"

"Whatever do you mean?"

Mrs. Einhorn laughed again. "Don't play coy with me. I see the two of you, thick as thieves whenever you think no one is watching. Have you gotten what you came here for?"

"Yes, dear madam. That, and then some."

"Ah, so you'll be returning home with a wife."

"What makes you think I'm in need of a wife?" His voice was teasing, barely containing his merriment.

"Oh, ho. So it's like that, is it?"

"I can't imagine your meaning. Shall I return you to your box and bring you a champagne?"

Helen remained in her hiding spot until she heard the usher making the rounds with his bell, signaling the end of the intermission. On wooden legs she managed to climb the stairs and was glad of the low light of the box as she sank into the chair beside Henry.

WINTER HAD TURNED harsh in Charleston. The wind off the ocean stung the eyes and cheeks and a haze of smoke hovered over the rooftops of the town.

Helen said good morning to her father when she entered the dining room and looked over the array of food on the sideboard. The smell of bacon was overpowering and she poured herself a cup of coffee and took her place at the table.

Her father lowered the newspaper and frowned at Helen's empty plate. "Not eating?"

"Just a cup of coffee first, Father. I'll eat something later."

He grunted. "Have you seen the paper?"

"No."

"Of course not." He pushed the paper aside. "Salisbury is going to have that boy hanged or be damned trying."

Helen took a slow breath and let her father's words pass without comment. She had long since learned the futility of trying to dissuade him from his rage against the British treatment of the Irish Republican Brotherhood. She knew he had been instilled with a strong sense of injustice from his childhood. His father, Trevor Fitzgerald, had fled Ireland in the wake of the failed uprising of 1848 and his son had nursed at the teat of his hatred and desire for nationalism throughout his hardscrabble youth. But mostly Helen didn't want to be reminded of the sons of Ireland this morning.

She had not seen or heard from O'Rourke for two weeks.

She meant to change the subject. "Any thoughts on what you'd like for the Thanksgiving? Do you think a large dinner is necessary this year?"

The door into the dining room opened as she spoke and the handsome widow, Mrs. Sybil Einhorn, sailed into the room. "Monty, darling. I hope I haven't called too soon." She turned to Helen. "A Thanksgiving feast? Sounds lovely."

Montgomery Fitzgerald rose to his feet and took Mrs. Einhorn's hands in his. They had known each other for many years. "Sybil. What a nice surprise. Coffee? Breakfast?"

Mrs. Einhorn feigned embarrassment. "Oh, dear, how rude of me. I shouldn't have been so impulsive as to disturb you so early in the day. It's just that I couldn't keep myself from rushing over to discover the news."

The Senator offered her a chair and she settled in, taking off her gloves as she did. "What news is that?" he asked.

"Why, I heard last evening that our dear friend Mr. O'Rourke sailed on the RMS Adriatic in the late afternoon." She watched Helen's face as she spoke. "Is it true, Monty? Have we lost our bonny lad of the summer and fall?"

"Oh, he was a bonny one, wasn't he? Well, I suppose if that's what it took to line his war chest, then so be it." He took a sip of coffee and made a face at the now cold brew. "But, yes, your news is correct. He sailed yesterday in hopes of arriving in time to consult on the situation of young Colomb McGuire. It's a nasty business."

"Yes, yes, of course." Mrs. Einhorn didn't seem much interested in the fate of the young Fenian set to hang for shooting a policeman. "It is such a pity, though I imagine his wife will be well pleased to have him home again."

She watched Helen as she spoke and there was no doubt of the gleam in her eye.

Helen stared at their guest, unable to turn away and unable to draw breath.

"Why, Helen, dear. You look dreadfully pale." The note of sympathy in Sybil Einhorn's voice did not ring true. "Are you ill?"

It took all her will but Helen lifted her chin and smiled. "I don't know. I do feel most strange. It could be that I've caught the pox from the Ainsworth twins."

"The pox!" Mrs. Einhorn sprang up from her chair. "Why ever would you not warn me?" She placed her palms against her cheeks as if she could already feel the scarring blisters rising on her face.

"That was most uncaring, Helen." She backed away toward the door as she spoke.

"In truth, I didn't really think of you, Mrs. Einhorn."

Monty Fitzgerald rose from his chair and laid the back of his hand on Helen's brow. "Are you unwell, Helen? Shall I send for the doctor?"

Helen watched as Sybil Einhorn disappeared through the door of the dining room. "No, Father. I am as well as I will ever be again."

THE PREACHER'S COLLAR sat askew on his thin neck. His hair bore the look of a brush hastily swept across his forehead. Mud caked his boots where he stood on the Persian carpet. He had ridden through the downpour in his small carriage and the damp had penetrated the enclosure. The coat he wore felt heavy and he feared it smelled of wet wool.

Helen Fitzgerald stood before him, paler than death. Senator Montgomery Fitzgerald stood to his daughter's left; a large florid man, a powerful man. His once handsome looks had long gone the way of excess.

Asa opened the Bible and glanced at the man to Helen's right, her soon to be husband, and suppressed a sigh of despair. He knew in his heart the truth of this matter but he didn't let that knowledge register in his expression. He spoke the words of the marriage ceremony with no hint of reproach in his voice.

"Will you take this man, Helen, to be your lawful husband?"

Silence.

The grandfather clock chimed the half hour, the deep melodious bong, bong, bong echoing in the still room. Asa watched her throat work but no words came forth. He lowered his gaze to the pages of the Bible. "Helen--"

"She does." Montgomery Fitzgerald fixed his dark gaze on Asa. "She damn well does."

Tears welled in Helen's violet eyes but they did not fall. She stared straight ahead and uttered not a sound.

Senator Fitzgerald gestured impatiently. "Get on with it."

Asa looked from father to daughter. The delicate lace of the bodice of her gown fluttered ever so slightly with her trembling. He cleared his throat and turned to the man she married this late night and he knew her suffering had only begun. The groom did not look at his bride nor did he touch her.

Asa closed the Bible after the final words of the ceremony and as he turned away, he saw Montgomery Fitzgerald place a heavy leather pouch into the hands of his daughter's new husband and he felt a great pity well up in his heart for this spirited, beautiful, young woman. He knew she would leave within the hour for a life far removed from anything she had known and that the stain of her sin would be used to torment her all the days of her life.

The wild, wide-eyed look on her face hardened. As she swept her gaze over the three men in the room, Asa saw defiance settle over her features. She would resist this man she had married in every aspect of their lives. Asa had no doubt of this. And he, in turn, would try to break her, subject her to his will.

Helen swept out of the room, the fragile fabric of her gown like gossamer wings in her wake. She was a bird in flight, one desperate to escape. Too late, Asa thought. Too late.

Montgomery Fitzgerald slipped several gold coins into Asa's hand as he escorted him to the foyer. If the fact that the Senator had not summoned a priest to facilitate this travesty wasn't proof enough, the heft and number of coins Asa now held in his hand confirmed his suspicions of this hurried affair.

A young negress strained to lift a large suitcase onto a stack of waiting luggage near the front door.

"Thank you, Asa. I trust you'll be discreet about the haste in this matter." The Senator removed a cigar from his breast pocket of his coat. "People will talk regardless of the facts."

"He has urgent business in the South, I believe, Senator. Your new son-in-law." Asa accepted a second cigar withdrawn from Fitzgerald's pocket.

"Yes. They travel to Alabama tonight." Fitzgerald rolled the cigar between his fingers and thumb. "I don't imagine we'll see her again for many years."

"She'll be missed."

Montgomery Fitzgerald didn't reply. He gave Asa a nod in parting and turned back to the drawing room.

THE CABIN JERKED as another car was coupled to the train, rousing Helen from her thoughts. She stared out into the moonless night seeing only her own refection in the window of their cabin. They had been traveling for hours now with barely a word spoken between her and her new husband. At least they had a private compartment. She was relieved that he had given that much thought to her comfort. But as the miles disappeared beneath the wheels the silence between them grew more and more oppressive. How can I endure this, Helen thought.

As if he read her mind, Luther put aside his newspaper and rose from his seat. "Would you care for anything? I thought I would go find the dining car, perhaps have a smoke."

Helen looked up at him but didn't quite make eye contact. "No. Thank you."

He hesitated at the door of their compartment. "You look very pale. Are you sure there's nothing I can get for you?"

"Nothing, Mr. Carroll."

"Try to rest then. We'll be in Atlanta by mid-morning."

He closed the door softly behind him and she crumpled across the seat. Her eyes were hot with unshed tears, her throat parched from thirst. She had been married less than eight hours. She had thought she could do this but now she realized it for the sheer madness it was. How could she endure another day much less a lifetime with this strange, quiet man who had watched her for months from the periphery of Charleston society? She should have run away, gone to Paris to her grandmother's people. She should have found a way. And now it was too late.

LUTHER MADE HIS way through the train. At the nearly empty dining car he took a table at the end and withdrew a cigar from his coat pocket. He rolled it between his fingers and thumb. It was a fine Cuban cigar, given to him by the manager of the Hotel Olympus in congratulations on his impending marriage to the daughter of the state's most eminent Senator. Xavier Mallory was the only person in Charleston to have befriended Luther in the nearly four months he had been in town.

He replaced the cigar in his pocket and signaled the waiter. He ordered a whiskey and when the white gloved colored boy placed it before him, he threw it back in one neat gulp. The drink seared his throat but did nothing to warm him. He felt encased in ice.

When had his mission to Charleston taken such a turn? He had set out to persuade Montgomery Fitzgerald to support an expansion of the Southern Railway to include a trestle bridge over the Tombigbee River at Road's End. Now he was a married man with a pocket full of gold.

He hadn't wanted the gold but he hadn't known how to reject it. The preacher had seen the Senator give him the heavy leather pouch of coins and Luther had felt the burn of humiliation for himself and for Helen.

From the first moment he had seen her he had wanted Helen Fitzgerald. She was so far removed from any woman he had ever met and his fascination with her had been immediate and all encompassing. In all the times their paths had crossed they had shared less than two dozen words and yet his infatuation had been obvious enough for Montgomery Fitzgerald to seek him out and propose their marriage. There had been the added hint that a rail line could be in the works for Road's End but the Senator hadn't known such a bribe was unnecessary. And now they were man and wife.

CHAPTER 9
JUNE, 1918

REUBEN OPENED HIS eyes and saw the gentle undulation of grayed and water stained canvas overhead. He shivered with cold and clenched his teeth to keep them from chattering. It took him a minute to realize he was in a tent. On either side of him beds lined the enclosed space. The man next to him lay with his eyes closed but with each breath he grunted, the sound like a litany, a marking of the clock of his continued existence.

He became aware of the odors around him, so different from that of the trench and yet the same. The stench that had caused him to vomit when he had first been deployed into the trenches was overlaid with the sharp astringent of antiseptics.

Knives of pain shot up his left leg with each beat of his heart.

Fear gripped him and he tried to sit up but couldn't muster the strength to do so. His head felt like a leaden weight. He had heard tales in the trenches of men who had lost a limb but still felt the pain of it, the ghost of it. He didn't want to be one of the miserable wretches he had seen when he first arrived in France, hobbling around on one leg and a crude crutch made of a tree limb.

The bravado left him almost as soon as they landed at St. Nazaire. The battalion quickly moved on to the training camps but in that brief window of time he had seen the devastation of shattered bodies, starving inhabitants of the town, lost children gesturing with their hands to their mouths, begging for a morsel from the kits of the newly arrived soldiers. This was what three years of war had done to the local population.

Reuben closed his eyes and shivered in spite of the fine sheen of sweat on his brow and turned away from the visions of the horrors he had seen. He set his mind to the rhythm of his pain. It was preferable to thoughts of what he had witnessed since setting foot on French soil.

HIS LEG WOULDN'T heal. The schrapnel struck him square on the shin of his left leg, tearing through the flesh and severing the bone. The break had mended though there was a knot at the joining of the bone, but the flesh around the wound played cat and mouse. It would respond to treatment for a while then it would begin to fester again. The skin around the wound remained a dark brown in the shape of a large oval along the length of his shin. With each setback his overall health became more fragile. Finally, in mid-August, the powers that be decided he was of no use to the war effort, just another mouth to feed, another demand for scarce medical resources and personnel. He was going home.

In the days before they set sail for home Reuben felt his health turn for the better. He had been removed from the front to Folkestone soon after the injury to heal, but the conditions there, while clean with the air free of the cordite haze of the battlefield, had not helped him much.

Two days before his departure, Reuben awoke and stared once again at canvas overhead but on this day in this tent there was no fever. His mind was clear. When the Sister leaned over him to check his temperature, he smiled.

"Well," she said. "This is a nice start to my day. How do you feel?"

"I think I'll live."

She caught the gold crucifix hanging from a thin chain around her neck and kissed it. "Then you owe a debt of gratitude to the maggots, young man."

His face blanched and regret swept across her features before she could regain her composure.

"I've never seen such a hardy lad so terrified of a little worm." Her voice held a teasing note but the undercurrent of horror at her error could be heard as well. "Must have been the fever."

Reuben was so far from the hardy lad he had been upon arriving in France that the Sister's words were a tease. There were times when the men in the trenches had moved past hunger, the lack of food moving them beyond appetite. Then a package from home would arrive and the soldiers in the unit would get a fair whack at the contents, starting the cycle of satiety to hunger to loss of appetite all over again.

Reuben mustered another smile for the nurse. She was so very young and she had meant well. In his fevered mind he had thought the worms climbing along his leg, eating at his wound, a nightmare. Although he no longer suffered the fever dreams, he continued to flail against the image in his sleep. No matter that the maggots had probably saved his leg and possibly his life. The corpses of the fallen, crawling with them as they lay rotting in the trenches, in the devastation of No Man's Land, haunted him whenever sleep overcame him. Like so many others, he fought against sleep, fearing his dreams more than he feared enemy fire.

THE CONDITIONS ON the ship were little better than the ones on his voyage over but Reuben didn't mind. In the few days he had been free of fever, he had eaten mutton stew and coarse brown bread until his stomach protested. It felt good to silence the nagging hunger. The good sisters had gotten him out of bed and moving as soon as they realized he was on the road to recovery. By the time they boarded, he could manage on his own for short distances with the aid of a crutch.

It was early in the morning of the second day at sea that the first deaths came. The ship carried few able bodied men other than the crew, only enough to help with the lame and ill. From the first, the coughing and gasping for breath had been a constant. In order to rest the men had to turn deaf ears to the sound, not a hard task for men who had endured the constant pounding of artillery fire and cries of the dying on the battlefield.

Reuben managed to find a spot on deck as soon as the ship left port. He felt he couldn't catch his breath below deck so he remained headstrong and refused to go below. The constriction in his chest set in on the afternoon of the second day at sea. By the end of the day he watched as the chaplain and the captain relinquished body after body to the keeping of the sea. The Spanish flu traveled with them and would not loosen its grip.

By the morning of the third day they carried him below. He hadn't the strength to resist and the ship was making slow progress in the face of a storm. He drifted in and out of a fever induced sleep between bouts to dislodge the viscous liquid slowly drowning him. What little health he had gained on shore quickly disappeared in the fight to draw breath. All around him men struggled as he did until the gurgle of death silenced them. Somewhere in the back of his mind he was aware that the beds around him were being emptied one by one. He dozed and dreamed the good Sister was leaning over him, the cross dangled from the chain around her neck and danced in the sunlight of his memory.

WOODROW BROUGHT THE telegram himself. He felt it only right that he undertake this task. Too many such missives had arrived in the past year and he didn't trust such a solemn duty to Harriet's boy.

Luther came out onto the front porch when he heard the old Ford wheezing up the drive. He could tell by the set of Woodrow's shoulders as he climbed down from his car that the news was bad and his thoughts flew to Helen and how she would survive it.

Anna came running. She had been down near the old forest when she heard the distant approach of a car. Her heart pounded and tears rolled down her cheeks even though she made no sound. She stopped abruptly when she rounded the corner of the house and watched as Woodrow handed the telegram to her father and touched the brim of his hat in silent tribute.

When Luther entered the sitting room he saw his wife in her favorite chair, her hands limp atop the linen cloth she was embroidering. There was no color to her. It was as if all life had drained from her. He knelt beside her chair. "Shall I read it first?"

She stared blankly at him then focused on the envelope before turning away. She trembled and nodded her head.

Luther opened the message and read silently. He cleared his throat. "He's in Boston. Alive at the time of the telegram but the ship's under quarantine. Influenza." He laid his hand on her forearm. "A priest—they didn't know—so a priest gave him last rites."

Helen stood. Her hands formed into fists at her side. "I must go. I have to."

Luther rose to his feet. "You can't. It's too late. There's nothing you can do." He touched her cheek with his palm. "You'll only expose yourself."

She drew away from his touch and took the telegram as she wiped away the threatening tears. She read it then curshed it in her hand. "I'll be ready in fifteen minutes. Get the buggy." She turned from him and left the room in a whirl of skirts.

Anna watched her father from the dimness of the dog-trot. She saw the fear and pain on his face. After a moment he followed her mother to the bedroom.

Helen glanced up from the case she was packing. "I'm going, Luther." She gripped the iron footrest of the bed with a white knuckled grip as she struggled to control her emotions. "I'm bringing him home. One way or another."

He crossed to her and took her in his arms. "I know, darling. I know." He gently rocked her back and forth until he felt her relax in his embrace. "I'll go with you."

Helen lifted her head from his shoulder and let her gaze linger on his face for a long moment. "Thank you." She took a deep breath and drew away from him. "But I'm going alone." When he would argue she shook her head. "If there's a risk of infection then it's better this way. There's Anna to think of."

"Then let me go."

"No. No, I have to be there." At last the tears began to flow. "He needs me and I *need* to be there."

ON AUGUST 17, 1918, the RMS Truvarna set sail from Folkestone with three hundred nine of America's wounded and weary. They were the fathers, sons, and brothers who had answered the call to duty and had paid a heavy price. But the fates were not kind. The loss of limbs and lungs, sight and hearing had not been enough. Over half their number were sent to the cold embrace of the sea, one hundred thirty-one were sent home in shrouds. On September 5, 1918, the quarantine was lifted and as Helen Carroll stood on the dock, her back straight and a porter with a wheel chair at her side, she watched as Reuben disembarked along with seventeen of the living skeletons who had cheated death.

PART TWO

Anna

CHAPTER 10
APRIL, 1941

LIGHTNING PIERCED THE night sky illuminating the outbuildings against the gray on gray landscape of the distant fields. The trees bowed before the wind. Rain pelted the window. Anna raised her hand and placed the palm against the chilled windowpane. Thunder rolled across the earth. The old house shuddered under the force of it. The din of the thunderclap had just begun to fade when another, equally as deafening, caused the glass beneath her hand to rattle.

"The windows, Reuben! The front windows!" Her mother's voice called from the bowels of the house. The sound of wood slapping against wood hurried the footsteps. Reuben's heavy tread and muffled response pulled Anna back across the river of time and quieted the hammering of her heart.

The storm had awakened her from a troubled sleep. A sleep in which the old dream held her paralyzed with fear. But this wasn't the killer hurricane of 1927, and she wasn't in a shotgun tenement house in Mobile. She wouldn't run into the hallway and out into the wild wind to find her husband impaled by a tree limb, her young daughter curling into the side of his lifeless body in terror.

With a sigh, Anna turned from the tempest raging around her. She was home, safe, her mother at the helm of the household, her brother Reuben the anchor that secured them. The childish voice raised in cries of anguish that had seemed so real, so immediate, was the past—the distant past that could no longer touch either of them. Down the hall her daughter Rose, now a grown woman, slept unfettered by memory of such horror or pain of loss.

Anna drew on a dressing gown and slid her feet into a worn pair of slippers. The wide, bare, boards underfoot were still cold this early in the spring. Without the aid of a light, she slipped into the hallway and made for Rose's room. Even in the smothering darkness of the storm she found her way unerringly through an interior she knew as intimately as her own heart. It was, after all, the heart and life of her existence.

At Rose's room Anna opened the door and stepped inside. A flash of lightning cracked open the night with a thin, jagged finger of white light that danced above the treetops for long, drawn-out seconds.

Rose lay on her back, arms thrown wide as if to embrace the world, her light hair sprawled in a halo around her head. The abandon of her pose reassured Anna that her sleep was untroubled.

Darkness returned and the floorboards again rumbled beneath Anna's feet with the reverberations of the thunderclap. Drawing the dressing gown more closely around her, she turned and retraced her steps.

She felt the seeping chill as the wind whistled around the house seeking out the cracks and crevices of the old, ill-fitting windows.

Her own turmoil matched that of the storm. She returned to the wide hallway that had at one time been a dog-trot. At the ancient desk she removed the accounts ledger. She knew that in the nature of spring storms, this one would soon blow itself out; she also knew she wouldn't sleep again. The vestiges of her dream and the anxiety over the events of the coming day had banished such hope. She had learned long ago that the best way to ward off unwanted thoughts, unwanted memories, was to stay busy, to labor until exhaustion numbed the mind and heart.

With a quilt wrapped snugly around her shoulders she sat at the dressing table in her room, the ledger open before her. The light of the lamp flickered once, twice, then glowed in an uninterrupted halo across the pages. She ran her finger down the long debit column: cotton seed; a plow shaft; chicken feed; Tucker Wallace for the new heifer; Flora's Dress Shop. Her finger stilled at this entry.

Rose could have done without the new shoes but Anna had wanted her to have them. Throughout her daughter's life she had never suffered from hunger or fear, even when the Depression forced half the countryside out of their homes and on the move. Even when the boll weevil had eaten its way through the cotton fields of the South, somehow they managed on Carroll's Hill. But Rose had known few luxuries and now that she was about to leave home Anna felt an almost desperate desire to hold her back, keep her close, pamper and spoil her.

She sighed. How foolish to think she could compete with Rose's new life. And that wasn't what she wanted. It was time to let go, time to send her only child out into the world to embrace the happiness and endure the sorrow that would surely come.

Anna let her gaze follow the column to the end and frowned at the lack of credits over the last six months. When Reuben paid Moses and Addie Mae their monthly wages there would be less than fifty dollars to tide them over the long summer until the cotton harvest. And they had to be paid.

Reuben couldn't manage in the fields without Moses's help. There could be no question of letting Addie Mae go. She was as much a part of the Carroll household as if she had been born into it. Anna couldn't remember a time when she hadn't been there, standing over the hot stove, scrubbing the front porch with Red Devil's lye after the dogs had been caught sleeping there, or turning the mattresses of their beds to air each spring. But mostly she remembered the smell of vanilla and the warmth of an ample bosom that soothed hurts, both of the body and of the heart. No, Addie Mae had to be provided for regardless the cost.

She drew a scrap sheet of paper from the drawer and began figuring the budget once again. There had to be something they could do without, something they could turn to cash.

The night faded to gray with the approaching dawn. Anna raised her gaze from the figures marching across the page. She rubbed the nape of her neck and rose from the stool. It would be morning soon and their journey would begin. She stared out at the trees and outbuildings of the farm as they slowly began to take shape.

No miracle had occurred in the waning hours of the night, no solution had magically presented itself. Her mother would have her way and that was that. Helen Carroll was set on making a grand production out of Rose's wedding and she would take the only avenue open to them.

Anna turned from the window and started attending to her morning toilet. From the back of the house came the small, hushed sounds of Reuben as he made his preparations for the trip. By the time the smell of brewing coffee began to seep through the house, Anna was dressed.

She paused at Rose's open bedroom door. The first rays of the morning sun slanted through the tall windows and danced in the pale tresses of Rose's shoulder length hair. She was so young to be taking such an important step; so young and yet so unlike Anna at that age. The tempest of emotions that had tormented the mother had thankfully left the child in peace and that calm had, over time, made Rose the glue that held this household together. A fierce protectiveness gripped Anna as she watched her only child sitting so quietly, the brush idle in her hands.

Rose was lost in thought, the nature of which marred her smooth, pale, forehead and turned down the corners of her mouth. Anna crossed the room and placed a hand on the fair head, trailing her fingers through the length of hair as she spoke.

"Why such a long face? And today of all days." She hesitated as her daughter looked up at her but didn't smile at the light teasing. "Are you having second thoughts, darling? It isn't too late to change your mind. Nothing is set in stone, you know."

Rose's forehead furrowed more deeply and she shook her head. "No, nothing like that, Mother. Quite the opposite, actually." She slid over a few inches to make room for her mother to join her on the old piano bench. With an impatient gesture, she tossed the brush onto the dressing table. "The truth is I can't stand the waiting. It makes me afraid."

"Afraid?" Anna placed her hand under Rose's chin and brought her face around so she could see her eyes. "Of what, darling? You know Marsh worships you. I've never seen a man more in love." She hesitated for the span of a heartbeat. "Have his parents done anything--"

"No, no, none of that. At least nothing in word or deed." Rose stood and moved to the window that looked out over the front drive to the sun riding the low distant hills in a burst of yellow and orange. "They're being very stoic about the whole affair." She ran her forefinger in a mindless circle over the wavery imperfections of the glass pane. "It's the war I fear. We listened to President Roosevelt on the radio last night." She looked at her mother. "Listening to him, I felt faint." She placed a hand at the base of her throat as if checking for a pulse. "I should have felt reassured. His words always calm me when the men have been talking of ships and guns and bombings. But last night," she glanced away, "last night I wanted to jump up and run from the room."

At the quaver in her daughter's voice Anna went to her. She slid her arm around her shoulders. "But there was nothing in his talk to frighten you, Rose. In fact, he was trying to soothe everyone's fears. Britain will hold, everyone believes it."

Rose shook her head. "I don't believe it. Marsh will go if there's war." Tears filled her eyes. "He laughs at me and calls me a silly girl for worrying but I can't help it." She wiped at the tear trailing down her cheek. "War will come, I know it."

"Darling--"

"It will come and he will go and something terrible will happen!" A note of barely contained hysteria threaded its way through her words. "I can't live without him, Mother." She turned her face into her mother's shoulder. "How have you stood it all these years? How could you bear being so alone?"

Anna ran her hand over her daughter's head, smoothing down her hair again and again. "But I wasn't alone, was I? I had you."

Rose lifted her head to scrutinize her mother's face. "And you'll be alone after the wedding. There'll only be you and Nanna and Reuben in this big old house."

Anna laughed softly. "You'll only be forty miles away, Rose. I imagine Mother and I will survive each other somehow."

The tension in Rose's features faded to an expression of sadness, the whiskey color of her eyes seemed to change, to become darker. "Has it been so terribly unbearable for you, Mother?"

Anna didn't flinch from Rose's steady regard. "I wouldn't change anything in my life, darling."

"Did you love him so very much? As much as I love Marsh?"

"Yes." She wanted to say something more but in the end she simply repeated, "Yes."

Rose swallowed back the threatening tears and turned to the chifferobe and rummaged through one of the drawers until she came up with a cloth lingerie bag. "This is my last pair of stockings. I almost hesitate to wear them."

"We'll buy new ones in Mobile. And anything else you need for your trousseau." Anna straightened the toiletry items on Rose's dressing table, aligning the brush and comb, placing the lid on the box of dusting powder. Her hand stilled over the framed photograph of Rose, herself and her long dead husband. She drew her hand back and glanced away, a weary note in her voice when she spoke. "Your grandmother is determined that the Ashcrofts not think they've gotten a sow's ear."

Rose stood in the center of the bedroom, the stockings in one hand. "I wish the wedding were tomorrow. Today, even. I don't care about going to Mobile to have a fitting for an elaborate wedding dress. I'd gladly walk down the aisle in my petticoat."

"I'm sure that would make a good impression on your new in-laws." Anna's voice deepened with a touch of humor.

"I don't care about them." Rose's hand knotted around the delicate silk. "Sometimes, I think my heart will break out of my chest if I don't do something. It's as if I can prevent the bad things if only I do what's needed." She looked at her mother, her forehead once again knotted with anxiety. "But I don't know what that is."

"You're exciting yourself for no reason, darling. If you're this upset maybe— Perhaps we should postpone the trip. We could wait until next week."

Rose took a deep calming breath and glanced down at the creased stockings. "No." She took another breath. "No. Liggy is expecting us. It's been so long since she was here. She says it's because of her arthritis but I think it's the way Nanna treats her." She placed the stockings on the bed and ran her hand along them to smooth the creases. "Besides, if I must wait six weeks to marry, then I might as well have the dress."

"If Liggy says she doesn't come because of her arthritis, then she doesn't come because of her arthritis. Nothing your grandmother could say or do would bother my cousin in the least. And as for the dress, trust me." She crossed the small space between them. "When you're old and grey," she smoothed back a pale lock of hair from Rose's forehead, "and you and Marsh are sitting on your front porch in your rockers, you'll be glad the day was special. No matter what the future holds, you'll always have those memories."

A blush crept up to darken Rose's pale cheeks. "You make me ashamed of myself. I should be thankful that Nanna has decided to sell the timber."

Anna smiled. "You're in love and impatient." She lifted the locket watch pinned to her blouse. "And you're late. Reuben will give us the silent treatment for the entire five hour drive if you don't hurry." From the chifferobe she took out a pale green dress of layered organdy. "Lord knows we've heard enough complaining about the fact that he has to leave the planting of the south field to Moses for the four days we'll be gone."

"Uncle Reuben will be happy enough when we get there. He can go look at tractors. You know how badly he wants one. Or go down to the cotton market and haggle over the price he'll get for this year's crop."

The mention of cotton prices caused a frown to settle over Anna's features. Talk of war had everyone speculating on the boon it would create for cotton farmers. She had heard such talk before. That was all it had been, talk. The only time Anna could remember when money hadn't been scarce was her childhood, before the banks failed and her father lost everything but the land. She set no store by talk of easy riches. And though Reuben might dream of a tractor she saw no hope of such luxuries in their future. She glanced at her daughter and forced thoughts of their money problems from her mind. Rose's anxiety had her worried and she wanted nothing to further mar the happy occasion of their trip. Once they were underway, Rose's spirits would lift. Anna held up the organdy dress. "Here, put this on."

Rose untied the sash of her cotton wrapper, draped it on the foot of the bed, and raised her arms as her mother eased the dress over her head.

"Now, you have ten minutes to finish with your hair and face and meet us in the kitchen." Anna didn't wait for a reply as she slipped from the room and followed her nose to the coffee.

Reuben sat at the kitchen table sipping coffee from a saucer. He glanced at the clock when Anna entered the room. "Don't suppose there's any need in pointing out the time."

Anna poured herself a cup. "She's feeling anxious this morning, Reuben. I'd ask you not to go on about the lateness of the hour if I thought it would do any good."

"Spoiled. That's her problem."

"She's worried about the war."

Reuben nodded. "And rightly so. Roosevelt will have us in it soon enough."

"Don't say such things."

"I'm only speaking the truth. He's a silver-tongued devil, that one. Talked until he got his way on the WPA and relief, didn't he? Got the draft, didn't he?" He poured more coffee from the cup into the saucer and blew on it. "Won't be much longer I reckon."

Anna pulled out the chair across from him and sat, her shoulders slightly rounded with the weight of Reuben's words. "Well, for Rose's sake can you keep your opinions on the matter to yourself? She's worried Marsh will be called up."

Reuben grunted and Anna had to be content with that. She knew he loved Rose. At least he did whenever he bothered to think about her. As for Anna, he was indifferent, but she didn't feel hard about that indifference for she understood her older brother well.

The only thing that mattered to him was farming. He was happiest plodding along in the wake of a pair of mules and the plow as it furrowed the earth into long dark ribbons that stretched away to the horizon. He understood the seasons and the tides of the earth, knew the habits of nature more intimately than those of his fellow man. She understood his reluctance to be away from it when the sap was rising and the soil waited expectantly for the seeds it would gestate.

She didn't allow herself to dwell on the thought of what the trip would mean to her or how she would endure it. But endure it she would. In the nearly twenty long years since Anna had last made this journey she had become a master at enduring.

Reuben finished his coffee in silence then rose from the table and left the room by the back door. At the sound of a soft tread on the bare boards of the hallway Anna straightened her shoulders just as her mother entered the kitchen. Helen Carroll placed a white envelope addressed in her strong, bold script on the table before turning to the stove to pour a cup of coffee. In the familiar pattern of their days neither of them spoke as the older woman settled in a chair opposite her daughter.

Helen's face softened as Rose burst into the room on a cloud of violet scent. She bent to kiss her grandmother's cheek and her gaze rested on the envelope lying between the two women. "Is that the letter, then? To the timber man?"

"Yes. I'll leave it in the mailbox for Rusty to pick up on his run today."

Rose slid into the chair beside her grandmother. "Should we be shopping just yet? What if he won't buy?"

Helen glanced across the table at Anna then quickly away. "Mr. Battle will buy. I've had letters now and again over the years. He's been itching to get at this lot. Battle's Mill always wants good mature trees."

The color was high in Rose's cheeks. "Will it be a good price, do you think? And will it be in time?"

"Mr. Battle is a fair man. He'll advance me the majority of the contract price. We won't have that riff-raff in here until after the wedding." She smoothed back Rose's hair with an age-roughened and spotted hand. "You buy a pretty dress with a veil. Shoes and stockings. A nice traveling suit. Whatever you want, Rosie."

Rose bit her lower lip. "Oh, Nanna. I'm so selfish spending money on foolishness when we need a new roof."

"This isn't foolishness, child."

Anna gave a small grunt of humorless laughter. "No, indeed. It's pride. Quite another thing altogether."

Helen gave her daughter a spare look. "It's respect. If we don't give Rose the respect she deserves, how can we expect others to do so." She covered Rose's hand with her own. "You must set out as you plan to go forward. In all things. Remember that." She patted Rose's hand, stood and moved toward the stove. "Now, you should eat something. It'll be a long day."

Rose shook her head and went to the kitchen window. "I couldn't swallow a thing, Nanna. Besides, there's Uncle Reuben. He's ready to go."

Reuben had brought the car around from the carriage house and it stood waiting, their suitcases already stowed away. Rose skipped down the wide front steps and along the brick path. No vestige of the storm remained but in its wake it had left the lawn and driveway strewn with the achingly white petals from the dogwoods and the pink of a lone crabapple tree. It was as if an unseen hand had shorn nature to adorn the path for the bride-to-be on this special occasion.

As she watched from the top of the steps, a hamper with their lunch clutched in her hands, Anna felt her spirits lift. The past was the past. She wouldn't allow it to take root in her enjoyment of her daughter's happiness. And Rose was happy. The doubts of the first dawning of the day had given way to excitement. She stood on the running board of Reuben's immaculately kept Hudson and smiled back at her mother. It made Anna's heart ache for a Kodak to capture the moment and she resolved that they would purchase one on this trip.

The Hudson, for all its weight, slipped and slid down the red dirt road leading from the farm-house. Anna sat in the back seat, the hamper clutched in her lap for fear it would be upended if Reuben failed to outmaneuver the muddy slope. She braced herself as best she could with her feet flat against the floorboard.

Last night's storm had deeply rutted the road with the force of the rain. Reuben muttered as he fought the steering wheel while Rose, seated beside him, laughed outright when he cursed a mud hole that threw up a red spray onto the pristine hood of the automobile.

Anna turned from the slippery road before them and stared out the window at the high clay embankment. The pasture grasses were heavy with moisture that heightened their green.

Ox-Eyed daisies leaned their showy heads toward the roadway and the pinkish white of Cherokee roses wound its way through the tall grass. Clusters of Sweet Alyssum perfumed the air and Anna closed her eyes to the scene. It had been just such a day as this when she had last journeyed from home.

That trip had also been occasioned by Rose. There, all resemblance ended. Although she struggled against it, the pain and humiliation of that day bore down on her. Her father's features, ashen with pain and disappointment, now played behind her closed eyelids. Her mother had stood at his side, her face white, her expression remote, emotionless as always.

The car swerved sharply and Anna's eyes flew open. They widened in fright as the narrow bridge over Fly Creek was suddenly much too far to the right of the automobile. Reuben could neither brake nor downshift the Hudson into obedience. Then at the last second it corrected and they hit the bridge straight on. They were over the creek and starting the climb up the next hill before any of them could catch a breath. Rose's laughter tittered nervously. Anna felt the tension in her neck and shoulders. It would be a long hundred-odd miles before they reached the paved highway that led down the state to the Gulf of Mexico and Mobile.

THEY STOPPED AT a gas station near McIntosh, the cinderblock building and pump separated from the highway by a narrow apron of red dirt and loose pea gravel. Automobiles swished by on the road as they sat in the Hudson and ate the contents of the basket Anna had packed. The slow, nerve-racking miles of dirt road in the aftermath of weeks of spring rains had them all tense with strain. Added to the rutted and slippery roadways had been the endless bottlenecks caused at different stretches along the way by first a tractor and then a number of log trucks. Even with the rains, loggers were working the woods, a good sign, surely, for her mother's hopes of selling timber.

Once they hit the blacktop the trip would go more smoothly, Reuben would be able to keep the Hudson purring along at a good clip on the two-lane highway.

Anxious to have their overly long journey at an end, Reuben ate quickly and silently and afterward raised the hood of the car to check the engine. He frowned as he watched each tick of the numbers as they rolled over at the pump where a slim-jim of a boy filled the gas tank.

REUBEN'S GROWING SILENCE as they neared Mobile made Rose decide to ride in the back with her mother after the stop. Her excitement was a palpable thing as they passed through the outskirts of the city. The closely spaced homes with their tidy lawns that lined Highway 43 set her to chattering about rose arbors and window awnings. This scenery gave way to heavier traffic and the warehouses and activities of the state docks. Two huge ships were anchored there and longshoremen unloaded great crates of bananas. The air was heavy with the smells of diesel fuel, fish, decay, and humidity. Sea gulls swooped and dove along the waterfront.

From Water Street they turned onto Government Street, slowed and gawked in awe at the entrance to the amazing engineering feat of the Bankhead Tunnel. When completed, it would run beneath Mobile River to connect the city to the eastern shore of Mobile Bay. Reuben muttered dire predictions of disaster and condemned the project as money wasted.

They quickly passed the courthouse, the LeClede Hotel, and the old LeVert home where it was said that Octavia LeVert once entertained Ulysses Grant. Rose marveled at the tremendous oaks dripping with moss that spread their ancient branches until the entire street was covered by a green canopy.

The homes along Government Street were much grander than any they had seen before, two-storied and elaborately finished with iron-work, masonry and imposing facades. Rose grew quiet in the face of such concentrated splendor.

Without the distraction of Rose's demands to know about every house and storefront they passed, Anna felt the years slip away as they followed the former path of the old street car line. The image of it traveled along beside them, the rhythm of the rails as audible in her memory as the last time she had ridden it.

At Rapier Street, they turned left, away from the noisy artery of the city, away from the stately homes of a mostly defunct elite, and into the quiet heart of the working class.

Surprisingly little had changed in the six-teen years since she had last followed this path although there were a few outward signs of relief from the bone-jarring poverty of the mid-twen-ties. A new car stood in a driveway; bright green awnings shaded the western windows of a house; a mother pushed an infant along the sidewalk in a shiny new buggy.

When Reuben turned onto Texas Street Anna felt each thump of her heart against her ribcage, the sound of each beat welling inside her until it drowned out everything else.

He pulled up in front of a narrow shotgun house with a postage stamp front lawn. Liggy, her tall, boney frame all angles and planes, stood on the stoop just as she had twenty years ago.

Little had changed in the picture she formed against the backdrop of the house. Not in the style of hair cropped off at her chin and shaped into an artificial wave on either side of her face, though now it was threaded with gray, nor in the smock that smothered her thin frame. The memory of the scent of her struck Anna full force.

CHAPTER 11
JUNE, 1922

LIGGY STOOD ON the front stoop of the long narrow house, her features revealing both joy and anxiety. Anna climbed down from the car while Reuben lifted her trunk from the rumble seat of the Ford. Her back ached from the long, six hour journey down the state and she felt three times her eighteen years.

Unable to contain herself any longer, Liggy flew across the small patch of grass that passed for a lawn and threw her arms around Anna. Immediately Anna was engulfed in the rotten-egg scent of hair fixative. The nausea, that had finally given way in the face of numbing exhaustion, rose in her throat. She swallowed hard and returned the older woman's embrace. Thin and boney as Liggy was, the feel of her arms was for Anna like finding her feet on a storm pitched ship. For the first time in weeks Anna felt the tension in her spine ease.

"Lord, it's so good to see you, child." She held Anna at arms length. "Just look at you, all grown up." Suddenly Liggy was drawing her up the steps of the frame house. "I've been on pins and needles all day. Nearly fried Thelma Jenkins hair this morning, I was that excited." She chuckled. "Not that it would have made much difference. Thelma has the wildest hair. Can't for the life of me imagine why she bothers with a permanent wave. But I don't argue, mind. Three dollars is three dollars, I say." She patted the large pocket of her smock with a satisfied smile. "Come on in the house. I closed up shop at noon so I could cook up a good dinner. Reuben must be empty to his boots."

As the screen door closed behind them, Anna heard the thud of the trunk as Reuben dropped it onto the stoop. After the long silent ride the sound jarred her into speech. "I don't know how to thank you, Liggy. I didn't know what else to do. As soon as I can figure something out--"

"Oh, pish. You're going to stay right here with me and that's the end of it. Your father's overrun with pride if you ask me. It's the Carroll in him. And after all, he's just a man." She linked her arm with Anna's. "Besides, I've been needing someone to help me in the shop. I just about worked myself into the grave during Mardi Gras. Talk about putting on the dog, honey. My fingers pure bled by the time Ash Wednesday rolled around."

They walked through the front sitting room and the bedroom. At the kitchen, an addition had been bumped out onto the original shotgun structure. Liggy held the door open. "Here, honey. Go on and wash up. Take your time. I'll just be getting the food on the table."

Anna closed the ill-fitting door behind her. She stood with her back against it in the confining space and stared at her reflection in the mirror over the wash basin. This was what the faces of hell looked like, she decided. Pale, drawn, without hope.

The chemical smell of Liggy's profession grew in the close room and Anna realized it came from the smock hanging from a nail in the back of the door. With a sudden rush she was ill. Silent tears of rage and frustration stung her eyes at her futile attempt to muffle the sound of her retching.

When she felt reasonably certain that the sickness had passed she rose from a crouch beside the toilet and ran water into the wash basin. She rinsed her mouth and washed her face, ran her damp hands over her hair.

The room was tiny but not airless. Its construction had left pinpoints of light at various joints and knotholes. Anna stared at the short tub and the naked wiring and piping. She could feel the stir of air through the thin rag rug on the floor. There was a coolness that she feared would be freezing in winter. But winter was a long way off. There was the whole of the long, hot summer ahead to be gotten through.

Although it was late in the day, Reuben started the long drive home as soon as he had eaten. For Anna his departure allowed her to give over to the fatigue brought on by the tension of the past weeks. She lay on Liggy's bed too exhausted to sleep, her mind a jumble.

Her brother hadn't condemned her nor had he sympathized with her plight. In the years since his return from the war in France he had remained a silent observer among them, more out of doors than not even when the fields lay fallow and no chore readily presented itself.

Sam blamed it on the war. Reuben had been one of the first to land in France with the American Expeditionary Force in July of 1917. He fought at Cantigny in June of the following year and later in the ill-fated Meuse-Argonne offensive where he was wounded.

Sam, fired with the propaganda Wilson's administration had put forth with its four-minute men, meatless Tuesdays and wheatless Mondays, had followed Reuben's lead. His stint in Europe lasted less than six months yet it left him no less affected than Reuben. He couldn't forget the stench of the trenches, the cold and damp, the constant presence of death.

He rarely spoke to Anna about the war except for a vague reference to dreams that would not fade, or to explain the sweats that came upon him suddenly for no good reason. But Sam hadn't lost his need of people.

Anna wondered how he would view her abrupt departure. She had made no attempt to contact him, not even a note. How could she have? What could she have said? That she loved him? Yes, that was true. That she hadn't loved him enough? Perhaps that was true, also. Better to let him think what he would, let the break be sure and clean. To do otherwise would be to give him hope where there was none.

ANNA LEANED OVER the woman's head and ran her fingers through her hair as she rinsed the slick concoction of bleach from it. The chemicals used to blondine were not as offensive as those of the permanent waves, but the harshness was the same. She turned off the water and squeezed the excess moisture from the length of hair, helped the customer to a sitting position, and wrapped her wet head in a towel with a deftness born of long weeks of experience. With the sore fingers of her reddened, raw hand, she massaged the small of her back. She felt Liggy's gaze on her and dropped her hand away.

"Honey, run on over to the kitchen and brew us up a pot of coffee. I'm dying for a cup." Liggy swiveled the woman in the chair around and studied her reflection in the mirror. "And I'm sure Charlotte is too." With nimble fingers she combed the hair on either side of Charlotte's face forward into a curl.

"I should comb out Mrs. Whitney."

"I'm practically done here, sugar. You go on, now. I'll get her."

Saturdays were the busiest time for the shop. Women came and went all day along the path that ran down the side of the shotgun house to the addition at the rear. Although attached to the house, it had a separate entrance.

Anna pushed open the screen and stepped out into the dappled light of the back yard. A large magnolia grew in the very corner of the small space and overhung the house blighting Liggy's hopes of a square of grass or a bed of flowers. But in its way that was a blessing because the deep shade kept the soil moist, and the combination produced a haven that was a few degrees cooler than the sweltering heat that gripped Mobile as summer extended itself well into September.

Anna longed to retreat to the wooden swing that hung from the tree's branches and put her swollen feet up on the seat beside her. If they weren't too tired after the last customer she and Liggy would sit out here in the evening and share a bottle of beer. But often the last customer didn't leave until nine o'clock, and then the shop had to be tidied, the curlers washed, combs and brushes sterilized, the floors swept and mopped. Even with Ida, the hired help, it was no wonder Liggy was bird thin.

Anna climbed the two steps to the dim kitchen. She emptied the coffee pot of the morning dregs and made up a fresh pot. Once it was on the gas stovetop she sat down, her feet up in a chair. This was, after all, the barely veiled purpose of Liggy's sudden appetite for coffee. With both hands Anna rubbed the swelling of her abdomen and sighed.

The work was hard but she didn't mind it. The worst part was the curiosity of Liggy's regular customers. Anna was nearly five months along and no longer able to conceal the fact.

In a no-nonsense manner Liggy explained that Anna's man had run off and left her. The first time Liggy told this lie Anna had flushed scarlet with shame. After work that day she insisted that Liggy not lie for her. Liggy's attitude was that it wasn't a lie. It was a fact that the father of Anna's child had left her and as to the matter of whether or not he was her husband should remain unspoken. Not telling someone what was clearly none of their business wasn't lying in Liggy's book.

Her bold statement fell short of satisfying the curiosity that seemed to hum through the shop, but Liggy had a way of pinning you with her small round eyes that made you think twice before crossing the line when she had drawn it. And Liggy wasn't timid about turning away business. The rules of her establishment were simple: no vicious gossip, no politics, and no religion. Few were willing to give up their standing appointment under Liggy's capable hands by abusing those rules. They considered egg money well spent for the look in a man's eye on a Saturday night or the envy in the tight lips of fellow parishioners on a Sunday morning.

Luck was with Anna and Liggy on this particular Saturday night. Sophie Westover's daughter ran off with a seaman and she was too hysterical to keep her seven o'clock appointment. By seven-thirty Anna and Liggy were sitting in the swing under the tree eating a shared plate of cold potato salad and fried chicken. On this occasion Liggy had brought out two bottles of beer instead of the one they usually shared at the end of a long and busy week.

"I'll be up all night if I drink this."

"Drink it. It looks like rain tonight. I won't hear a thing."

"Umm. Dog days. I'm truly sick and tired of rain every single day." Anna rubbed the cold sweating bottle against her forehead.

"Be thankful. It's the only thing that gives us some relief from all this heat. We can sleep late tomorrow morning." Liggy looked up through the branches of the tree but no stars were visible in the overcast sky. "The rain'll pass off soon enough. I've never known it to be so wet this late into September. It can't keep up much longer. You'll see, there's dry, clear days ahead."

Anna felt a little bubble of movement in her abdomen. "Oh." She placed her hand over the spot.

"What?" Liggy sat forward. "Are you all right?"

"Yes." Anna smiled. "Yes. It's the baby."

"Glory," Liggy's voice dropped to a soft whisper, "she moved."

Anna took Liggy's hand and placed it on her abdomen. "She *or* he moved."

Liggy held her hand still but nothing happened. "What will you name her?"

"Rose." Anna stared at the rectangle of light that fell across the ground from the kitchen doorway. "If it's a girl."

"It's a girl. You're carrying low, all belly." Liggy patted Anna's abdomen then sat back in the swing. "And thank the Lord for that. Under the circumstances."

"I'd think a boy would fare better. In the long run."

"Not a bit of it. Men can't handle shame. As for women, well, it's their lot, isn't it?"

They sat in silence for a while. Anna took no offense at Liggy's words. None had been intended. Life was life, it was as simple as that. It would take a fool to pretend otherwise.

"Why did you leave, Liggy?"

She smiled as she gave the question some thought. "Because I liked dance halls and beer and handsome men." She took a sip of beer. "Not that there was a huge crowd lining up at the kitchen door, mind. But Luther took it in his head that I was going to ruin without the influence of a father. With Papa's death the baby brother appointed himself the head of the family. I expect it was simply out of concern for me and Mama. There's a lot of good in him, Anna. It's just that he loved your mother too much. It changed him from the boy he once was." She sighed. "Well, anyway, he decided we should move into the house on the hill so he could supervise my activities."

Liggy chuckled. "I was eighteen and headstrong. I also had a little money from Papa's insurance. So, come the day before the move, I caught the mail truck to Demopolis and the train from there."

"Have you ever regretted it?"

Liggy remained silent for a moment. "No. There was a boy back home. Like me, he wasn't much to look at. I could have married him, had kids." A tree frog began to sing somewhere over their heads. "But I couldn't bring myself to do it. I kept thinking there was something more, something I was missing." She smiled. "And there was. For a time I took my fill of pleasure at the dance halls. Every Friday and Saturday night there was a dance at the Elks Lodge at Government and Joachim. Enjoyed the company of a number of not-so-handsome men. Even after I opened the shop I was never too tired to frolic on a Saturday night."

"Were you ever in love?"

Liggy's forehead furrowed. "Other than the boy back home, no. There never was a man I felt I could give myself over to. I suppose that comes from growing up a Carroll. Mama never had one thought that was her own, never committed a single act without taking into account the possible displeasure of some man. Papa, Grandfather, Luther." She pushed her foot against the ground and set the swing into motion and her voice held a note of humor when she spoke. "I guess I'm just too darned selfish to allow myself the love of a good man."

The latch of the gate to the side yard clicked and both women turned to watch the shadowy figure approach. At the kitchen, a man stopped in the spill of light.

"Sam." Anna's hand went to her throat.

Sam pulled the hat from his head. "Anna. I thought I'd find you here." The surprise in his voice belied his words.

Liggy rose from the swing and collected the plate and the two beer bottles. "I'll wash up the dishes."

Sam didn't move until the screen door closed behind Liggy. He twirled his hat in his hands. "I never thought of Liggy until old Fiske came into the store the other day." He approached the swing. When he was three feet from her he stopped. "Have you been here all these months?"

"Yes." The word came out in a whisper.

He looked down at the hat in his hands, swallowed hard and cleared his throat. "Why, Anna?"

Anna couldn't think. She hadn't expected him to show up like this. Before this there had been no evidence that he had even looked for her. She was totally unprepared to answer his questions.

When she made no reply, he looked around the darkened yard and up into the branches of the tree. "I thought," he cleared his throat. "I figured after what happened to Claire— I know you blame yourself but I don't know why. What happened— It's not your fault, Anna." He lowered his gaze to the hat in his hands. "Is that why you left?"

He took a deep breath and let it out slowly. "When no one would tell me anything about where you were I thought— Well, you know what I thought. I'm ashamed that I could have considered— But I know now it wasn't anything like that." There was hope in his voice.

He said nothing more and with the growing silence Anna felt her chest tighten painfully.

At last he threw the hat onto the swing and dropped to one knee before her. "I won't push you Anna, you know that. If you're not ready to get married then we'll wait. But for God's sake tell me what I did to make you run off without saying a word. I've been out of my mind--" He reached to take her hands from her lap and he suddenly went very still.

He placed a hand on either side of the swelling of her abdomen. "Oh, Anna." Tenderly he followed the curve of her belly with his hands. "My God, Anna, why didn't you tell me?" He swallowed hard. "It isn't—" He looked up into her face, his expression pleading. He lowered his gaze. "That's why you left."

He took a deep shuddering breath. "I'd have married you, Anna. We could still--" Something he saw in her expression when he glanced up must have told him this could not be. Time seemed to stop then a strangled sound tore from his throat. "Oh, Anna. Anna." He buried his face in her lap.

Anna felt him tremble then his shoulders began to shake and she realized he was silently crying. She ran her hands over his head, weaving her fingers through his hair again and again. "Sam, Sam." Her throat closed. She could say nothing more. There was nothing to say.

Finally, he grew still. He raised his head to face her. "I love you, Anna. Don't you understand? I love you."

She swallowed against the tightness. "I know, Sam. I know."

"Then tell me it isn't so. Tell me--"

She turned away. "Please don't. Please."

"It's his, isn't it?"

Anna had never heard such despair. It made her want to tear at her hair and cover herself with ashes. How could she do this to Sam? How could she?

He stood abruptly. "Does your father know?" He made a guttural sound in his throat. "Of course he does. That's why none of them would tell me anything. I should have known." He averted his eyes. "But I did know, didn't I?" He took a faltering step backward. "Do you still see him?"

"Stop it, Sam."

"Do you love him?"

She didn't answer. She couldn't answer.

The silence grew. Finally, he gave her a long searching look. "I see." He turned from her. "I see." And he walked away.

As Anna watched him go, she saw him stagger like a man drunk or suffering from a blow to the head.

"Sam." The whispered word rose on a sob.

CHAPTER 12
MAY, 1941

SALLY DAN TROTTED along at Joseph's heels as they made their way down a long narrow corridor of lumber stacks. When Joseph stopped to make a notation on the clipboard at a particular juncture, Sally Dan sat back on his haunches and waited. They had been making the tour of the yard for close on to two hours and in that time the dog hadn't once succumbed to the temptations of the men who called or whistled, the stray cat that lived in the nether regions of the yard, or the call of nature.

Sally Dan had picked out Joseph on the day he first wandered into the yard half starved and in bad need of worming. No one understood the attachment, except perhaps the dog. Joseph had made no particular attempt to endear himself to the part Jack Russell terrier and who-knew-what. The attachment remained a mystery to everyone, including Joseph's daughter. She had christened him Sally upon first seeing him and had declared him as her own. Joseph had taken the dog home a few times in an effort to establish him as the household pet but Sally Dan preferred the life of the yard. Each morning after these relocations Joseph would arrive at the yard to find Sally Dan patiently waiting by the locked gate.

It had been decided by the men that the name Sally might have a detrimental effect on the dog's psyche so they had added Dan to his title. He had been called Sally Dan since.

When they reached the yard office, Sally Dan sat outside the closed door while Joseph sat at his desk and stared out the window.

The intense green of the lone dogwood beside the building punctuated the sense of melancholy that came upon him more frequently these days. He didn't know why this should be so, only that it was. Other people reacted differently to spring, felt a sense of renewal, new beginning. In fact, he couldn't remember when he had last anticipated anything. Age, he decided. Or at least that's what his wife had suggested. Lately she had taken to following him with her eyes, as if fearful of what might happen if she let her guard down.

A light rap sounded against the milky glass of his door. Joseph straightened and faced forward as Harry Battle stuck his head around the door. "You busy, Joe? Got a minute?"

Harry was the only person who ever called him Joe. "Sure, Harry. What brings you to the mill today?"

Harry shuffled into the office and brought with him the smell of age, stale cigars, and Vicks Vapor Rub. He grunted. "Had to get away from Martha before she nursed me to death." He sat heavily in the chair across from Joseph and threw several envelopes onto the desk between them. "These were in my mail. Don't know why that girl didn't give them to you straight off."

That girl had been Harry's secretary for some forty-odd years and the old man had never once, in Joseph's memory, called her by her name.

Joseph picked up the three envelopes. They were all addressed by hand to Harrison Battle. "Business?"

"Yes. The first two, old timers looking for favors, jobs for a grandson and a nephew if I remember rightly. The other is an old customer from years back. Did business with the man of the house. Dead now."

Harry coughed violently around the unlit stub of a cigar. It was a deep, phlegmy spasm of coughing that left him short of breath and his face flushed. It took him some minutes to recover. His hand shook as he wiped a handkerchief across his mouth. He took a deep wheezing breath. "It's an old family, land poor. Need to sell some timber."

"We don't need it, Harry. We've got lumber we can't sell. There isn't even a market for pulp right now."

Harry nodded. "I know. I'm not asking you to buy, just see to it personally. Go down there and explain the situation." He rubbed his hands together, the papery thin skin making a dry rustling sound. "They wouldn't be asking if they weren't desperate."

Joseph frowned. He knew too well the plight of folks who had relied on the fact that if times got really bad there was always timber to sell. Battle's Mill had done well on that assumption and that need. This was the part of the business Harry had always handled, until his first heart attack two years ago. Now the thought of having to tell a desperate widow that he couldn't buy her timber made Joseph's stomach ache. Perhaps this was the source of his recent malaise, the reason Sarah watched him all the time and his son and daughter grew quiet whenever he entered a room.

"I know you don't like this, Joe."

"Yeah." Joseph couldn't bring himself to look at Harry. It was as if the older man was somehow responsible for the dilemma he now faced. It was an irrational thought. Harry had been a good father-in-law. Joseph had known and worked for him the greater part of his life. Harry had made it easy for him to shield himself from the unpleasant side of the acquisition of wealth. All the property and holdings that were Battle's Mill would some day come to Joseph through Harry's only child, Sarah. It was a little late in the game to start suffering pangs of a long dormant conscience. "Don't worry, Harry. I'll take care of it. Personally."

Harry rose unsteadily. "They're good people. I hate it. But we have to watch our backs. There's a war coming."

Joseph let that old dog lie. It was true their inventory was high and things were slow. Try as he might, he couldn't convince Harry that war was indeed coming, that they needed to be stockpiling for the demand it would bring.

Harry had spent too many years struggling to cover a payroll, to keep a roof over his family's head while he built his business. He wasn't going to risk his capital in these uncertain times.

Joseph picked up the letter on the top of the stack and stared at the return address. He felt his stomach drop and didn't hear Harry's parting comment.

SARAH WAS IN the kitchen at the sink when he got home. Water splashed over the early corn they would have for supper. She sang along with the Andrews Sisters on the radio and bobbed her red head with the music every now and then as she worked. He watched her as she swayed her slightly plump hips in time with the melody. She glanced up in surprise at the sound of the back door closing solidly. A blush tinted her fair cheeks a pale pink as she wiped her wet hands on her apron.

"Joseph. You're home early." A frown replaced the look of surprise and she reached up to the window ledge and turned off the radio. "Is anything wrong?"

"No." Joseph leaned against the door. This had been a mistake. In his frame of mind he should have gone anywhere but home where he was confronted with the irrefutable facts that were his life. He couldn't endure Sarah's concern so he lowered his gaze to the brick floor and said the first thing that came into his head. "Nothing much going on at the yard so I thought I'd come on home."

He glanced up to see her reaction. Her expression warned him that this would be chalked up as another sign of his *mood* and her scrutiny of him would intensify.

He crossed the room to the Frigidaire and took out a cold bottle of Pabst. This brought his wife to his side and for a moment he feared she might check his forehead for a temperature. He was a man who never came home early and a beer was reserved for hot Saturday afternoons when he had just finished mowing the lawn or cleaning the gutters. He had to get out of there. "I'll be in the workshop."

Sarah stood in the open doorway as he crossed the back yard. Joseph could feel her eyes on him and knew that her shoulders would be slumped with worry. As soon as he was out of sight she would be on the telephone to her mother to discuss this latest puzzling behavior.

Stairs ran up the outside of the shed he used for woodworking and storing gardening tools and supplies. He placed a hand on the weathered, splintered railing then slowly began to climb to the loft above. The cramped, airless space above the shed contained only three things: a Windsor chair with one of the spindles broken out of the back, a standing lamp with a torn shade, and an upright travel trunk. A layer of thick dust covered everything.

He couldn't remember the last time he had entered this hot, musty attic. He sat in the rickety chair and placed the sweating beer bottle on the floor then fished a key ring from his pocket and unlocked the trunk. There was no need to turn on the lamp. The dim light from the small window under the eave gave enough illumination for he knew the contents by heart—an old baseball mitt, his mother's Bible, three dog-eared novels and a Whitman's Sampler tin.

He removed the tin and sat back in the chair. With his thumb he traced along the edges of the container but he didn't open it. To do so would be to re-open the wound, to relive Sarah's betrayal all those years ago.

The tin and its contents had come into his possession quite by accident nearly six years before. Sarah had wanted more closet space and in the process of emptying the cupboards in the upstairs hallway he had discovered it. She had blushed and stammered when he confronted her. It hadn't been intentional, she had said. He had been so ill after his accident and she so concerned with his care that the letters had slipped her mind. She had forgotten and then it had been too late. And what did it matter now, she had asked. It was all so long ago.

Yes, so long ago. Twenty years now. Twenty long years since that spring on Carroll's Hill. And next week he would return there.

He had often wondered what Anna's life was like, if she ever thought of him. Before the discovery of the candy tin he had assumed her feelings had not matched his, that those five weeks had been nothing more than a mild infatuation, one she regretted. Now there was no way of knowing.

The cold of the beer bottle felt good in his hand and he drank down the remaining contents in one long pull. He studied the empty bottle before replacing it precisely in the wet ring on the dusty floor of the attic. He closed and locked the trunk but didn't return the candy tin to its place. Instead, he took it down the stairs and out to his truck where he placed it in the glove box. He was about to start the motor when his son Harry came running across the yard.

"Dad, Dad!" He hopped onto the running board and grinned at his father. "Did you come for my game?" The freckles stood out across the bridge of his nose and tiny beads of perspiration dotted his upper lip. "Coach is letting me pitch. For the first inning, anyway."

Joseph felt a pang of guilt. "Sure, Champ. I wouldn't miss the star pitcher in his first game."

"It's not the first game, Dad." Some of the enthusiasm faded from Harry's expression, a subtle reminder of all the games Joseph had missed over the years.

"No, but it's the first you're pitching."

His son's smile returned. "Can I drive the truck? Just to the ball park?"

Joseph glanced toward the kitchen windows where he could see Sarah looking out at them. "Not where your mother can see. She thinks thirteen's a little young to be driving." He motioned with his head. "Go tell her we're leaving and I'll let you drive from the end of the block."

"Thanks, Dad!" Harry jumped from the running board and ran into the house, the screen door banging behind him.

Joseph watched the pantomime as Harry informed his mother of their destination. The exchange took longer than it should have, and he knew Sarah was still struggling with the unsettling events of the afternoon. She followed after their son as he raced back across the yard to the truck. Joseph had the motor running by the time she reached his side.

"Daddy's on his way over. He was going to give Harry a ride and watch the game."

"Tell him we went ahead."

"He could ride with you."

And decide what was going on with me, Joseph thought. Well, not today. Besides, he had promised Harry he could drive. It was little enough to assuage his conscience. "Why don't you and Melissa come with him?"

Sarah studied his face then glanced at the workshop before looking down at the ground. She understood. After his discovery of the unmailed letters he had retreated to the refuge of the workshop. For months afterward he had spent his evenings there. A frown drew down the corners of Sarah's mouth. "What about supper?"

It was obvious the thought of another break in the routine of their lives was more than she could take in one day. She was very near tears. Joseph put the truck in gear. "We'll be home by seven." He backed out of the yard and into the street. Just as he rounded the corner he caught a glimpse of his father-in-law's Cadillac easing down the street toward their house. He popped the clutch and caught rubber. To hell with Sarah's worries. Let her father deal with them for a change.

JOSEPH SAT AT the kitchen table, the newspaper before him and a neat glass of whiskey in his hand. The controversy over the passage of Roosevelt's Lend Lease Plan held no interest for him tonight. He ignored the headlines as he nursed the whiskey with a growing sense of appreciation. It had been a long time since he had enjoyed the sharp, oaky flavor and he realized it was a taste the palate remembered without difficulty.

He had been contemplating his upcoming trip, deciding how long it would take for his letter to arrive, then allowing a couple of days before he appeared on their doorstep. On Mrs. Carroll's doorstep. The widow Carroll. Wednesday, he figured. He would leave in the morning on Wednesday and arrive by mid afternoon.

He wondered what had brought about Mrs. Carroll's need to sell timber. Had the crops failed? Did Anna's older brother still farm the place? Or was it inhabited solely by Luther Carroll's widow? Would he learn anything of Anna while he was there? He thought of the letters in the candy tin in the glove box of his truck and took a large gulp of whiskey.

A shadowy movement near the doorway caught his eye but he didn't look around. Sarah came slowly into the kitchen. She had made an effort to hide the fact that she had been crying. She wore a new gown with a matching duster, pale yellow and cool looking. She hesitated, her gaze on the bottle of whiskey next to the unopened newspaper. Finally, she looked at him.

"What's going on, Joseph?" She eased into a chair across from him and clasped her hands together on the table. "I don't know what to do when you're like this."

"Like what, Sarah?"

A half-sob caught in her throat. "Don't do this to me, Joseph. Please." She placed a trembling hand to her forehead, shading her eyes. "Can't you ever forgive me? Will she always be between us?"

Joseph watched his wife struggle for control and felt shame wash over him. Like him, she was no longer young but she remained soft and fresh and ever optimistic. Except when he was in one of his moods, except for that time six years ago. But, as she had said, all that was so long ago.

No one had made him marry Sarah Battle. For five years he had nursed his wounded heart. Then one day he had looked, really looked, into Sarah's eyes and saw the love there. What man could resist such a woman? A woman who had been brought up to anticipate a man's every need and cater to it ungrudgingly, with gratitude even. And, he had reasoned, why should he resist? Anna was gone from his life; passion had gone with her. Why not accept the comfort of one in whose eyes he saw only himself reflected? He hadn't wanted to go through life always alone. So he had asked and she had accepted.

Perhaps she truly had forgotten to mail his letters to Anna all those years ago. Who could say that if she had mailed them it would have made any difference.

"I don't mean to upset you, Sarah." He pushed the glass of whiskey away. "It's work. Nothing more."

"Is it? Tell me, Joseph. Tell me what's troubling you. Then perhaps I can believe you."

Joseph looked into her teary eyes and realized he wanted her to believe him. Suddenly it was terribly important that she not guess his true state of mind. He didn't want her to suspect what he planned to do. Until that moment he had not clearly known what he intended. Now he did.

He would return to Carroll's Hill and learn whatever he could of Anna. It had been the uncertainty that had kept him and Sarah in a kind of limbo since the discovery of her deception. He had felt all that was behind him with his decision to marry. And it had been. For a time there had been a contentment in his life, a pride in his wife and home, his children. Maybe, by going back once more, he could regain that peace of mind.

But how could he convince Sarah that his behavior of the afternoon and evening had been solely due to business, especially when they had never been completely honest with each other?

He had never really believed her when she said she had forgotten to mail his letters. It had been there in her expression the day he confronted her with them. Guilt. Though she hadn't opened the letters she had realized their significance when, unable to rise from his sickbed, he had asked her to mail them.

That she had manipulated his and Anna's fate was a wall between them, one he had felt no desire to scale. That, too, was part of their problem. He needed to let go of the past for both their sakes but he couldn't. Not until he made one more trip to Road's End.

"I have to go see one of your father's old customers." He lowered his gaze to the newspaper. "They want to sell and we can't buy. He wants me to go see them in person."

"Why? Why not simply write a letter?"

Joseph raised his eyes until he held hers with his steady regard. "It's the Battle way. When you take away a man's last hope you should be big enough to do it to his face."

"You hate that don't you, Joseph? The dirty end of Daddy's business."

He didn't answer.

"Maybe this customer isn't so desperate; maybe he simply wants to sell some timber." Her expression turned to one of pleading. "Maybe that's all it is."

"Nobody sells when prices are this depressed unless they're desperate."

"But that's going to change if there's war. You said so yourself. Maybe you can buy it. Especially if the price is low."

"Your father won't take the risk. It's his decision."

"Must you go then?"

"Your father asked."

Sarah didn't question this statement just as she didn't reproach Joseph over the whiskey. In her world such things didn't happen. If her father wished something it was done. If her husband drank whiskey at the kitchen table until all hours of the night, that was his right. "When will you go?"

"Next week. Wednesday, maybe."

"Will you be gone long?"

"Several days. I thought I'd make the rounds of some of the buyers, see if things might pick up soon, maybe go on down to Mobile."

He marveled at the casual way this thought voiced itself. It had only just formed in his mind. The trip to Road's End could be accomplished in one day, two at most. But he wanted the freedom to stay or go as he chose, something he hadn't done since his days as a bachelor. He wanted, quite simply, time to himself.

JOSEPH GLANCED INTO the rearview mirror. Sally Dan sat in the bed of the truck, his face to the wind as they drove through the heart of Bedlam. He wasn't sure why he had allowed the dog to accompany him but when Sally Dan jumped into the truck bed that morning Joseph hadn't seen fit to eject him.

He pulled into the Phillips 66 station and stopped beside the gas pump. The proprietor leaned against the storefront in a straight-backed chair. He brought the chair upright and stood to amble over to the pump.

"Afta'noon."

Joseph nodded. "Fill'er up."

The man took the cap off the gas tank and began to pump gas as he read the name of the mill on the side of the truck. He squinted at Joseph. "Fixin' to do some logging 'round these parts?"

Joseph shook his head. "Just passing through."

The man eyed him up and down. "Good piece from home." He pointed to the side of the truck.

Joseph nodded.

"Where ya headed?"

"Across the river."

"Where 'bouts 'cross the river?"

Joseph whistled to the dog and he jumped to the ground. "Not far." He turned on the water faucet to a steady trickle and Sally Dan lapped at it. "Got any cold Co-Colas?"

"Sure thing." He topped off the gas and replaced the nozzle in the pump housing. With a jerk of his head he motioned Joseph toward the store. "Come on in."

A long, wooden table, scarred and battered from years of use, served as the counter, an assortment of favored products lined up along the surface. Joseph took an ice cold bottle of Coca Cola from the ice box and selected a package of Planters Peanuts. "What do I owe you?"

The proprietor took a stub of a pencil from behind his ear and licked the point. He used a brown paper sack to figure on. "Two dollars and fifty-five cents."

Joseph inhaled the dry, stale air of the store while the man made change for a five dollar bill. "Thanks." He stuffed the change into his pocket and started from the building.

"You gone finish that Co-cola?"

Joseph dug a nickel out of his pocket. "I'm in a hurry. I'll take the bottle." He flipped the coin at the man who caught it with a deft flick of the wrist then followed after Joseph to stand in the open doorway watching. Joseph whistled Sally Dan into the truck and they headed down the road toward the Tombigbee River.

As the truck crested the high point of the bridge Joseph looked over the railing at the slow moving brown water. Rumor had it that a man who had worked on the construction of the bridge was forever buried in one of the pilings. He had slipped and fallen into the mold for the structure as the concrete was being poured and nothing could be done to retrieve the body from beneath the tons of sludge.

Joseph felt as if the later part of his married life had been a struggle against just such sludge. That if he ceased to fight he would lose the man he had been and become as permanent a fixture in the world of his wife and father-in-law as the man imprisoned in the piling of the bridge. And just as that poor soul had slipped into his fate, Joseph had also.

The town of Road's End came into view as he coasted down the far side of the bridge. A ferry had once served the local farm community as a means of transporting goods and people across the river in the days before the construction of the bridge. The town had grown up around it and for want of a better name the locals had called it by its location, at the road's end. The ferry had ceased to function with the arrival of the bridge which gave easy access to all that lay on the other side but no one saw any need to change the name of the town. It was Road's End to this day.

A man stood in front of the post office, mail in hand. He followed the progress of Joseph's truck with his eyes. A lean, white dog of indeterminate heritage barked and chased after them. A couple of men sat on the wide, sagging, front porch of Toxey's General Store. They also watched Joseph's passing. Nothing else stirred in the small community. The Baptist Church was closed up and the half dozen homes that lined either side of the county highway lay quiet in the afternoon heat.

Joseph didn't stop. His destination lay nearly two miles further. With a quickening pulse, he left the town behind and began to climb the series of low hills that would eventually lead to Carroll's Hill.

Little had changed in the years since his last trip. The timber that Battle's Mill had harvested twenty years before had been taken from deep within the property, away from the county road. It would have reseeded itself and be a mature stand of trees now. Not old growth like what he saw from the truck window but good saw logs. He wondered if Mrs. Carroll planned to harvest the same area. It would be a shame to cut the older forest. Some of the trees looked better than a hundred years old. There were some good hardwoods scattered among the pines. In good times the Carrolls stood to make a lot of money from those trees. But times were not good.

His stomach muscles tightened when the mailbox came into view. It wasn't marked in any way to indicate the residents of the house, unseen from the road. He shifted into low gear and turned into the driveway. After seventy yards it curved around a stand of pecan trees and the house came into view. Joseph slowed to a crawl as he scanned the scene before him.

It looked much the same, a little more tired with the paint peeling and the tin roof rusted in spots. The barn had been extended and a new, small outbuilding stood off to the right of it. Nothing moved except the slow swish of a cow's tail as she stood in the shade of the barn.

He pulled into the loop formed by the drive as it doubled back on itself and stopped the truck. From there he studied the house. The wide dog-trot had been enclosed with some sense of style. A large door was topped with a fanlight and long, narrow windows flanked the door. In the distance he could see that the fields were still under cultivation.

He stepped down from the truck and whistled to the dog. Sally Dan relieved himself on the tire and followed Joseph as he approached the house. When they reached the bottom of the steps the screen door opened.

Joseph's heart jumped into his throat. Before him stood a young woman, a smile on her face. It was as if he was reliving the past, as if he had somehow been transported back across the years. The hair was lighter and the color of her eyes was not blue but everything else was the same.

"Hello."

That voice, low and mellow, seared through him and weakened his knees like a straight shot of whiskey.

"Anna."

CHAPTER 13
MARCH, 1922

THE OXEN STRAINED in their harness and Joseph swore under his breath as his foot sank into the red, clay mud of the road. It sucked at his boot as he struggled to lift his foot free. He had worked some remote pieces of property in the years he had been with Mr. Battle but this was the most inaccessible he could remember.

The county road was so hilly that even if a work crew had touched it in the past year, which he doubted, it had done little good. The run-off of each rain rutted the surface into small valleys that caught at the wheels of the heavily laden wagons of equipment. Grunting and cursing, he and his men pushed from the rear while the oxen teams pulled against the dual forces of gravity and the clinging mud.

He looked up and saw the mailbox on the right of the road. It was unmarked but Joseph felt this had to be the place. Surely nothing existed beyond this remote hilltop.

"Hold up, Jack. Hold up there, Jonesy." The oxen came to a halt and Joseph looked up the driveway. He could see nothing ahead but pecan trees and crepe myrtle.

With a bandanna he wiped at his forehead and hands. It did little good. Both were covered with clay thrown up by the wheels of the cart. He looked back down the line at the men and animals that struggled up the last of the incline. One of the men came up beside him.

"This it?"

"I reckon. Can't hardly be much else beyond here."

"And thank God Almighty for it. I'm plumb tuckered."

Joseph stuffed the bandanna into his back pocket. "You wait here with the men."

As he made his way up the sloping curve of the driveway Joseph tried to stomp some of the muck free of his boots. He stopped when the white house came into view.

It was a big, old house with a central dog-trot. The tin roof was high pitched with a deep porch all around to keep the sun out. The way it sat astride the very top of the hill spoke of permanence. At one time there had no doubt been money, too.

At the steps he hesitated, looked down at his mud-caked boots, then rapped against the handrail.

Giggles and the rush of feet accompanied two dim figures who ran from a door at the far end of the dog-trot and stopped in the center of the large opening. The two girls wore long aprons over straight cotton shifts. The smaller one giggled again.

The first thing he noticed was that they were barefooted. The second was that they weren't girls at all. In fact, the taller of the two, with her dark blonde hair and deep blue eyes, was very much a woman. Neither of them spoke.

Joseph cleared his throat. "I'm from Battle's Mill. With the logging crew." He suddenly remembered his manners and pulled his hat from his head.

The taller woman turned her face slightly away from him, not quite in profile. She observed him with a slanting look. "Hello."

The sound of her voice surprised him. The depth of it didn't match the lightness of her hair, eyes and complexion. It held a deep, mellow note, like well seasoned whiskey.

Heavy footfalls sounded against the wooden floor and a tall man, his blonde hair swept back from his forehead, appeared to tower over the two women. He glared at Joseph. Mr. Battle followed behind him to join the trio.

"Ah, Joseph. You've arrived. Everything all right?"

"Yessir. Crew's down the road."

"Good, good. Mr. Carroll's son will show you where to set up. It's a ways off still. A road will have to be cleared."

Joseph figured the man with Mr. Battle had to be Luther Carroll. He shifted from one foot to the other as he endured the blatant scrutiny of the tall, erect master of the house. Luther eyed him from head to toe and the corners of his mouth turned down even further. Joseph felt the tension in his shoulders ease when Carroll's cold regard was diverted by a giggle.

Luther Carroll's head snapped toward the sound and for the first time gave notice to the two women. His cold, blue eyes flicked down them and up again as his face reddened. "Anna! What do you think you're doing?" His nostrils flared. "Parading before strange men like a slattern!" His hand drew back so swiftly that Joseph was unprepared for the slap when it was delivered.

The print of his hand on the blonde's cheek stood out starkly against her pale face but she didn't cry out. A fleeting look of astonishment gave way to no expression at all. Her companion's eyes rounded with fright and she fled back down the hallway.

"Get in the house!" Carroll's voice shook, whether with rage or something else Joseph couldn't tell for Mr. Carroll's expression was also one of astonishment or perhaps regret.

Joseph watched Anna turn and walk stiff-backed down the hall. His gaze traveled from her blonde head to her bare feet. She had small feet and slender ankles.

When he looked away from her retreating figure he found himself under the most malevolent scrutiny he had ever experienced. Luther Carroll eyed him with a look of cold, unguarded hatred. It took a moment to realize Mr. Battle was introducing him.

"--my best man. He'll oversee the crew and keep them in line." Mr. Battle smiled down the steps at him. "Joseph's my right arm."

Luther Carroll looked down his long, straight nose at Joseph but he spoke to Mr. Battle. "Keep that lot away from the house. I've women up here.

Decent women. I won't have the likes of that," he nodded in Joseph's direction, "slipping around my back door."

The smile faded from Mr. Battle's face and his expression hardened. "Don't you worry about my men, Mr. Carroll. They keep to camp. And Joseph here is like my own son. You deal with me, you deal with Joe."

Luther Carroll made no response, he simply looked from Joseph to Mr. Battle and back again before turning into the house.

Harry Battle's cheeks flamed red as he came down the steps. "What that man needs is a good kick in the pride."

Joseph grinned. "Forget it, Mr. Battle. The likes of that don't bother me none."

"Doesn't bother me."

"Yessir."

Harry slapped him on the shoulder. "Come on, son. Let's go see about the boys." He grinned. "Wait 'til you see this stand of timber. The trees are so thick a hummingbird couldn't fly through it sideways. We're going to make a killing off the hardwood alone."

Joseph recognized the false bravado in Mr. Battle's voice. Few people knew that Battle's Mill survived from day to day by the sheer force of Harry Battle's will. Many a payday had been covered by a frantically arranged loan from the local bank at a usurious rate. The big lumber companies had tried to squeeze all the independents, the *wood-peckers*, out of the business. But with the introduction of trucks to the industry, the independents could now compete. Areas once too remote to have been timbered and transported by the traditional means of water and rail could now be marketed. And that was when men like Luther Carroll turned to men like Harry Battle.

More than one such landowner had looked down his long, aristocratic nose at the man who was like a father to Joseph. Harry always shrugged it off. On such occasions he would remind Joseph that few people could afford such pride in these hard times. When banks began closing their doors to their customers in '21, it squeezed the mighty as well as the lowly.

A door banged and both men looked back toward the house. A tall, dark-haired man came down the steps toward them. He appeared to be several years older than Joseph's own twenty-two years. They waited for him to join them.

"Joseph, this is Reuben Carroll, Mr. Carroll's son. He's going to show us where to clear the road."

Reuben glanced at him then stared into the distance. "We'll skirt the fields for the first part of the way. After that, it gets rough."

Joseph thought of the three day trip he and the men had just endured. It had taken a dozen crossings on the ferry to get everyone and everything across the river. Two of the oxen had jumped from the platform near mid-stream. Joseph had jumped in after them without thinking and nearly drowned when his boots filled with water. Like the docile creatures they were, the oxen placidly swam in the wake of the ferry while he lay with his head over the side puking. His stomach growled in hunger. "How far to the actual site you reckon?"

"Three miles as the crow flies." Reuben jerked his thumb over his shoulder.

Joseph looked in the direction indicated and saw the woman named Anna running beyond the barn toward a distant field that was just greening with new growth. Her bare feet seemed to skim the earth and her fair hair blew out behind her as the loose shift billowed around her slender figure. As he watched, he realized she held something in her hand.

THEY MADE CAMP on a low rise at the far edge of the cotton field. It hadn't taken much effort to clear the few seedling pines and scrub oak. The men and animals were too tired to do more. Reuben hovered until they finished setting up for the night. He reluctantly agreed the site would serve until the road to the desired stand of trees was finished, but he tersely warned Joseph to keep the men and animals clear of the fields.

The first tent they pitched was the cook tent. The aromas from their supper of roasted chickens lingered in the air though the embers of the fire pit had long since died. Ester hated cooking over an open pit but she would have to manage until the permanent camp was established. As much as the men liked their meals served up hot, none of them were willing to unload the heavy, black, over-sized, iron cook stove for the few days it would take to clear a road.

The men had washed up in a small creek fifty yards downhill from the campsite, eaten their fill, and although the sky was just beginning to streak with reds and pinks, they were settling into their bedrolls. Life on the road was hard and they slept when they could. It was only the first week of March and the sweet spring air was dry and cool, too cool yet for mosquitoes or redbugs.

Joseph took his bedroll to the base of an oak several yards from the campsite. He positioned it so he could watch the western sky as the late afternoon began to blur with the first signs of the approaching dusk. This was his favorite time of day. He leaned against the tree trunk and rolled a cigarette. As he smoked, he surveyed the landscape. Across the rolling cotton fields the homestead stood out on the rise of the hill, crowned in a slant of fading sunlight. It looked unreal somehow, as if nothing could be quite that perfect. The thought spoiled his enjoyment of the landscape so he rose to his feet and wandered down to the creek.

A gnarled old water oak disrupted the path of the small, clear creek and a pool had formed amid the tangle of roots. Here, he and his men had bathed in the natural basin. The silt had resettled after their visit and he could see the dark shapes of tops of the overhead trees reflected on the surface of the water. He surveyed the surrounding area and his attention settled on a narrow path that led away from the pool on the other side. He waded across and followed it.

Halfway up the embankment wild ferns grew over the trail and as Joseph continued he felt a drop in temperature as the vegetation became denser, the trees taller. The density gave way to a spacious corridor of tall sentinels that towered overhead.

Silence enveloped him and the thick carpet of pine needles absorbed his footfalls. The trees were the largest he had ever seen. Virgin longleaf pine. Some of them had to be over two hundred, maybe three hundred years old. Their sheer size had produced a natural selection that smothered out all the scrub growth and the wiregrass that was the natural companion of the longleaf.

Far overhead where the branches didn't quite meet, Joseph could see small patches of a sky purpling with the coming dusk. The tree trunks lurked in the thickening shadows and he turned to retrace his steps. That's when he saw it.

The white of the page seemed to draw the remaining light to it. He knelt beside the book and lifted it from the forest floor. Darkness came down rapidly around him and he could make nothing of the words. With a gentle slapping sound he closed it and turned in the direction of the camp.

By the light of a lantern he read the cover page. Written in a neat, strong script were the words, *For Anna with deepest affection, Sam.* He read the short introduction then the first of the poems. They didn't make much sense to him. He flipped through the book, stopping to read a line or two here and there. Finally he raised his eyes toward the homestead. Light fell from the windows. Near the barn a pale shadow moved about illuminated by the glow of a lantern. Someone was in the barnyard.

He hesitated then rose to his feet. It probably wasn't her but if it was he could use the book as an excuse. There could be no harm in that. Mr. Battle wouldn't object. Mr. Carroll wouldn't have to know. If it was one of the men or a field hand he would simply leave the book where it could be found.

Though the distance was well over a quarter mile, his long gait covered it in short order. He stood beyond the circle of light and watched, suddenly unsure what had compelled him to be where he wasn't wanted, where he wasn't supposed to be.

Anna was humming under her breath, a patriotic tune he had heard on the radio. Light from a kerosene lantern formed a warm bubble around her. She milked a cow in one of the stalls attached to the side of the barn, her forehead leaning into the side of the animal's belly.

She must have sensed his presence for she looked up and stared into the night.

"Hello," he said.

"Jesus, Mary and Joseph!" The stool flew backwards as she sprang to her feet. She snatched up the lantern and held it high to see who was there.

"Didn't mean to scare you."

She pushed a lock of hair behind her ear. "What did you expect? Sneaking up like that!"

Joseph didn't know what to say so he simply stood there.

"Well, what do you want?"

He felt his throat close on the words he had intended to say. He felt unbalanced, out of his element. He lowered his gaze to the straw strewn stall unable to form words to answer her question. He simply shrugged.

"Didn't you hear my father? He'd like nothing better than to find you here."

Joseph could tell that the prospect of his discovery intrigued her and he raised his eyes to meet her steady regard. She lowered the lantern and moved a half-step closer. He held up the book. "I found this."

Anna looked at it and recognition spread across her features. "My book." She frowned. "Where did you find it?"

"In the woods."

Her eyes bored into him as if she would look through him. Then a hint of panic or fright, maybe, caused them to widen. "The old forest? That's where you found it?"

"Yes."

"What were you doing there? No one said--" Her voice wavered. "You're not—you're not going to log it?"

"No." He shrugged. "Least wise, that's not what Mr. Battle says."

She turned her profile to him and was silent for a moment. "You're not afraid? Of the old places?"

"Old places? You mean that section where I found the book?"

Her gaze dropped to the book then back up at him. "Most people are afraid of it. They say the spirits of the Indians and runaway slaves inhabit it."

"You trying to say it's haunted?"

"Maybe."

Again Joseph shrugged. "I guess it's kinda spooky, the way there's no sound 'cept just the wind high up."

"Don't go there anymore."

There was a note of accusation in her tone and, like the look her father had given him earlier, it angered him and grounded him. He suddenly felt himself, a man who knew his abilities and his limitations but a man nonetheless. "It's just woods. Look, you want this book or not?"

Anna reached for it but he maintained his hold an instant before relinquishing it.

"The night air would have ruined it. The dew and all." He didn't want to be angry with her because her opinion of him suddenly mattered. "I could've just left it there."

Anna clasped the collection of Emily Dickinson's poetry to her chest. "You're right and I thank you. It's just that that particular place is— It's special, private."

Joseph felt the heat rise in his face.

She glanced away then back. "I didn't mean to give offense." She hesitated. "How did you know it was mine?"

"Your name's wrote in it."

She went very still. "You read it?" She stared at the bedding of the stall.

He could tell the thought offended her and the feeling of defensiveness grew. "I can read. How else was I to know whose it was? Besides, it don't—doesn't make much sense. A lot of talk about Shades and dying."

She ran a finger along the spine of the book. "You think she writes about death?"

"Don't you?"

"No. Not always.

He had her interest again and that made his heart give a little flutter. If only he could keep her talking. "What then?"

For a moment he thought she wouldn't answer but finally she looked up at him. "Freedom, I think." Her words held a note of uncertainty. She drew her brow into a frown and hesitated. "Yes, I think she writes about being free." A smile touched her lips and she turned back toward the cow patiently chewing its cud and lifted the bucket of milk.

The silence grew between them, stretching painfully across the seconds. Joseph knew he should leave, there was nothing more to be said. But for some reason he couldn't bring himself to make that move. "You think death is freedom?"

Her brow furrowed then smoothed again. "I hadn't thought of it that way. Not exactly."

He waited for her to say something more but she simply stood there studying him. He endured her silence and watched her in turn.

"Why did you come?"

He stared straight into her dark blue eyes. "I hoped it was you." He glanced away then back. "This afternoon—I felt bad about—well, what happened on the porch."

She turned her head and watched him with that funny slanting look. "Don't." Her shoulder lifted in a dismissive gesture. "My father isn't like that." She started to turn toward the house then looked back. "He doesn't know what to do since the bank failed. It's like--" she shook her head.

Joseph felt his face darken with anger. "He had no cause."

"You don't understand. He doesn't mean it. In fact, he's never hit me before. Ever." She paused. "You're a strange one."

He nodded. "I suppose."

She laughed, a deep, delicious sound. It sent a shiver over him.

"Chocolate cake."

Anna's eyebrows shot up. "What?"

"Your laugh. It puts me in mind of chocolate cake."

She laughed again.

"Chocolate's my favorite."

The laughter died away but didn't leave her face entirely. "You are the strangest man."

"Why, because I like chocolate cake?" He couldn't repress a grin.

"No." She turned the book over in her hand and studied the cover. "Because you have the imagination to associate it with— I don't know. Men don't usually think that way. I didn't expect--"

"You didn't expect a dumb hick to know when something is beautiful."

Color washed over her throat and face but it was a blush of pleasure. "Is it?"

"What?"

"Beautiful."

"You know it is." He crossed his arms over his chest and for the first time felt himself to be on familiar ground. A slow smile lifted the corner of his mouth. "You know you are."

A rustling sounded in the corncrib at her back and Anna took a step sideways and glanced around.

"Rats."

She nodded but looked toward the house. "You should go."

"Will I see you tomorrow?"

"Why would you think you would see me tomorrow? Or any other day for that matter?" The amusement had faded from her voice. What he heard now was surprise and perhaps a little interest.

Indeed, what excuse could he offer? He nodded toward the book. "I thought you might want to teach me to make some sense out of what it says there. You know, freedom and all."

"I don't think so."

"Why? Because of your father?"

"I do as I please." She shifted her grip on the pail of milk. Without so much as a glance she passed within a hair's breadth of him and marched across the muck of the barnyard toward the house.

ANNA BRUSHED HER hair as she stared into the mirror over the washstand. Claire yawned and slipped between the sheets of the bed situated under the stairwell that led to the attic. "Hurry up, Anna, and come to bed. I'm dying to know what you saw."

"What do you mean?"

"Oh, don't try that with me. I know you ran off to our lookout in the pecan tree to see what they were up to." Claire hugged her knees to her chest. "Isn't it the most exciting thing? I mean, all those men going to live right here on your door step for weeks and weeks." She giggled. "I'm so glad you invited me to stay the week. Won't we have fun spying on them?"

"Well, I don't know about spying."

"One of them's real cute. He came near the chicken coop when I was feeding up. Looking for the pump to draw some water for the mules, he said."

"Since when did you take to feeding the chickens, Claire Milkisen? As many times as you've slept under this roof you've never set foot in the pen. Afraid of getting doo between your toes!"

"Shhh! Your pa'll hear." Claire looked anxiously toward the door. "Put out the light and come to bed so we can talk."

With a practiced deftness, Anna plaited her hair into a loose braid, lowered the wick in the lamp and blew out the flame. She climbed into the narrow three-quarter bed beside her cousin and they giggled as they snuggled down into the feather mattress.

"What did you think of him?" Anna whispered close to her cousin's ear.

"Well, he has big brown eyes, the most perfect straight teeth and blonde hair--"

"Blonde hair? Who're you talking about?"

"The fella with the mules. Who'd you think?"

"Joseph."

"The fella that cost you a smack on the cheek?"

"I didn't get the smack because of him."

"Well, why else?" Claire bunched the pillow and rolled onto her back. "If you ask me he wasn't worth it. At least not that you could tell, all covered like he was with red clay."

Anna chuckled deep in her throat. "He washes up well enough."

The room fell silent. Claire rose onto her elbow and looked down at her cousin in the pale light of the half moon. "Get that notion out of your head right this minute, Anna Carroll."

"What notion?"

"Hankering after the likes of that. Mama was right. That restlessness of yours is gonna get you in trouble. Some things soap and water can't wash away, Anna. Handsome or not, these men are a rough sort. Your papa would strap both of us raw if he even thought--"

"Just listen at you. One minute you've got goose bumps because one of them dared come near you and the next you're afraid of them."

Claire plopped back onto the pillow and hugged her arms across her chest. "It's exciting and frightening all at the same time, isn't it? They're so— Oh, I don't know. Besides, there's Sam."

Anna frowned in the dark. "Yes, there's Sam."

Claire sighed. "You make it sound like a curse. Lord knows half the women in Road's End would give just about anything to have Sam a'callin'." She giggled. "Mama says if it wasn't for Papa, Sam Stone could park his shoes under her bed anytime."

Anna laughed. "She never did."

"Swear to God. She and Aunt Lena were shelling snow peas out on the back porch and didn't know I was listening. You should have seen Aunt Lena bobbing her head in agreement."

The image of Claire's Aunt Lena in all her ungainly glory made both young women burst into a spasm of giggles. Lena had been cursed with the Milkisen's strong family characteristics of a long neck, prominent Adam's apple, and receding chin. To Anna's mind, she very much resembled a chicken scrambling after its feed when she let herself go to the thrill of a good gossip.

Their giggles subsided and Anna lay in the dark considering Claire's words. She did care for Sam, very much. By all rights they should be planning a wedding. She had been out of school for a whole year, idling away her time between chores and the social obligations of the small community. So why did she feel as if she might burst out of her skin at any moment? Why did the prospect of being the wife of one of Road's End's most upstanding citizens leave her with the urge to run mindlessly until she couldn't draw breath? His love sometimes frightened her. It felt so fierce.

As if reading her thoughts, Claire broke the silence. "Why don't you want to marry Sam?"

Anna didn't respond immediately. She stared up into the darkness trying to decide if there was an answer to her cousin's question. "It's not that I don't want to marry Sam. It's just that I want something else, something more."

"What?"

"I don't know. Sometimes I think he loves me too much."

Claire sighed in exasperation. "Loves you too much? Will you just listen to yourself. How can someone love you too much?"

Anna thought of her father, the soul wrenching way he sometimes looked at her mother when she was unaware. That longing to be loved in return burned away at him day and night. Did Sam love her that intensely? That love had made her mother unkind. Anna sometimes thought she didn't even realize how her indifference tore at her father's heart.

Claire sighed again. "Isn't that what every woman wants? To be loved like that." She settled more deeply into the mattress. "Honestly, Anna, sometimes you say the strangest things. It has to be more than that."

"Maybe." Anna yawned. "Maybe I just want to be free."

"Free? Of what? To do what?" Claire's voice rose an anxious notch. "You're a woman, Anna. Women don't want to be free." She pulled the sheet more tightly around her shoulders. "You don't know how lucky you are. Me, I'll probably be an old maid. There isn't a man within three counties I'm not related to." She grew silent. When she spoke her words held a soft note of pleading. "Women *want* to be married."

Anna knew her words fell far short of expressing what she felt. The truth remained that she didn't know why she couldn't commit herself to Sam Stone. Every time she was with him she wanted to be his wife, truly wanted it. But the minute he left her sight, anxiety settled over her and the prospect of spending the rest of her life in domestic bliss in Road's End frightened her to the point of fainting.

She swallowed against the panic and focused on the need in her cousin's voice. "Well, there's always the handsome blonde with the perfect teeth. Wonder why he came all the way to the house looking for the pump to fetch water when there's a creek no more than fifty yards from their campsite?" She goosed Claire in the ribs.

Claire giggled. "Stop it, Anna. He probably didn't know about the creek."

"Oh, yes, he did. They all washed in it."

"They didn't!" Claire inhaled sharply. "Anna, *you* didn't!"

Anna snuggled down into the mattress and didn't respond. Her eyelids drooped and she yawned.

Claire yawned, also. "Besides, they're not our kind. Rough men like that. Uneducated. Living on the road." She turned her face toward the window and stared sleepily at the moon. "Common."

Yes, Anna thought, common but exciting.

FOR THREE DAYS Joseph and the crew cleared a road toward the logging site. Each night after everyone had washed up and eaten he took the dog-eared novel, *The Adventures of Huckleberry Finn*, and retreated to the creek bank. It had been given to him by Sarah, Mr. Battle's daughter, before they started out on this job.

He had known her since she was a little bitty thing for it seemed he had worked for Mr. Battle all his life. For months now she had been helping him with his reading, gently correcting his grammar and generally polishing his rough manners, something his pride wouldn't have tolerated for anyone else.

Patiently he picked out the words in the fading light as he waited, hoping that Anna's curiosity would overcome her better judgment. For three days there had been no sign of her on the path on the other side of the creek.

The road was nearly finished. Felled and lopped saplings created a roadbed so the heavy trucks and wagons wouldn't bog down in the aftermath of the spring rains. Monday the campsite would be moved. The men would build sheds and set up the large band saws on roughly constructed stands and Bummer carts would bring the felled trees out of the forest to the new site. The softer pines would be milled on the spot but the hardwoods would be hauled off on logging trucks to Camden for finishing. Once the operation started Joseph wouldn't leave the camp for weeks.

He closed the book with a soft slap and settled more firmly against the trunk of the water oak. He hadn't expected to see Anna after their encounter in the barn but past successes with a certain kind of woman had caused him to hope.

Bigger fool he. She wasn't like anyone he had ever known. High born. Haughty. Not for him. Mr. Battle wouldn't approve. Her father certainly wouldn't. Apparently, neither did she. But the thought of the slender turn of her ankle and an elusive something in the depths of her blue, blue eyes caused him to stir uncomfortably. It wasn't the same stirring he had felt for other women, that immediate, easily sated response to a fragrance, the turn of a cheek, the trill of a laugh. This was something altogether different and for that reason alone, uncomfortable.

He rose and forded the creek. His feet carried him along the path to that ancient place, to Anna's place. He hadn't intended to intrude on her domain again but he couldn't help himself. He wanted one more look at it, to see what she saw, to try to understand its importance to her. For it was important to her. He knew that much from her reaction.

The cool descended on him as he wandered among the giant trunks in the shadowy world of the trees. Even at mid-day little sun would penetrate to the forest floor for though the tree branches only occasionally overlapped, they grew so tall and uniformly that the ground could never see more than brief snatches of sunlight. High above, the breeze soughed in the pines, whispering in an unintelligible language.

Joseph felt ill at ease, an intruder. The mystery of the place would not be revealed to him. Not today. The ancient trees kept their own counsel and any hopes he had harbored of running into Anna vanished. Joseph made his way back to camp. Tomorrow he would take the company truck and ride to Road's End to telegraph Mr. Battle about their progress. On the way, he would report in to Mr. Carroll. Just as a courtesy.

JOSEPH STRUGGLED WITH the top button of his best broadcloth shirt. He hadn't worn it in over a month, a month in which hard physical labor had enhanced the muscles of his arms and shoulders. The tent flap opened and the bright light of mid-day pierced the dim interior. Lucky stepped through the opening and stopped with a low whistle when he saw Joseph.

"What's the occasion? I ain't seen you so spruced up in a month of Sundays."

The button slipped through the buttonhole and Joseph smoothed the front of his shirt as he peered into the small rectangle of mirror that served both men for their toiletry. He wished for a fresh collar but resigned himself to doing without.

"Just going into town to telegraph the boss, let him know we'll be moving camp tomorrow." He ran a hand over freshly shaved cheeks and frowned at his reflection.

Lucky watched his preening from the corner of his eye as he rolled a cigarette. He licked the paper, sealing in the tobacco, and dangled the finished product from his lips before turning his full regard toward Joseph.

"Uh huh." He struck a match against the denim of his britches' leg and held it to the cigarette as he inhaled deeply. "Don't imagine you'll be looking in at the big house." Although he didn't smile, the small lines around his eyes crinkled with amusement.

Joseph felt himself coloring. "Just to speak to Mr. Carroll. He'll want to know how we're getting on."

Lucky took the wash basin from the makeshift table of saw horses and boards and threw its contents through the open tent flap. "I think I'll ride along with you.

Joseph stared at him as he poured fresh water from the bucket into the basin. "I don't have time to wait around for you. I need to get on into town."

Lucky splashed water over his face and hair. "Where's the fire? It's Sunday and there's nobody up at the house 'cept that colored woman. I understand our Mr. Carroll is a Justice of the Peace and an upstanding pillar of the community. They'll all be at the church for a good half hour yet." He began to lather up his face. "Besides, the telegraph office don't open 'til after dinner."

"And why are you suddenly so anxious to go into town? It ain't nothing more than a squat in the road."

"Squat or no, it's more'n there is in these woods." He grinned over his shoulder at Joseph. "Besides, you never know what undiscovered beauties there are in these little hick places."

"Just what're you up to?"

Lucky looked Joseph up and down. His grin widened. "Same as you, I reckon, 'cept the one I'm hankerin' after has red hair instead of yellar."

Joseph's forehead creased. "And how would you be knowing anything about that?"

Lucky went about shaving as he answered. "The bee always finds the sweetest flower."

"You've been up at the house, ain't you?"

Lucky chuckled.

Joseph's face reddened with anger. "You know how Mr. Battle feels about such as that, Lucky. He'll fire you sure if he finds out. He don't like none of his crew mucking about at the houses where we set up."

Lucky washed the remaining soap from his face and dried it with a limp scrap of towel. "Who says I've been up at the house? I've been keeping to camp like everybody else."

"Then how come you know so much about what's going on up there? How do you even know there's a redhead in these parts?"

Lucky took a shirt from the cardboard suitcase at the end of his cot. "I ain't blind. And like I said, the bee always finds the brightest flower."

"Here you mean? She came here?"

He grinned and cocked an eyebrow at a rakish angle. "Not *here* exactly. Let's just say the young lady enjoys walking in the woods."

"Mr. Battle ain't just gonna fire you, he's gonna kill you."

Lucky laughed good-naturedly. "Don't you worry about Mr. Battle, Joseph. What he don't know won't hurt him."

Joseph turned toward the opening in the tent. "It's not Mr. Battle I'm worried about."

Lucky followed after him, pulling on his shirt as he went. They took the truck and skirted along the edge of the fields toward the house.

Joseph had already begun to regret this sudden impulse as he stood for some minutes after he had knocked before a small, gnarled, colored woman came along the dog-trot toward them. She looked beyond them to the truck parked in the drive and drew herself up to the full of her height.

"What you want?"

"I'd like to see Mr. Carroll." Joseph stood with his hat in his hand.

The woman stared coldly from one to the other of them. "Well, get on 'round the back then. He'll be along bye the bye."

As she retreated back down the dog-trot Joseph heard her mumbling under her breath about white trash and trouble. He clenched his jaw and turned toward the front steps. Lucky, rolling another cigarette as he went, followed after him to the rear of the house.

Behind the main house stood the kitchen that emitted smells of fried chicken, greens, and bread baking. Beyond the kitchen a workbench encircled a sprawling live oak. From the look of it, it was used for skinning and cleaning game. They continued on to the garden gate and watched as Reuben labored on his knees at the far end of the enclosure.

"Looks like one of the family ain't so religious." Joseph rested his forearms on the fence.

"He's the only one not scared of the old man. Not since he came back from the war, anyway."

"You're just chock full of information, ain't you."

"Claire told me."

"Claire, is it?" Joseph eyed his companion and wondered if he should wire Mr. Battle about the obvious familiarity between Lucky and a member of the family. It was his job to keep the men in line. But wasn't he here in this very spot for the same reason?

Damn Lucky. Women were crazy about him and for the life of him, Joseph couldn't see why. For all his strength Lucky was a slight man whose lack of stature was emphasized by what Joseph could only term as a limberness of the spine. And in the honky tonks he could all but make love to a woman on the dance floor.

Joseph was still worrying over the problem of Lucky when he heard a car motor as it labored up Carroll Hill. He ran a hand over his hair. Lucky grinned at his actions, causing the heat to rise in Joseph's face. The two of them started toward the house when the cook appeared in the doorway of the kitchen with two steaming plates in her hands.

"Might as well eat while you wait. He," she jerked her head in the direction of the main house, "don't do no bizness on a empty stomach."

They accepted the offering and sat on a bench that ran beside the kitchen door. They heard the car come to a halt on the other side of the house and Joseph could hear the heat in Mr. Carroll's voice even though he couldn't make out his words. Sitting as they were, looking down the dog-trot and through the house, he watched Luther Carroll's approach. As he mounted each of the front steps, the sun at his back made his image appear to levitate.

Joseph felt his stomach muscles clinch as he realized he had made a mistake in coming here. As quickly as the thought occurred to him, he pushed it aside. He had business here, legitimate business. He set his plate on the bench beside him and stood. Once inside the open hallway that divided the house, Luther Carroll stopped and fixed his gaze on Joseph.

Even from this distance Joseph knew what his reception would be. It was there in the rigid manner of Carroll's stance, in the way he turned to the slender, graying woman at his side and silenced her with a glance.

The woman walked through the house to the end of the hallway, casting a glance at Joseph and his companion before calling across to the kitchen, "Addie Mae, Mr. Carroll will have his dinner in ten minutes."

She was a beautiful woman. Joseph could see the daughter in her face and pale complexion. And the eyes, those indigo blue eyes were Anna's eyes. But where Anna had blonde hair like her father, her mother was dark headed.

She caught a small rope attached to the clapper of a bell mounted on the wall and rang it twice before turning back into a room on the right side of the house.

Luther Carroll took off his hat and placed it with careful, controlled movements on the bureau that stood between two doors to his right. He adjusted the stiff white cuffs of his shirt where they protruded from the sleeves of his coat before he cleared his throat and approached the rear of the house and the two men waiting there.

Reuben appeared in the small alleyway between kitchen and house just as his father came to a stop at the top of the steps. He glanced in Joseph and Lucky's direction with a brief nod and began washing up at a pump beside the kitchen door.

Lucky looked up from his nearly empty plate, his mouth stuffed with food. He wiped the back of his hand across his mouth and stood beside Joseph.

"What are you doing here? Didn't I make myself clear that you're to keep away from this house?"

"I needed to speak to you about the timber, Mr. Carroll."

"Good God, man! Do you know what day of the week this is?"

It's Sunday, Mr. Carroll. And I wouldn't have called except--"

"There are no exceptions. If Battle needs to discuss business with me then let him do so, not some," he looked Joseph up and down, "ignorant, back-woods--"

"I thought you'd like to know where things stood. We're ready to move--"

"Enough." Carroll's chin rose a notch higher. "I refuse to sully my hands like a common money-changer on the Lord's day."

Every muscle in Joseph's body was taunt as a wire. "The boss expects me to send him a telegram today. He needs to know how we're getting on with the job."

Carroll stared at him. "You impudent fool. Battle's *job* exists only at my discretion and it can also disappear at my discretion. The timber is mine to harvest or not."

Pride goaded Joseph and his voice seemed to have a mind of its own. "But the money is Mr. Battle's." He was now so angry he was beyond prudence, angry that he had been deemed beneath contempt, beneath even the notice of the members of this household. "And he says how and when we conduct business."

Carroll started down the steps, his voice cracking with rage. "Get away from this house before I take a whip to you!"

Reuben stepped forward and caught his father's arm but his attention was focused on Joseph. "Best go on about your business." His regard was as unheated as if he were discussing the weather. "The telegraph office opens at one on Sundays."

Joseph's fists were clenched at his side, he had been ready to spring. He suddenly realized Lucky was pulling at his arm. Without another word he jerked free of Lucky's grasp and stormed down the alleyway and along the side of the house toward the truck. His fingers trembled as he turned the starter. Lucky jumped onto the seat beside him and hooted with laughter as he banged the passenger door closed.

"Bastard." Joseph thumped his palm against the steering wheel and the truck jerked forward as he let out on the clutch.

THEY ROARED INTO town and sent up a spray of loose pebbles as they skidded to a halt in front of Toxey's General Store. A cloud of dust rose and settled around the truck as they surveyed their surroundings.

"This is a one-horse town if I ever saw one." Lucky pushed his hat onto the back of his head. "Wonder what folks in these parts do for fun on a Saturday night?"

Joseph was still in a temper. He knew he would be in trouble with Mr. Battle when he learned of his confrontation with Luther Carroll. His only response was a grunt.

Lucky chuckled. "You'd best get over that gal, Joseph. I see nothing but trouble on the horizon over that skirt." He suddenly straightened in his seat and adjusted his hat as he grinned broadly. "And speaking of which--"

Joseph looked around from his contemplation of the storefront and followed Lucky's gaze. He, too, sat up straight. Standing on the front porch of a house not fifty yards from where they sat were Anna and Claire. They came down the front steps and turned in the direction of the store. Between them walked a tall man with sandy hair. As he watched, the man took Anna's hand and laced her fingers with his. The taste of fried chicken was suddenly greasy and heavy in Joseph's stomach.

"Looks like you've got some competition, boy." Lucky lifted his hat and smoothed back his hair before replacing it. "While I, on the other hand, see nothing but smooth sailing." He opened the door of the truck and went around to the front where he leaned against the hood and waited for the women and the tall stranger to reach him.

Slowly Joseph got out of the truck and joined Lucky. Anna watched him as she drew nearer. Her regard was cool and distant and she made no effort to withdraw her hand from her companion's. In contrast, Claire seemed ready to burst at the sight of Lucky.

Joseph and Lucky removed their hats as the party came abreast of them. Claire was the first to speak. "Well, hello. Imagine seeing you here." She cut her eyes from Lucky to Joseph then to Anna and her companion.

The man glanced at the lettering on the side of the truck. "You know these men, Claire?"

"They're the timber men. You know, Sam. The ones cutting Uncle Luther's timber."

Sam's nod of acknowledgment was barely perceptible.

Joseph stepped forward. "I'm looking to send a wire to my boss." He nodded at the sign hanging from the eave of the store's porch. "I understand the telegraph office opens at one."

"Yes." Sam extricated his hand from Anna's and dug in his pocket. "I was on my way to do just that." With the key in hand, he mounted the steps of the store.

Claire started up after him, followed by Lucky. As Anna turned to follow suit, Joseph caught her by the arm.

"I thought I might see you sometime. Around the place." When she looked up at him, he thought his heart would stop.

Anna shook her hair back from her shoulder and pulled her arm free. "Really?"

That single word was more a statement than a question and without another glance, she skipped up the steps.

Joseph stood in the edge of the dusty road and watched the sway of her skirt where it just skimmed her slender ankles as she disappeared into the dimness of the building. He felt the heat in his face and looked down at his battered boots for a long minute before he slowly followed.

CHAPTER 14
MAY, 1941

JOSEPH FELT DISORIENTED, as if he were experiencing a waking dream. But this young woman, this replica of Anna, was no dream. He scrutinized her features. So very like Anna except for the eyes. The color was wrong. And the hair, much lighter than Anna's. But that voice. It was the voice from his dreams, a voice that was as familiar to him as his own breathing. She was laughing, that warm, delicious sound. He forced himself to concentrate on what she was saying.

"—Rose. Anna's my mother."

But he had known that. There could be no other explanation for this striking similarity.

"We didn't expect you so soon." She smiled down at him. "But forgive me, I've kept you standing there as if I had no manners at all. Won't you come and have a seat?" She motioned toward one of the rockers on the front porch. "I would invite you inside but Nanna has Addie Mae and Bess turning the house inside-out in preparation for the wedding."

The quiet excitement in her voice struck Joseph. He realized he hadn't spoken a word beyond that of Anna's name. He cleared his throat. "Wedding?"

"Yes. I'm to be married in a few weeks."

Hence the letter to Harry Battle, Joseph thought. The mystery of what had prompted Helen Carroll's desire to sell timber was solved. He looked at the young woman so like Anna that the sight of her made his heart ache. It would be difficult for anyone to deny her anything she desired. And who would wish to? With his hat in hand he climbed the steps and stood before the rocker. "I hope it's not inconvenient. My arrival, that is."

"No, no, not at all. I'm delighted and Nanna will be too. Please have a seat and I'll tell her you're here."

The screen door sang on its hinges. "I'm not deaf, child. At least not yet." There was strength in the voice that sounded from the shadow of the hallway. Helen Carroll stepped across the threshold onto the porch, her hair almost completely white now, but her spine as unrelentingly straight as Joseph remembered. She peered at him through small, round, wire-framed glasses. "I'm Helen Carroll."

"Mrs. Carroll." He watched her closely for any sign that she remembered him. There was none. "Mr. Battle sent me in response to your letter. His health is such that he couldn't make the trip himself." He paused. "I'm Joseph Holt."

"Joseph." Helen adjusted her glasses on her nose and looked him in the eye. "Yes. Yes, it is. Well--" She hesitated then made an impatient gesture with her hand. "Sit down, sit down." She turned to her granddaughter. "Fetch us some iced tea, child. And some of Addie Mae's teacakes."

Joseph waited until the widow Carroll was seated before taking the offered chair. "I thought you'd have received word of my arrival several days ago."

Helen waved her hand dismissively. "Rusty Johnson still drives the mail truck these days and it's a wonder anything gets through. It does no good to complain, though. His brother's the county commissioner." She tilted her head toward the door and listened. When she spoke her voice was low. "So. I hadn't expected this."

"No, I don't imagine you did."

"You've worked for Mr. Battles all these years?"

"Yes. In fact, he doesn't have much to do with it anymore. His health isn't good."

She studied Joseph's face in the manner of someone trying to bring forth an image, a memory.

"What did you have in mind, Mrs. Carroll? Your letter only stated that you wanted to sell timber." Joseph knew he should tell her straight out that Battle's Mill couldn't buy. It would be heartless to lead her on, to allow her to hope. But then, he would have no excuse to remain here and learn what he could of Anna. "Was it a large tract you had in mind?"

"Large enough. It's the same lot you cut before. I'm in need of a good return, times being what they are." She looked off down the driveway but it didn't seem to Joseph that she saw the curving line of crepe myrtles not yet in flower. Nor did she appear to notice, as Joseph did, Sally Dan trotting down the gravel drive. "Your involvement complicates things."

"Yes, I imagine it does."

A silence fell between them. Joseph had no doubt that if Battle's Mill didn't buy what Helen Carroll offered, someone else would. Someone who saw what the coming war would mean, someone willing to take the risk that demand would soar when America decided to join the fray. And they would go to war regardless of Roosevelt's promises before the election that he wouldn't send America's sons into battle unless we were attacked.

Roosevelt wanted to go to England's aid. Joseph heard it in his voice each time he spoke on the radio and what Roosevelt wanted, he usually got.

Joseph studied Helen Carroll's profile for a moment trying to decide what approach to take. He cleared his throat. "I'd have to see the stand, of course. Any decision would depend on the size and density, if it's still reasonably accessible."

"Of course." Helen shifted to a more settled position in the chair. "Reuben will take you to the plot." She rubbed her aged and spotted hands together. "The road's still passable. Reuben's kept it that way." Footsteps sounded in the hallway.

Joseph noted the barely concealed desperation. It was obvious that Helen Carroll was prepared to offer up anything she had to give her granddaughter a wedding and what a woman of her time would consider a suitable trousseau.

Relief from the depression was only just beginning to be felt with the demand from a war-torn Europe. There was money to be had and he didn't doubt that she wouldn't stop with Battle's Mill's refusal to buy. Even if it meant selling Anna's woods. He knew that war or no war, there would be plenty of takers for such prime, virgin timber. And, as she said, his presence complicated things.

Ice tinkled against crystal as Rose arrived with a tray bearing refreshments. She placed it on a low wooden table beside her grandmother. "You've come all the way from Camden today, Mr. Holt?"

"Yes. I had an early start."

"Indeed, you must have. I doubt you've had time or opportunity for anything to eat. Addie Mae's teacakes should help but I'm sure you'd have no objections to a good hot supper." She handed a glass of tea to her grandmother then one to him. "Being country folk we generally eat early in the evening." She glanced at her grandmother. "We'd be pleased to have you join us."

"You're very kind but there's no need. I plan to be in the area a day or two so I thought I'd look around for a place to stay before it got too late." He sipped the tea. "Some place with meals."

"Lena Milkisen's." Rose nodded as she spoke. "Down in Road's End. She and her brother take in the odd traveling man now and then."

Rose took a seat in the swing suspended from the porch ceiling. "But you will stay to supper? Addie Mae already sent Bess out to kill a chicken."

"Mr. Holt has other plans, Rose. Lena will be cooking for Percy."

Rose frowned. "Nana. Help me convince Mr. Holt to stay. It'll be so nice to hear what's going on outside our sleepy little town."

Joseph cleared his throat. "I couldn't impose. I'm sure I'll be very happy at Ms. Milkisen's."

"That's just silly. Addie Mae is already cooking supper and you wouldn't want to hurt her feelings. She has the reputation of being the best cook in the county."

Joseph glanced at Helen Carroll. "Well. How could I refuse such enticement."

Rose laughed. "Good. Now tell me, Mr. Holt, have you worked for Battle's Mill very long?"

"Most of my life it seems."

"Really? Then you must remember when they logged the lower range before." She blushed. "But probably you aren't that old. My mother was only a girl then."

Helen set her rocker in motion. "She was your age."

"Yes, I remember." Joseph stared straight ahead.

Rose clapped her hands together. "Of course you do! You know my mother, you called me by her name. How silly of me."

Joseph sat very still, his face forward. The rocker beside him slowed to a stop and he could feel the intense scrutiny of Mrs. Carroll. When he turned to face her, he saw misgiving in her expression.

Rose hadn't noticed the charged atmosphere. She continued to chatter on and he forced himself to listen.

"Don't you?"

Joseph cleared his throat. "Pardon?"

"Grandmother. You must remember her, too."

"No." He glanced in Helen's direction again before turning his full attention to Rose. "That is, we never formally met."

"But you remember Mother. How odd."

"Not really. Your mother was a beautiful woman. And I was not such an old man then as not to notice." He smiled at Rose. "Unless memory fails me, you are very like her."

"You flatter me, Mr. Holt." She turned away from his scrutiny and suddenly sat forward. "But your memory is true. My mother was and still is very beautiful as you shall see for yourself." With that she sprang up from the swing and hurried down the steps and along the drive.

Joseph looked beyond Rose. Someone was approaching on foot up the long curving drive. He could see a dusty-gold head appear intermittently between the foliage of the crepe myrtles. His heart thudded once against his chest, hard. His hands gripped the arms of the rocker and he must have made some sound.

"Yes, Mr. Holt, it's Anna." Helen Carroll sank against the back of her chair. "If I had known you would come--" She paused. "If I had known I would have written anyway." With an effort she drew herself into her former erect posture. "It's for Rose, you see. It's all for Rose. Her life has been hard enough and I won't let you spoil things for her." She caught his arm with claw-like fierceness. "Whatever you came here for, remember my words. You will not hurt Rose."

Rose approached her mother who held out her hands and drew Rose's arm through hers. Joseph watched as Anna laughed at something Rose said then grew still as her attention settled on his truck. Suddenly she turned in the direction she had come from as a tall, slender man came into view. Sally Dan trotted at his heels carrying a stick in his mouth. The man joined Anna and Rose, took in the truck and the occupants of the porch in a sweeping glance, then caught Anna's hand in his. She seemed to lean into him for a fleeting second before the three of them turned to follow the path to the house.

Joseph drew in a deep breath. He had never believed he would see Anna on Carroll's Hill. He had dreamed of it but had never truly believed it would happen. Now all those daydreams were shattered by a long shadow from the past, the shadow of Sam Stone.

"She doesn't know." Helen Carroll's words brought him back to earth.

"What?"

"She doesn't know you came looking for her all those months after she left. No one knows."

Joseph stared at the widow with disbelief. He thought of the letters in the glove box of his truck and the injustice of it all enraged him. "How could you not tell her?"

"It was already too late." Helen focused her attention on the trio as they neared the house. "I saw no reason to subject her to further hurt."

"Hurt?" Joseph's voice dropped to a low menace. "I never hurt her, I loved her."

When Helen looked at him he was surprised to see unshed tears standing in her eyes. "Didn't you, Mr. Holt? When you disappeared never to be heard from again what do you think it did to my daughter?" She blinked away the evidence of her weakness and her voice once again was strong with accusation. "You have no idea the harm you caused."

"You knew my reasons."

"Yes. But not until after the fact, not until it was too late." Her voice softened. "If you truly loved her, Mr. Holt, don't hurt her again. Do not hurt her or Rose."

There was nothing Joseph could say because Anna, Sam and Rose had reached the steps. He stood, his gaze fixed on Anna. Rose had been right. Anna was still beautiful. In fact, the years had given her a softness very like the patina of a rare and treasured object.

She kept her gaze focused on the steps as she mounted them and only when she reached the porch did she slowly lift her chin and look at him. It seemed to him she trembled ever so slightly; it was there in the barest movement of a wisp of her hair, the flutter of her lashes, a quiver in her lips.

"Hello." She tried to smile but failed.

Joseph couldn't find his voice. He felt the scrutiny of Sam Stone and knew he had to say something. "Mrs. Stone--"

Rose drew in a soft breath and Sam stood stock still.

"Moreland. Anna Moreland." The smile, although strained, stayed this time.

"I'm sorry. I thought--" He glanced at Sam and stopped in mid-sentence. "You've changed so little."

Anna drew herself up straighter and Sam's arm came around her shoulders. "I see you remember Sam."

With an effort Joseph tore his gaze from Anna and confronted the guarded concern in Sam Stone's expression.

"Yes. Mr. Stone. Good to see you again."

"It's Joseph Holt, isn't it?" Sam didn't offer his hand.

"Yes. I'm surprised you remember."

"The spring Battle's Mill logged Carroll's Hill was quite an occasion around here. Nothing since has quite lived up to that event." Sam escorted Anna to the swing then sat beside her, his arm resting protectively along the back of it.

Joseph stood a moment longer then became aware that Rose had perched on the top step. "Please, Miss Moreland, take the chair."

She smiled up at him. "I'm quite comfortable, Mr. Holt."

"Yes, well." He sat down and stared at Sally Dan sitting on his haunches at the foot of the steps.

A strained silence stretched over several seconds until Rose spoke. "Tell us about Camden, Mr. Holt. I visited there once with a friend when I was about twelve. It was the first time I'd ever been to a movie theater. Is it still there?"

"Yes. Still there." Joseph searched his mind for the title of the latest film but couldn't think of it. "A western is scheduled for this week, I believe. Randolph Scott in a white hat."

Rose smiled. "Randolph Scott always wears a white hat. I would love to live in a town with a movie house. I'm quite mad about picture shows."

"You want to be a movie star then?"

"No, nothing like that. I just love seeing far off places and people. I've hardly ever been more than thirty miles from this hilltop."

"That's not true, Rose, and you know it. You've only just returned from Mobile." Helen's quick gaze glanced from Rose to Joseph to Anna as she spoke. "Besides, it's only the war and all this constant talk of far-flung places in Europe that has you talking this way. You're better off here, at home, where you're safe. We all are."

All pleasure faded from Rose's expression. "We're not safe, Nanna. None of us. Even here in Road's End. When the war comes we'll all suffer for it."

It was obvious to Joseph that Helen's words had touched on a sore subject. The already tense atmosphere seemed charged. He cleared his throat. "So you've been to Mobile. How did you like it? I believe they have two movie houses."

"Yes, and we went to see *Gone with the Wind* twice! We also attended an afternoon tea given by my fiancé's aunt. She's one of the Tacons and lives in the most splendid mansion. It must have twenty rooms. And there was a colored girl in a white uniform who did nothing but walk around serving crab cakes and champagne." Excitement crept into Rose's voice as she talked. "And that's not all. It was the week-end after Easter. The end of Lent. Walker took me to the most fabulous ball. It was like something out of the movies. One of the Mardi Gras societies puts it on every year at the same time, right after Easter."

She hugged her arms to her chest. "Walker's sister, Maddie, let me wear one of her gowns." Her eyes glittered with remembered pleasure. "It was the most divine thing I've ever seen. I felt like Cinderella." She laughed. "We danced and ate and drank champagne. Walker is the most divine dancer! He says we must attend again next year. And there are lots more balls and parties before the beginning of Lent. Parades, too, right through the middle of town with everyone dressed in costumes and bands marching and playing." She sighed.

The gentle creaking of the swing had stopped and Anna stared at Rose, her face ashen. Helen sat motionless in the rocker, her gaze also riveted on her granddaughter's happy face. The silence grew and the air seemed to thicken.

Joseph cleared his throat. "Well, I imagine Walker will take you to a lot of those parties next year, especially since the two of you will be married then."

Rose had been staring into the distance, her attention seemingly fixed on the horizon. Joseph's words brought her head around. Her mouth formed a little O and color flooded her throat and face. "Oh." She glanced quickly at her mother then her grandmother. "No. I mean--" She looked down at her clasped hands. "Marsh is my fiancé. He couldn't go with us to Mobile." Her shoulders lifted in a small shrug. "We'd gone to buy the wedding dress, you see." A nervous little laugh escaped. "Walker was just being kind. He's Marsh's cousin. He was simply entertaining the country bumpkins."

Helen set her rocker into motion once again. "I don't imagine Rose will visit Mobile much once she's married. Marsh has his father's company to run. There won't be time or money to waste on trips and such."

Rose's back straightened but she didn't look up. "I like Mobile. It's such fun there with lots to do. You can simply walk out in the evening and go to a restaurant or the picture show or the theater, even. And there are parties all the time with everyone all dressed up in such wonderful clothes. The women never go anywhere unless they're all dressed up in stockings and hats. Silk stockings. Even the men wear suits, during the day I mean, for no occasion. I think I would like to live there." She raised her head and addressed her attention to Joseph. The light of defiance radiated over her whole being. "I was born there, you know, but we came back here to live when I was just four and I don't really remember much. I sometimes wish we had stayed, even after--"

Anna stood abruptly. "Rose, I think we should see how Addie Mae and Bess are coming along with the cleaning."

"Oh, they don't need--"

"And there's supper to see after." Anna's face was still quite pale as she crossed the porch to the front door. "You'll stay for supper, Sam? And Mr. Holt, of course."

"Miss Moreland already invited me but if it's too much trouble--"

Anna cut him off. "Not at all. I'm sure you've had a very long day. We wouldn't dream of sending you off without a good meal." She held the screen door open. "Rose?"

An expression of confusion mixed with defiance clouded Rose's face. With a hesitant look at each of them, she stood and followed her mother.

The trio remaining on the porch fell silent. Sally Dan stretched out on his stomach, his tongue lolling from a grinning mouth as he panted. The rocking chair creaked and Helen rose to her feet. "Reuben should be in from the fields by now." With that she turned and followed the path of her daughter and granddaughter.

It wasn't until the bell clanged, that same summoning peal from years past, that Sam spoke.

"Will you be staying in Road's End for very long, Mr. Holt?"

Joseph sat back in the chair and allowed himself to openly study the other man. Little had changed except the graying of his sandy hair at the temples and the usual facial lines that suggested more pleasure than hardship in the years since their last meeting. "No. Mrs. Carroll called me here on business. It shouldn't take long for us to determine a course." He felt in his shirt pocket for a cigarette that hadn't been there in years.

"Yes, I know about Helen's desire to sell timber. Anna told me."

There was a certain note in Sam's voice that caused Joseph to look up from the contemplation of his dusty boots. Did he somehow know what had passed between Joseph and Anna that spring so long ago? Was this a warning that he wouldn't again quietly yield the field? No, Joseph decided. Anna wouldn't have shared the fact of their love. It had been too special.

"She doesn't have to do this. Rose is very special to me, like my own daughter. I would gladly give her anything she wanted but Anna can be stubborn. Stubborn and proud."

"Yes, I seem to remember that about the Carrolls."

"I wonder what else you remember about that spring, Mr. Holt."

Joseph hesitated for a split second before he responded. "Red bugs, mosquitoes the size of crows, and boots that stayed damp for weeks on end."

REUBEN JOINED THE men on the porch. His gaze lingered on Joseph for a long moment before he glanced at Sam then offered his hand in greeting. A discussion of the proposed logging gave way to a desultory conversation about politics. Joseph felt relieved when Rose finally appeared in the doorway to summon them to the dining room.

The long oak table held a deep gleam from years of polishing. The sideboard was loaded with food that perfumed the air and made his mouth water. It had indeed been a long day and he was hungry.

Reuben sat at the head of the table and Joseph was seated at his right, Helen Carroll to his left. Sam's place was at the opposite end with Anna on his right and Rose on his left. The positioning afforded Joseph the chance to watch Anna without being too obvious. He couldn't help but note that the seating arrangement established the relationship between Sam, Anna, and Rose as effectively as a wedding ring on Anna's finger could have.

Joseph's appetite soon vanished in the face of Helen Carroll's wordless scrutiny and Anna's marked avoidance of any direct comment to him. It was left up to Sam and Rose to keep the meal from passing in complete silence. The talk centered on Rose and her wedding plans.

"Heavens, listen to me, going on so." Rose laughed softly. "Tell me, Mr. Holt, are you married?"

Joseph's hand stilled in the process of cutting into a plump, crisp chicken breast. He glanced down the table at Anna and saw that she sat perfectly still, her attention fixed on her dinner plate. He cleared his throat. "Yes. Yes, I am."

"And do you have children?"

"Two." He returned his attention to his food and speared the chicken with his fork. "A boy and a girl." When he next looked up, he realized the tension had eased a bit around the table. All except for Anna. She still wouldn't look directly at him and he noticed that Sam watched her.

They made it through dessert and coffee and the women began clearing the table. Before joining the men once again on the porch, Joseph went in search of the bathroom. As he was coming out, he found himself alone in the hallway with Anna as she carried the last of the dirty coffee cups to the kitchen. She hesitated but would have passed him by if he had not reached out and touched her arm.

"Can't you bear to look at me, Anna?"

Her arm quivered beneath his light touch and the coffee cups clinked against one another. "I don't know what you mean."

"You didn't look at me once during dinner. Is it so painful to remember."

She had been staring at his chest. Slowly she raised her eyes to meet his. "There's nothing to remember."

"Isn't there? I remember, Anna."

She moved away from his touch and her eyes blazed at him. "Then you are no gentleman."

"I never claimed to be a gentleman. That was always Sam's provenance." He reached out to touch her cheek but she turned from him and he dropped his hand to his side. "And look what it cost him."

Without looking at him again she started down the hallway. "Excuse me. I must get these dishes to Bess so she can finish up and go home."

JOSEPH WATCHED AS Lena Milkisen straightened the corner of the quilt for the third time. Her glance skittered around the room and she nodded to herself in satisfaction. She had already ascertained that Joseph was in Road's End on business with Helen Carroll, that, yes, he had been with the crew that logged the property twenty years before, and, no, he didn't find the place much changed. He had been shown the facility at the rear of the house, the washbowl and pitcher of water in his room for his more immediate convenience, and the spacious armoire. The window had been raised a couple of inches and the extra quilts in the trunk at the foot of the bed pointed out in the event of a freak cold snap during the night.

"Well, if there's anything else you need, Mr. Holt?"

"Thank you, I can't think of a thing."

She nodded again and crossed the room to the door. There she paused and looked back at him. "Two or three days you say?"

"Yes, ma'am."

With her hand on the doorknob she paused again. "There's a telephone at Toxey's store. In case you need to call anyone, family or such."

"Thank you."

Still she wavered on the threshold. "Sam opens up around five-thirty ever' mornin'. The coloreds sometimes stop in to buy a Neighi or some such to take to the fields." She twisted the glass doorknob. "'Course in an emergency you can fetch him and he'll open up. Lives in the big white house at the fork of the county road and Grist Mill Road."

"I'll remember that."

Finally she stepped across the threshold but she wasn't ready to give up. She looked back into the room. "Percy has his breakfast at six-thirty after he feeds the chickens and pigs but you needn't worry about that. I keep a pot of coffee and a pan of biscuits on the back of the stove and it's no trouble to fry up a couple of eggs and some bacon whenever you like."

"Six-thirty's fine. I'd like to get an early start."

"Well," her gaze traveled around the room once more, "good-night, then."

"Good night, Miss Milkisen."

With the door finally closed between them, Joseph sank onto the edge of the bed. He ran his hands through his hair and stared at the pattern of the rag rug on the floor. Sam Stone had made sure Joseph understood he was the man in Anna's life now. A self-deprecating grunt of amusement escaped him. Nothing had really changed after all those years. And Anna. Her cold reserve shouldn't have surprised him, he supposed. Helen Carroll's confession that Anna had never known he had returned for her still burned in his chest. She had been hurt by his apparent abandonment. And in the face of that hurt what more could he have expected? That she would see him and rush into his arms? No, he hadn't been that foolish at least. In truth he hadn't expected anything.

The fact that she was in residence on Carroll's Hill, that she had been for nearly fifteen years, had been something of a blow. If only he had made one last attempt to contact her before— But what good would that have done? She had been married then, hadn't she? Moreland. Was that who she had run off with all those years ago? Had to be. And she hadn't wasted any time. Rose looked to be eighteen. Surely she was at least eighteen if she was planning to marry. Helen Carroll had been right. By the time he had healed enough to come looking for her, Anna would have been married to this Moreland.

He sighed and went to the mirror hanging over the washstand. For the first time in a long while he looked at his reflection with more than the intention of simply shaving or combing his hair. He really looked at the face staring back at him. His dark brown hair was more gray than not. The lines around his nose and mouth looked drawn. When had he gotten so old?

He turned from the mirror and began to undress. It had been a long day and it had taken its toll. He turned out the light and crawled between the stiff, clean sheets. Tomorrow he would get an early start and finish his business in Road's End. It was time he got on with his life.

His thoughts turned to his family and guilt washed over him. Sarah would be putting the children to bed about now. Harry would resist as he always did but the minute his head hit the pillow he would be sound asleep. Melissa would need a bedtime story, a trip to the bathroom, a glass of water, and finally, to be tucked up again. He smiled in the darkness.

Sarah was a good mother in the mode of her own mother. She cared, cosseted, and comforted but rarely questioned. The things she had done, she had done for love. He had known it all along only it hadn't been excuse enough for him. Now, it would have to be. Tomorrow he would tell Helen Carroll that Battle's Mill couldn't buy her timber. But first he would visit Anna's woods one more time. Just once more before some future generation of Carrolls found it necessary to sacrifice it to their needs and wants.

Beneath the window he heard Sally Dan as he turned around and around seeking just the right position for the night. The chirping of the crickets and the occasional call of the whip-poor-will relaxed Joseph to the edge of sleep. This was what he missed most about the old method of on-site logging and milling, this closeness to nature.

His eyes drifted shut and he imagined he could hear the soughing of the pines high overhead, the soughing of Anna's pines in her woods. He smiled and suddenly the image of the distant branches against a clear sky was replaced by a halo of deep golden hair and eyes, the blue of which rivaled the sky, as she leaned down to kiss him.

ANNA PACED THE floor of her bedroom though she was exhausted. The evening had been pure disaster. With an iron will she suppressed a bubble of laughter that threatened to escape her tight throat. Indeed, there was no humor in the situation in which she now found herself. If ever there was a need to play a cool hand, this was it. But she had to keep up the facade on so many fronts! Sam, Rose, Joseph. Even her mother. None of them must guess the truth. Especially Rose.

If she somehow discovered Anna's great lie after all these years, what would she do? And with the wedding so close at hand it could all be ruined. Or had it been already? Did Rose somehow know that Joseph was a part of her mother's history, the key to her most guarded secret? All through the evening she had been so animated, talking of Walker, of the excitement and pleasure of the ball and all it entailed. So much so that Joseph had mistaken Walker for her fiancé.

It was as if Rose felt a need to include Joseph in her happiness, to make him a part of it. And she had seemed so reluctant to see him go. Fate could not be so unkind. She had to keep them apart. One wrong word and everything would unravel.

She took a deep calming breath and tried to quiet her fears. There had been nothing there, nothing to be read into Rose's behavior except the pleasure of a stranger in their midst, someone to alleviate the monotony of their days. Rose loved Marsh. It had been only natural that she would welcome an audience to all her plans and expectations. Yes, that was it, youth and the excitement of this happy time in her life.

Anna stopped pacing and stood perfectly still. And how did she feel about Joseph's presence? Had it been fear or something else that caused her to go weak in the knees at the sight of him? No, she loved Sam, truly loved him. She ran her fingers through her hair and resumed her pacing. This couldn't be happening. Not again.

She had to get rid of Joseph. His presence was a menace to the happiness of them all. Like a house made of cards, one false step and it would all come tumbling down. And what would he do if he discovered the truth? Would he tell Rose? Or Sam? His arrival in Road's End all those years ago had been the catalyst that irrevocably altered the course of Anna's life. She couldn't let it happen again. There was Rose to consider now. And Sam.

She slumped onto the stool at her dressing table and studied her reflection in the mirror. Her face was devoid of color, her eyes huge against the paleness of her face and hair. This would never do. Anyone who looked at her could see that she was terrified to the point of being sick. She took a deep breath and went back over the evening.

During supper Sam and Rose had sustained the conversation. Sam had sensed her distress and with his usual quiet manner insulated her from Joseph's presence and probing regard. She allowed herself a little smile. Sam knew her so well. Joseph could not have mistaken the message. He would know not to trespass there. But his behavior in the hallway: why couldn't he have left the pretense alone?

She ran her hand through her hair yet again. Well, tomorrow he would tour the proposed timber and be gone. There was little chance she would see him after that. On-site milling was a thing of the past and Joseph had risen above the calling of a lowly laborer. Far above.

Her gaze drifted to the rose colored silk cord draped over one of the spindles of her dressing table. From it dangled a small key. With trembling fingers she lifted the ribbon from the spindle. She held it in her hand for a long while before she opened the bottom drawer of the dressing table and took out a metal box. The key fit the lock and turned smoothly.

Anna lifted her gaze to the window and the darkness beyond. Did she really want to take this journey through the past again? After the trauma of the day, was she up to it? Yes, she decided. It was necessary to fortify herself, to be reminded of the danger.

She opened the box. First she removed Rose's baby shoes. She smiled as she fingered the tiny scraps of leather. Next came a pincushion made of Rose's hair when she had been only a year old. Finally, she lifted out the large envelope-shaped leather pouch. This she took to her bed where she propped herself against the headboard and pulled her feet up under her.

Often she had considered destroying the contents of this pouch but had been unable to bring herself to do it. She untied the cord and opened it. The book fell out onto the bed. With her forefinger, she traced the title on the cover, then she set it on its spine. It fell open to the well remembered page but she didn't read the passage there. She was no longer a silly school girl to be easily swayed by the syrupy sentiments of Robert Dunne. She needed only to remember the occasion when Joseph had given her this slender volume.

After all those years she could still feel the strength of his arms about her as they lay snuggled together in the hayloft. He had vowed he would return just as soon as Mr. Battle could spare him from the new job site. He would return for her. Then he had kissed her. Anna rested her head against the banked pillows and allowed herself to remember that kiss. It had been so sad, so sweet, then so urgent.

Her eyes flew open. Such sentiment would not do. She dug in the pouch and withdrew the envelope. It was addressed to her in Liggy's cramped handwriting. Anna smoothed the frayed missive against her thigh. Dear, dear, Liggy. She had meant only to help, to stop the torment. How Anna missed her. How she needed her now, her dry wit, her common sense, her placid acceptance. What the short term called for, Liggy would say, was a beer. And the long term, well, that would take care of itself. It always did.

Anna withdrew the letter and the newspaper clipping from the envelope. The letter she didn't bother with. It had been much read over the years. The newspaper article she held by the very edges, as if it still had the power to wound. With a deep slow breath, she read:

On Saturday, June 12, 1927, Miss Sarah Elizabeth Battle was wed to Mr. Joseph Holt. Miss Battle is the daughter of Mr. and Mrs. Harrison Battle of Camden, Alabama. The couple will reside in Camden where Mr. Holt is employed at his father-in-law's lumberyard, Battle's Mill.

She read no further. There was no need, the details were forever imprinted in her mind. So, Joseph had achieved all he desired. She wondered if it had taken him those five years to win the hand of the coveted Miss Battle or if he had needed that much time to bring Harry Battle around.

Perhaps Mr. Battle had not been so easily charmed. But then Mr. Battle had been a man of the world while Anna had been naive, sheltered, and gripped with a restlessness that bewildered and frightened her. Joseph had seen that restlessness in her. And he had known what to do, how to draw her to him, to tempt her with the illusion of freedom that the unknown and forbidden promises.

She opened the back cover of the book of poetry and picked up the pressed rose. She brushed it across her lips as the tears welled up in her eyes. Yes, he had certainly known what to do.

CHAPTER 15

MARCH, 1922

NNA STOOD NEAR the window in the far corner of the store and fingered the brightly patterned fabric. But she didn't appreciate the floral design or the fine texture of the weave. Her attention was divided between Claire and Lucky who stood on the front porch of the store drinking Coca Colas, and Joseph Holt who sat on the corner of the table that held the telegraph machine. Sam busied himself in the no-man's land in between. For this she was thankful.

Although she felt Joseph's gaze linger on her from time to time, she didn't return his regard. The memory of his touch when he caught her by the arm fueled the restlessness she felt, a restlessness that had started in the deep cold of winter and had only increased with the coming spring. It was a feeling close to panic and because of it she had shied away from Sam's every reference to the future. Their future. The days had slipped away with her hardly knowing what she had done to fill them.

And now a touch—Joseph's touch—had stirred that restlessness until Anna thought she would run from the building, run all the way to Carroll's Hill. There was something forbidden yet exciting about the heightened state she found herself in. It was as if his hand still lingered there, like a dream half-remembered, a fragrance already fading. Claire's gentle laughter floated through the open window and the sound, like the touch, spoke of secrets and pleasures. Forbidden pleasure and secrets that were not part of Anna's world.

Here, in this overly warm, dry-smelling corner of Road's End, this was her world, her life. She would marry Sam, have his children and keep his home. That was what her father wanted, what her mother wanted for her, an orderly, ordinary existence with Sam. She watched Sam from beneath lowered lashes and her heart thumped in her chest. She did love him. If he would only take her in his arms and kiss her, right here, right now, she wouldn't feel so disoriented, so unanchored.

She placed her warm forehead against the cool pane of the window and watched Claire and Lucky. Although they stood at a perfectly respectable distance from each other in full view of all of Road's End, there was something between them, something Anna couldn't put her finger on.

Claire was innocent enough. A feeling of true affection softened Anna's features. Claire was so naive, so unguarded in her openness to the world. Perhaps that was what troubled Anna for she saw nothing innocent in Lucky. It was there in the undercurrent of his low murmured words, in the ease of his stance, as if he had all the right in the world to be standing there gently teasing and tantalizing one of Road's End's prized daughters.

The telegraph machine began to clatter and a sense of relief washed over Anna. With the answer to their telegram these men, the one slight and fair, the other solid and dark, would go. They would leave her sphere and take with them this unsettled feeling.

She didn't turn around at the sound of Joseph's boots against the bare boards of the floor. She continued her vigil at the window and watched as Lucky leaned close to Claire's ear and whispered. A pretty blush ran up Claire's cheeks and she giggled as Lucky followed down the steps after Joseph.

The truck roared to life and she saw Joseph shift gears. Just when she thought he would be gone he turned and looked directly at her. It was as if he touched her.

With a small intake of breath she turned from the window only to find Sam standing right behind her, so close he almost touched her. His expression was pensive and she felt she should say something, anything to dispel the doubt she saw forming there. But before she could say or do anything Claire danced into the store.

"Anna, can I come home with you? When Sam drives you home can I come? I could stay until Uncle Luther brings us back for Wednesday night prayer meeting." She danced to a stop in front of Anna. "Wouldn't that be fun?"

Anna frowned. "I don't think so, Claire."

"Oh, Anna. We'd have such fun!" Claire's lips formed a pout. "I could help with the early peas. Uncle Luther wouldn't mind and Aunt Helen never cares."

"But you always get so bored at the house, Claire. The last time you came we walked all the way back to Road's End after only one day."

"Oh, forget about that. Uncle Luther was being mean and I wanted to come home." She bounced on the balls of her feet. "Let's do, Anna. I promise I won't be bored."

Sam took Anna's arm and they turned toward the door. "I imagine it would be all right with your mother, Anna." He smiled down at her. "The loggers are moving camp tomorrow. It'll be better than three miles away from the homestead so all the noise and turmoil will be far away. You and Claire can enjoy each other's company. Everything will return to the way it was."

The smile didn't touch his eyes and it seemed to Anna his reassurance was more for himself than for her.

ANNA STOOD ON the path that led from the creek and looked across its now still water to the place where the loggers had been encamped. Nothing remained of their occupation but the muddied prints of men and animals. Even the debris of the cook fire had been thoroughly scattered.

The absence of sound left in the wake of their departure was as noticeable as the noise and activity that had preceded it. Her gaze traveled over the desolate scene before her. The scent of bruised pine rent the air. Even in so small a space as the clearing for the campsite the legacy of the loggers was like a raw wound on the landscape. Anna felt the weight of their occupation of the land and was glad the site of destruction stood so far from the homestead. She knew she would never visit it again. She wished she would never have to see the loggers again. At least they were gone from sight and hearing.

Anna should have felt a greater sense of relief but she didn't. Claire had been gone from the house for over two hours. It was imperative that Anna find her before her absence was noticed, before the wrath of her father rained down on both their heads.

Once again Anna scanned the horizon. Could Claire have gone so far as the new campsite? Would she have acted so rashly, so foolishly? Anna feared she would—and had. Since the arrival of the loggers she had been completely infatuated with them. Her head was filled with them; she could talk of nothing else. Anna felt a mild rush of panic. What was she to do?

She stared into the clear, smooth surface of the small pool in the eddy of the creek. She had looked everywhere she could think of and she was afraid to call out. That would draw attention to the fact that Claire had not returned to the house after setting out to feed the chickens. The day was growing late.

A twig snapped and Anna's head flew up. On the other side of the creek stood Joseph.

"What are you doing here?" Anna felt her heart hammering in her chest. She didn't know how long he had been watching her. "I thought everyone was gone."

He tore a twig from a sweet gum. "Just checking behind the men. Mr. Battle don't allow us to leave a mess."

Anna wanted to ask what, exactly, constituted a mess in his estimation. What did he think the flattened campsite represented? But her greater fear dictated her words. "Where's Claire?"

His brow furrowed. "Claire?"

"Claire! Claire!" Her voice rose with each repetition. "Have you seen her?"

"No. Not since yesterday. In town." He put the end of the twig in his mouth and chewed on it. "Why would I?"

"Because." She looked away from his scrutiny. "You know very well why. Lucky."

"Lucky's at camp."

"Is he?"

He clenched his jaw then relaxed it. His eyes narrowed slightly. "My men keep to camp. That's the rule. Mr. Battle don't cotton with any fooling around. Keep to camp, keep away from the house, or keep on going." He folded his arms across his chest. "That's the rule."

"Well, Mr. Battle isn't here, is he? And you're not at camp so how do you know where Lucky is?"

Color stained his cheeks beneath the beginnings of a beard and he glanced in the direction of the new camp. He shifted his weight from one foot to the other. "Lucky knows the rule and he abides by it. If your cousin ain't where she belongs, it's not because of any of my men."

There was a lack of conviction in his voice and Anna felt her panic increasing. "How can you say that when it's as plain as the nose on your face that she's infatuated with the whole--" she waved her hands to generally encompass the area around them, "with the whole notion of strangers in our midst, of excitement and—and--" Anna saw the shadow of a smile play around his lips. Mortified, she sputtered to a halt.

"And?"

She felt the blush traveling through her and willed it to stop to no avail. "Claire isn't accustomed to socializing with— with strangers, strange men. She's very—innocent. She doesn't understand--" Anna hesitated.

"Understand what?"

"Oh, for pity's sake don't pretend you don't realize what's going on." He was goading her, she knew. He wanted her to say what she feared, to admit there could be an attraction. "Claire is like a spoiled child. She acts on impulse, without thinking. Right now she finds Lucky's charm, his worldliness, intriguing." She paused, wondering how to continue.

"Lordy at the words you use." Though the lilt of his voice suggested amusement, all humor had left his expression. "If by all that you mean the little lady has taken a fancy to Lucky, well, Lucky's like that," he paused for a heartbeat, "intriguing."

"Look, I think Claire is with your friend and he isn't the kind of man— Well, I don't imagine he'd be too concerned about the situation she found herself in if--"

"If it was known she was hankering after the likes of him?" His anger flashed like quicksilver. "I wouldn't worry too much if I were you. If she's such a lady, well, she wouldn't stoop to such as Lucky, now would she? And he ain't off chasing after her. So if she's with him, it's because she wants to be."

Anna wanted to slap him. "That's the problem. She doesn't understand men like Lucky. She doesn't know what she wants."

"Unlike you."

"What's that supposed to mean?"

He started across the creek. He had only taken a couple of steps when the sound of her name reached their ears.

"Annn-naaa, Annn-naaa."

She snatched up the skirt of her dress and started up the slope at a run. She could hear him splashing through the water.

"Annn-naaa."

At the top of the rise, she could see the homestead. Claire stood at the end of the farthest stock pen, her eyes sheltered by her hand as she scanned the horizon.

"I believe that's your missing cousin."

His voice, so near, made her start and turn toward him. He was staring down at her with a look she couldn't read. Without another word, he turned and retraced his steps. Anna watched him until he disappeared below the slope of the rise.

Damn Claire! Anna hurried toward the house. She had just put herself through all that humiliation for nothing. At least she hoped it was nothing. Where had Claire been for the past two hours?

By the time Anna reached her, Claire had climbed into the fork of the pecan tree that stood at the corner of the pen. She leaned her back against the trunk and swung a foot back and forth as Anna approached.

"Where have you been Claire?"

"I went to feed the chickens."

"For two hours?"

Claire looked away toward the horizon. "Oh, don't scold, Anna. I got bored shelling peas." She examined her stained and tender thumbnail. "I didn't know there'd be so many."

"So where were you?"

Claire's brow furrowed and her lower lip extended in a pout. "Nowhere. Just taking a nap." She wouldn't meet Anna's gaze. "Down in the saddle house, in the back of the hay wagon."

Anna looked west to where the saddle house sat outlined against a sky streaked with pinks and reds. She could see the wagon parked beneath the roof of the low, open shed. It was a perfect place to escape for a nap or to read unmolested by the members of the household. Had Claire really been there all along? Studying her face, Anna couldn't decide.

Claire jumped down from the tree and skipped a few steps ahead of Anna. "Come on. It's almost time for supper and I'm starving." She waited for Anna to catch up with her and slipped her arm into her cousin's. "Let's play charades tonight."

"But there's only the two of us."

"That's okay. We can guess for each other." She looked away from Anna but not before Anna caught the traces of a smile. "You'll never guess mine."

ANNA LAY ON her back in the swing, the book open across her chest. Her eyes were mere slits against the lethargy induced by a heavy mid-day meal. Claire had given in completely to the need of a nap and slept in Anna's room.

In the distance Anna heard the straining of a car motor as it labored up Carroll's Hill. Even when it slowed, she didn't let it disturb the somnolent ease of the early afternoon. She thought it was probably Rusty Johnson delivering the mail to the box at the end of the long drive. But then the sound of the engine changed to a low striving and she realized someone had turned into the drive.

With a yawn she sat up and reluctantly tied the laces of her shoes and buttoned the top button of her blouse. She was smoothing her hair when Sam's truck swung into the curve of the driveway.

He got out and lifted a bundle of greens from the truck bed. Anna went down the steps and met him halfway across the lawn.

"Sam. This is a nice surprise."

He smiled at the pleasure in her voice and held up the bundle of turnips. "I got these in trade this morning and thought your mother might like some."

"It'll make a nice change. Where did you get them?"

"Old Fiske cut the last of his crop."

"Fiske?" The mention of Aaron Fiske always made Anna think of her cousin Liggy. Whenever the dark rumors about Liggy were being bandied about by the local wags, her name was invariably linked with Fiske.

Liggy had run off to Mobile when Anna was only eight, but Anna remembered the carefree young woman who laughed easily and was generous with her time and talents. Anna had loved Liggy and her abrupt departure had hurt in that indefinable way which children cannot explain.

As she got older, the innuendo puzzled Anna. Fiske, even in his youth, had resembled more her image of Ichabod Crane than a love interest. She couldn't imagine her fun-loving, independent cousin being paired with him. But then she had never thought of Liggy as plain, either.

"Yes." Sam's response broke into her reverie. "I was surprised, too. I believe this is the first time I've seen him since the fall. He's become a regular hermit."

"Well," Anna slipped her arm through Sam's as they started up the steps, "I'm glad you came. It's been very quiet around here today."

His eyebrows rose and his words held an undercurrent of amusement. "Oh, and what of the chief pea sheller?"

Anna laughed. "She's having a nap. Shelling peas can be so exhausting, you know." She leaned close and whispered loudly, "I expect she'll give up this new enthusiasm long before the early corn is ready."

"Or as soon as the fascination with the loggers fades." He laughed. "Poor Anna. How will you manage?"

"Quite well, actually." She smiled up at him and thought how right it felt to be arm in arm with him. His strong jaw was softened by the ready smile and the warmth of his light brown eyes. He was a man of conviction and compassion. Only a fool would want more. "I'm glad she's napping. We can have a nice, long walk. It's such a beautiful day."

He looked away from her regard and blinked, his smile widened. "Well, let's drop off old Fiske's offering and be on our way. He says they're at their peak. There isn't going to be another frost to speak of this spring and greens won't be worth eating in that case."

"But Easter is still three weeks away. We always have a cold snap around Easter."

"Not this year." He shifted the bundle so nothing would drop onto the floor of the dog-trot. "At least not according to Fiske. A wet February, March beginning so fierce. No, our Fiske is a great believer in the signs of nature. He predicts spring will be mild and the summer hot and wet."

"I'm glad." Anna went ahead of him down the back steps and across the alley separating the house from the kitchen. "I'm so tired of winter, of the cold. Maybe I'll be warm at last."

"You've come to the right place if you want to be warm." Her mother's voice addressed them from the dim depths of the kitchen. "Addie Mae's taken it into her fool head to bake this afternoon."

The warmth enveloped them as did the comforting smell of bread rising. Sam inhaled deeply in appreciation. "Smells wonderful, Addie Mae. Don't suppose I could talk you out of a loaf?"

"Ummmh." Addie Mae grunted as if annoyed but her expression gave away her pleasure at his compliment.

"Sam's brought you some turnips, Mother." Anna took them from him and placed them in a washtub.

"That's very kind of you, Sam. You'll stay to supper and enjoy them with us, won't you?"

"I'm afraid I can't, Mrs. Carroll. Lena's watching the store for me and she gets antsy about Percy's supper toward the late afternoon."

"It seems a shame to come all this way and go straight back again." Helen Carroll wiped her hands on the skirt of her apron as she spoke.

He grinned. "Well, I hadn't planned on going straight back. I thought Anna and I would take a walk first."

"Well," Helen nodded, her gaze going from one to the other, "that would be nice. It's such a lovely day."

Anna turned from the room and hurried down the steps. Sam caught up with her halfway to the side gate and slipped her hand in his arm. They continued in silence until they reached the row of wild plum trees that followed the road to the fields.

"Which way shall we go?" He looked toward the fields then along the path down to the old well. "I think this way would be better."

"Yes." Anna leaned closer in toward him and followed his lead along the sun-spangled trail to the old well. The dogwood and maple were coming into leaf, filtering the sunlight that sought the wild irises and violets that grew in the protected shadows of the trees. They drew the eye with their vivid yellow and blue.

They had reached the gnarled oak that marked the half way point along the old, worn pathway when Sam spoke. "Are you happy, Anna?"

She felt the ease created by his visit, by the lazy afternoon, slipping away with his question. "Happy?"

"You've been different lately. For a long while, in fact. All winter I've felt a distance between us." He stopped and turned her to face him, his hands gently gripping her upper arms. "And at the store the other day I--", he folded her into his arms, "Anna, I love you."

Her slender arms went around his waist and she pressed her cheek to his chest. "I know." His heart beat in a steady, comforting rhythm at her ear and she experienced a surge of caring that made her own heart thump erratically for a brief moment. "And I love you."

She felt the tension ease from his embrace and heard the relief in the soft sigh. He kissed the top of her head before he removed her to arms length. "Then say you'll marry me."

Anna wanted desperately to say the words. As she looked into his face, shining with hope and promise, she wanted nothing more than to live forever at his side. But the words would not come. It was as if her throat closed against her own will, against her own desire.

Sam's grip tightened on her arms. "Say it, Anna. Say yes. Yes, Sam, I'll marry you."

She swallowed against the constriction in her throat, and at the growing hurt in his expression, tears began to well up. She tried to return to the comfort of his arms but he held her fast, his eyes burning into hers.

"You say you love me." He swallowed. "Do you, Anna? Do you really?"

"Yes." The admission whispered from her lips and with it he relented and took her into his arms again.

His lips touched her hair then the top of her ear in a feathery kiss. "What do you want me to do, Anna? What do you want?"

She ran a hand across her cheek and sniffed. "Oh, Sam, I wish I knew." When she sniffed again he drew a handkerchief from his pocket and handed it to her. "When we're together, I can't imagine life without you."

His hand came up and he caressed the back of her neck with his long, slender fingers. "That's because we were meant for each other. I think I've always known it and I've waited for you, Anna. I've waited for you to learn to love me, too."

"How can you be so sure, Sam?"

He took her hand and held it against his heart, and smiled. "I feel it here, like a physical thing." He was silent for a long time, as if gathering his thoughts. "In France when I was cold and frightened, looking into the face of death on the battlefields, I knew I would survive. Fate intended that we be together and therefore I couldn't die. My love for you is what brought me safely home."

"You believe in fate, then."

"Yes."

Was it truly fate? Would her life be dictated by some unknown, unseen hand that cared little for the uncertainty, the fear she felt? The fear that she was like her mother? That she would destroy Sam the way her mother had destroyed her father? The thought made the panic rise in Anna's throat. "Can't people escape their fate?"

"Yes, I imagine people can if they want to. Look at Reuben."

Anna blushed scarlet and hid her face against his chest. Sam, her best friend, her life-long confidant, knew all her secrets, her trials, her triumphs. He also knew what she had witnessed between Reuben and Mara Duardo in the hayloft when she had been only ten. "Maybe he didn't really love her."

"Maybe. But I think he did. I think that's why he joined the army, because he couldn't bring himself to believe that Mara was his fate. And look how unhappy he is."

"Is he?"

"You tell me. He buries himself out in the fields with virtually no human contact. With each passing year he grows more and more withdrawn. Before you know it he'll be just like old Fiske."

"But I thought you said it was the war that had changed him so."

"In part. A man can't experience something like that without being changed forever." Sam hesitated. "Perhaps it's only the war, after all." He cleared his throat. "Am I your fate, Anna? Do you want me to be?"

She couldn't tell him what he wanted to hear so she said what she knew to be true. "I do love you, Sam. So very much."

He held her a moment longer before he released her slowly, as if reluctant to be parted from her. "Are you afraid of married life, Anna? Of living with me as my wife? Do you think I'll be unkind or--"

She placed the fingers of her hand over his lips to still the words. "I trust you completely, Sam. And when we're together like this I want be with you the way--" she glanced down at his chest. "The way Reuben and Mara were."

"Anna." He kissed her then, kissed her with all the passion of years of restraint and as he crushed her body to his, she felt desire stir like a column of smoke curling skyward. Yet even as her body yielded, her mind resisted. How could she explain? How could she tell the companion of her lifetime, the champion of her heart, of the strange attraction of another man, of the resentment of a life long planned for her? With those doubts the panic deepened and she broke free of his embrace.

"Anna."

She held up her hand in protest of what he might say. She felt defenseless against his logic, his caring, his calm acceptance. "I'm sorry. I can't."

The muscle in his jaw flexed then relaxed. "All right." He looked away down the path for a long while before he spoke again. "All right, Anna. I'll wait." A corner of his mouth turned up in mock humor. "It'll be easier now that I know you feel some attraction to me."

"It was never a question of desire, Sam."

He stared into her eyes. "Not a question of desire, not one of love." He searched her features as if the answer could be gleaned from the set of her mouth, the tilt of her chin, the depths of her blue eyes. "What then?"

Anna realized he deserved the truth, as much of the truth as she herself knew. "I try to imagine my life, the future, and I can't see it, Sam. I want you to be there but the picture doesn't come." She turned from him and picked a twig of new green growth from the ancient oak and her voice held a bleak quality when she spoke. "All I see is--"

"What do you see?" He spoke so softly, his voice filled with caring.

"I see my mother, sitting in the front pew of the church, the ever dutiful wife. I sometimes used to wonder why she married my father but lately I've come to realize that she had no choice, did she? It's a woman's place to marry, to be dutiful and obedient. Like my mother, like Aunt Maree." Her eyes narrowed. "And then I see my father, I see his pain when he looks at Mother." Her brows drew together in a frown. "Love isn't supposed to hurt like that, is it?"

"But that's not our future, Anna."

"Isn't it?" She threw the twig away. "Road's End. So final, so--" she shook her head.

"And you see nothing else?"

"The river and the other shore, so near and yet so far away. Do you never want to leave here, Sam? Just go without a thought as to where or why?"

"I've been away, remember?" Sam leaned against the trunk of the tree and stared off into the distance. "Men are the same whether they're in Paris or New Orleans or Road's End. No one place is any safer than another."

She shivered. "Safe. Is that what you feel here, Sam? That you're safe in Road's End?"

"It's not the place, Anna. The only thing a man can control is what's here," he placed a closed fist against his chest. "This is the only place anyone is safe."

Was that what she wanted, she wondered. To be safe? Then why didn't she feel safe with Sam? "If it's not the place, then it's me. All I have here," she placed her hand over her heart, "is uncertainty and—I don't know—darkness. I don't know how to explain it to you, Sam."

He caught her by the shoulders but she wouldn't look at him. "I can't say that I know what you're feeling. Maybe men are too different from women. But you have to realize that all men aren't like your father. And all women aren't like your mother."

"I know. I know." She turned to him. "Dear, dear, Sam. What would I do without you?"

"I never want you to have to find out. I'll always be here for you, Anna." He kissed the top of her head. "I've been in love with you since you walked into the store one Wednesday afternoon, your hand in your father's. I felt it then and I feel it just as sharply now."

"On a Wednesday, was it?" She smiled despite the gravity of their discussion.

He lifted her chin so that she had to look at him. "Yes." He gave her an answering smile. "And you were all of eight years old."

"You wouldn't have been but fourteen then. You couldn't have known."

"Perhaps I didn't know what it meant then, but I have for a very long time. I still feel that sharp prick of awareness every time I look at you. I've never felt it for another woman." He paused. "Like I said, fate."

"Yes." She felt the tears forming so she hid her face against his chest. "Fate."

He smiled again, a sad smile but one not void of pleasure. "Then I can wait. For as long as necessary."

"GET UP THERE, mule!" Joseph slapped the reins against the animal's backside. "Come up, there! Come up!" He whistled sharply and the skidder stacked with long boards began to move. Perched atop the load with his feet apart, his knees flexed, he balanced himself as they covered fifty yards of cleared ground. At the partially finished building on the edge of the clearing, he reined in the mules. "Whoa, whoa."

Ester stood in the doorway of the roughly framed structure, her hands on her wide hips. "Where my stove?"

Joseph hopped down from the platform and tethered the mule team to one of the roof supports. "Next load, Ester. I want to get the roof on first. Benny says we'll have rain before the week's out."

Ester squinted up at the cloudless sky but grunted in acknowledgment. Benny's left hip was an unfailing predictor of foul weather. "Just so's you gets it in 'fore them fools wall me up. Las' time we had to take down the back side."

"I can't help it that your stove's too big to fit through the door, Ester. They'll know better this time."

"They better. I's tired a stooping over a open fire just so's this lot can have hot biscuits." She rolled her dark eyes in the direction of the men overhead putting the roof of the camp cookhouse in place. "No stove, no biscuits."

Lucky leaned over the roof's edge to take the boards Joseph was handing up to him. "You don't mean that, Ester. Why, the whole lot of us would quit this lousy job if we didn't have your biscuits to look forward to."

Ester shook her head and clucked her tongue against the roof of her mouth. "Get away from me, Mr. Lucky. That sweet tongue don't work on this here colored gal."

Lucky's laughter was punctuated by the slap of boards against boards as he continued to pitch the lumber onto the roof.

Joseph grinned as he extended the last of the boards skyward. "Now, Ester, you know you've got every man here wrapped around your little finger. What would we do without you?"

"Huh." She turned and with her head high, angled her sizable girth through the framework where the door would later be hung.

Still grinning, Joseph unhitched the mule team and hopped back onto the skidder, reins in hand.

"Joseph!"

He looked in the direction of the call and waited as Benny hurried toward him with his gimping gait.

"They're at it again." Benny wiped the sweat from his brow with the sleeve of his shirt. "That jack from up North done started in on Woody."

"*God* dammit!" Joseph jumped off the skidder and tied up the team before he started toward the line of trees that marked the site of the initial logging. "Any blood?"

Benny gasped for breath as he tried to keep up with Joseph's long strides. "Not much—yet."

Joseph ground his teeth. "Well, there will be."

A group of men had gathered around the combatants and the air no longer sang with the sounds of saws biting into wood. The shouts of encouragement slowly died as Joseph pushed his way through the crowd.

The big Swede stood his ground, his fists raised in classic pugilist fashion. Blood trickled from his nose and a gash over his left eye. He revolved slowly as he followed the movements of Woody who crouched and circled him, his teeth bared and fire in his eyes. Except for a dark red spot on Woody's right cheekbone, he appeared unscathed thus far. Joseph stepped between the two men and shoved Woody into the arms of the crowd.

"Hey!" Woody struggled against the restraining hands, the cords of his neck stood out and he blinked a couple of times as his charged senses took in the situation. His outrage changed focus. "Stay outta this, Joseph!"

Joseph ignored Woody's protests and turned his full attention to the Swede who continued to maintain his stance. "Pack your things."

The Swede shook his head, his eyes still on Woody, his lower jaw hanging slack. He raised his fists a notch higher. "Come to me you little woodpecker."

Joseph wasn't sure whether the Swede was addressing him or Woody but it didn't really matter. He felt his stomach muscles tighten with the sick anticipation of pain and he swung a hard uppercut to the man's right jaw. The answering blow in his gut made him suck air and only the supporting arms of the circle of men kept him from going down. Before he could regain his balance, the Swede landed a blow to his left temple. Joseph rocked with the force and pain of it.

He wasn't sure how the peavey came to be in his hand but he didn't stop to think about it. As he straightened from the blow, he brought the long pole up across the Swede's mid-section with all his might. The peavey quivered in his hands with the force of the impact and Joseph heard the sickening sound of bones cracking. The Swede staggered and dropped his left shoulder to protect his middle. Joseph brought the pole down over his back and the big man dropped to one knee.

The shouting men fell silent as the seconds ticked away. Joseph stood there, swaying slightly, the pole balanced in his hands. The Swede took a ragged breath and attempted to rise.

"Don't." Joseph panted with exertion and pain, his vision blurred. He poised the pole like an overlong baseball bat. "I'll kill you if you get up."

His adversary cut his eyes upward and scrutinized Joseph. Finally, he laughed and sat back on his heels, a grimace of pain causing the smile to falter briefly. A ripple of answering laughter made its way through the assembled loggers.

Joseph relaxed his stance only slightly. The Swede was a bully and troublemaker who should have been cut loose long before. It no longer mattered how good he was at his job. Joseph couldn't have his team at each other's throats every time his back was turned. The man had to go. "You know the rules, Davin. Pack your gear."

Davin nodded. "You'll regret this, Mr. Boss Man. You not get so good a worker as Davin again."

"Maybe not so good, but a lot less trouble."

Davin grinned. "Yah, this is true." He lifted his hand in a gesture of acquiescence as he slowly got to his feet. He stood, his right hand cradling his left side. "But there is no spice, either."

Joseph stabbed the sharp tip of the peavey into the ground then leaned his weight against the long pole. "That suits me."

The Swede laughed again and made his way through the gathered men toward the camp.

Woody stood at Joseph's shoulder, his face still red with anger and exertion. "You shoulda left him to me, Joseph. It was me that got insulted." Woody wiped his sleeve across his nose. "Talking 'bout my mama that way."

"Get back to work, Woody." Joseph gingerly felt his left temple then looked at his fingers. No blood, thank god. "These trees ain't gonna jump on the bummer cart all by themselves."

Woody picked his hat up off the ground and slapped it against his knee. "Shoulda left him to me," he muttered as he turned toward the lopped logs waiting to be loaded.

Joseph shook his head to clear it and started across the clearing toward the skidder. It was common knowledge among the loggers that Woody's mother had, in her prime, worked the roadhouses. It was a fact that she had ignored her marital status, often being gone from home for days at a time, and had left all the domestic responsibilities, including the rearing of her son, to her doormat of a husband. But you wouldn't know it from Woody's ramblings about her.

To him she represented the finest of woman-hood, a good cook, loving mother, and dutiful wife. Everyone in the crew generally indulged Woody's fantasies but not the Swede. Once someone let him in on the truth he made it his business to call Woody on it every time he opened his mouth about his mother. Which was often. Joseph was glad to be rid of the headache and that was a fact.

Lucky fell into step beside him. "Head still ringing?"

Joseph gave a grunt of acknowledgment.

"Well, I know just the cure."

Joseph sighed and closed his eyes briefly. Lucky's remedies generally involved things that, if not downright illegal, were at the least illicit. "No, Lucky."

Lucky assumed a hurt expression. "How can you say no when you haven't even heard what it is."

"Because knowing you, I know what it is."

Lucky chuckled. "Not this time, you don't. All I'm saying is, come Saturday night we should head out to this club I heard about over near Finley. They got good hooch, I hear."

Joseph grinned and shook his head. "And what's new about this *cure*? It's the same as you always come up with."

"Only this time I figure we'll take along a little company."

Joseph stopped in his tracks and caught Lucky by the arm. "What're you up to, Lucky?"

Lucky lifted his shoulders and spread his arms in appeal. "What? I'm just saying how it would be nice to have someone to dance with maybe. You know, some nice young ladies."

"You don't know any nice young ladies."

Lucky's grin spread slowly. "Now there you're wrong, Joseph. I happen to know a couple of very nice young ladies. Beauties, too."

"Not Claire."

"Why not Claire?" He shrugged defensively. "If she's willing."

"Because it's against the rules, Lucky." Joseph punched at Lucky's chest with his forefinger. "You remember the rules, don't you? Keep to camp, keep away from the house, or keep going?" He jabbed again. "Is that what you want, Lucky, to lose your job?"

Lucky shoved Joseph in the chest. "I know the rules. I been keeping to camp and I ain't been to the house except that once with you." He flexed the muscle in his jaw. "The rules don't say nothing about otherwise."

"Don't start threading the needle with me or else you can follow the Swede."

Lucky took a step back and lifted his hands in resignation. "Okay, okay." He grinned. "So what do you say? We can still go across the river to the club. I 'spect there'll be a lass or two that won't object to our company."

Joseph felt the tension ease from his shoulders and he nodded in concession. It wouldn't hurt to sip a little white lightning and rub up against a soft body on the dance floor. The image of Anna in his arms flashed through his mind and he quickly dismissed it. What he needed was a dark headed beauty with lots of round places to take his mind off his troubles and Anna Carroll. "Sure, Lucky. Why not?"

THE CAR HIT a rut and Claire squealed as she and Anna bounced against each other. "We'll have so much fun, Anna. You haven't stayed with me in ages." Claire glanced toward the front seat and Luther Carroll and lowered her voice. "I can hardly wait for Saturday."

Anna studied her cousin's face. She seemed ready to burst with barely restrained excitement. "It'll be nice to see Sukey and the baby but I didn't think you got on so well with Gerald."

"Oh, well," Claire waved her hand dismissively, "they'll only be there for the day. It's a long drive to Meridian. He'll want to start back soon after dinner. Besides, he'll probably bury his head in the newspaper or go 'round to the store to see who he can impress bragging about his job at the bank." She giggled. "Everybody knows he's only a clerk."

"Don't be mean, Claire. He is your step-brother."

"So? That doesn't mean I have to like him. Besides, he's so much older than I am that I hardly know him. I can't imagine why Sukey married him."

"Maybe she was impressed with his job at the bank."

They both giggled until Anna's father cleared his throat loudly. After that, their exchanges became mere whispered comments until they pulled into the church parking lot in Road's End.

The churchyard was empty when they arrived. Anna took the flowers she had picked inside and fashioned an arrangement for the low table in front of the pulpit. Claire wandered the pews in an aimless fashion, occasionally picking up an item she found there; a fan advertising Brown Memorial Insurance, a prayer book, a hymnal from which she hummed a few bars before replacing it. Luther disappeared into the small office behind the pulpit. Anna's mother hadn't accompanied them into town for Wednesday night prayer meeting due to a sick headache. Reuben never attended church services of any kind, not since his return from the war.

When the flowers were finished, both girls went out onto the front steps to enjoy the early evening and watch the approach of the citizens of Road's End. They visited with each arrival, chatting of crops, the weather, and the upcoming visit of Claire's half-brother. Oddly, there were few comments about the loggers on Carroll's Hill. Anna assumed that was in deference to her father.

Luther's pride was well known around the county as was his temper and his influence as the Justice of the Peace was more than a little feared. The fact that few of them understood the politics of government control of the railroads and its effect on stocks made the loss of the Carroll's money base more puzzling and therefore a more intriguing topic of conversation.

They understood when the bank closed its doors against its customers. Most of them had experienced some loss on that score when the banks in Montgomery and Birmingham began to fail. But true wealth, in their minds, existed only in the land they owned and the crops that land yielded. Pieces of paper that were worth a king's ransom one day and worthless the next were a mystery to them. And even though they were willing enough to question the wisdom of such investments, no one dared gossip about Luther's financial woes within his hearing.

Sam was one of the last to arrive, the scent of Pears soap and a clean-shaven jaw attesting to the fact he had closed shop early in order to go home before church. Mrs. Bramley was already at the piano, attacking it as if only a full out offensive would yield the required notes. Sam took Anna's arm and together they entered the church. She was aware of the covert glances cast in their direction from the pews that lined the aisle and could guess the thoughts behind each of those pairs of eyes. There was approval and acceptance in the kindly faces. It seemed everyone held a claim to the course of Anna's life. Everyone but her.

Anna paid little attention to the sermon. She opened her Bible obediently when those around her did and she mumbled the correct responses when required. But her mind was on the man beside her. He would never be like her father, cold and distant, his passion expressed only in bursts of anger. No, with Sam she felt cherished, protected. It would be good to be in Road's End for a few days, good to be close to Sam. Everyone was right, it was time she quit straddling the fence. Before she returned to Carroll's Hill she would come to grips with this reluctance; she would get on with her life.

A calm settled over Anna with this decision. It lasted through the church service and a late supper.

It was only as she and Claire were preparing for bed later that night that panic struck once again. It stared at her from the wrinkled and stained sheet of paper. She read the missive through once again before she raised her eyes to meet those of her cousin. "You can't mean to do this, Claire."

Claire's chin lifted and the fire of determination burned in her eyes. "I most certainly do."

Anna turned from the mulish stubbornness she saw in her cousin's expression and tried to think. "This is impossible. How can he think you would do it? Your father would kill you before he let you go."

Claire snatched the note from Anna's hand and carefully folded it along the already much creased lines. "Father won't know. Neither will Mama." She looked up at Anna. "Unless you tell them."

"I should."

"But you won't."

"I will if I have to."

"No you won't."

Anna turned to the window and stared out into the night. What would she do if she couldn't dissuade Claire from this recklessness? "You can't seriously consider going to such a place. They'll have liquor and—and who knows what. It's the kind of place where no respectable woman would be seen."

Claire caught her by the arm and turned Anna to face her. "There'll be *dancing*, Anna." Her whole body seemed to hum with excitement. "How I long to dance." She clasped her hands together. "Lucky says they have a colored band that plays and people come from all over. Respectable people, too."

"And who is he to judge whether someone is respectable or not? Think about who he is, Claire. Rough, common. The very words you used not more than two week ago."

"But I didn't know him then."

"And you don't know him any better now."

Claire's lips formed a pout. "I most certainly do."

Anna lifted a mocking eyebrow. "From one little encounter on the porch of Toxey's store?"

Claire turned from her and flung herself onto the bed. "No. Not one little encounter."

"What's that supposed to mean?"

Claire smiled and toyed with a curl but still wouldn't meet Anna's eyes. "We happened upon each other a time or two on Carroll's Hill."

Anna felt the blood leave her head, and her heart gave one hard thump. "You little fool."

Claire sat up and glared at her cousin. "I am not a fool! Lucky likes me. A lot. And he wants to take me places, show me off." Her chin came up a notch higher. "It's not as if I were still a little kid. I'm seventeen."

Anna eased herself onto the rocker, her attention no longer fixed on her cousin. "The saddle house. It was a lie. All a lie while you were off with him." She sat forward in the chair. "What were you doing with him, Claire?"

Claire's gaze dropped to the patterned linoleum on the floor. "Just walking in the woods, talking."

Anna took a deep, slow breath. "Nothing else?"

"I told you, we walked and talked." Her expression softened. "He took me to a place where I could spy on the men while they worked." A childish giggle bubbled from her throat. "Some of them stripped down to the waist. It gave me the funniest feeling in the pit of my stomach. Kinda like when Lucky--" She stopped abruptly.

Anna rose from the chair and sat beside Claire on the bed. "What? When Lucky what?"

"When he kissed me." She looked up into Anna's troubled face. "I *have* been kissed before, you know. But not like this. I wanted him to keep kissing me." Color suffused her cheeks.

"Did he touch you?"

Anger sparked in Claire's regard. "Of course he touched me. I just told you he kissed me, didn't I?"

Anna took her cousin's hand in hers. "But Claire, did he—" she watched the subtle changes in Claire's face as realization dawned.

"No." She stood and began to undress. "He didn't take advantage of me, if that's what you're asking." She turned to stare down at Anna. "He isn't like that."

"How can you know what he's like? He's a stranger, uneducated, coarse. What if he had tried something else? What would have happened with you off in the woods like that, alone, unprotected. He could have done anything."

"He only kissed me and just the once." A small frown marred Claire's forehead. "He didn't even try to take advantage of me."

Anna felt weak with relief. "At least he hasn't been that bold. Yet." She stood and caught her cousin's hand in hers. "But that doesn't mean he won't, Claire." At the protest she saw forming on her cousin's tongue, Anna rushed on. "Men like him, grown men who've been out in the world", she struggled for the words that would turn Claire from this folly, "they've had experiences with women. They know how to go about getting what they want. A girl like you--"

Claire jerked her hand free. "I told you, I'm not a girl! I'm a woman." Her eyes glittered. "Lucky appreciates that I'm a woman."

Anna had no doubt that he did. "You can't be alone with a man like him. With any man." She forced herself to remain calm, to sound rational. "Women have nothing but their reputations to offer in a marriage. Do you want to destroy your chances? Do you want people talking about you like they do about Liggy?"

A pout formed on Claire's lips. "This is different."

"How? People talked about her because she liked to go dancing in such places as Lucky's suggesting. They talked until no one would consider her for a wife."

"Fiske would."

"Would you settle for the likes of Fiske?"

Claire threw her petticoat onto the floor in the corner of the room. Her voice was a wail of protest. "But I want to go dancing! It's so unfair."

Anna began to unbutton her dress. "I know. A lot of things are unfair if you're a woman." She hung the garment on a peg in the armoire. "But at least you see why you can't go somewhere alone with a man, a virtual stranger."

Claire didn't respond but there was a pensiveness in her expression. Anna didn't like it but she decided she would leave off for the moment. Tomorrow, when she had had time to sort through this mess, she would gather her arguments into a more persuasive assault. Surely, Claire would give up this foolishness once she understood the ramifications of such actions.

They were snuggled into bed, the lights out, but neither of them slept. Anna knew Claire was still awake by the sound of her breathing. She wondered how different it would be to sleep in the same bed with a man, with Sam. Did he snore as her father did? Or would his slumber be as quiet as Reuben's? Would he be a restless sleeper like Reuben, up often in the night, pacing the front porch in his bare feet?

"Wouldn't you like to go dancing, Anna?"

With her mind miles away, her thoughts unguarded, Anna's reaction to the question sent a little shock through her. Yes, she wanted to go dancing, to wear something pretty and have men look at her. She gripped her hands into fists and tried to push away the desire to have a man's arms around her, a strange, dangerous man; to have him pull her close against his body. Anna pulled her clinched fists into her abdomen but the shameful feelings and thoughts wouldn't go away. "I don't know how to dance."

"Neither do I but it can't be that hard. Lucky said he would teach me."

Anna turned her flushed, heated face into the pillow. "We aren't supposed to dance."

"Only because the preacher says so. It's not really a sin. Lucky says lots and lots of Christians he knows dance and think nothing of it."

Anna opened her eyes and rolled onto her back. "Lucky knows a lot of Christians, does he?"

"Don't be sarcastic, Anna." There was a huff in Claire's voice. "You don't know him."

"So you keep saying."

Claire turned onto her side so that she faced Anna. "If you came with us, you would get to know him, then you'd see. He's really a gentleman."

"No, Claire, I won't go with you. I'm not so eager as you to throw away my reputation."

"It wouldn't be throwing away anything if no one knows."

"How do you think you're going to manage that? You have no idea where this place, this club, is. Or how you're to get there and back without being missed."

Claire rolled onto her back. "Don't worry, I've got that all figured out and the club's over near Finley."

"That's across the river. You'll have to take the ferry and then everyone will know."

"I'm going with Aunt Lena when she take's eggs to Grandma Saturday afternoon. We'll stay the night just like she always does and come back across the river for church on Sunday morning." She snuggled further under the covers. "It's as simple as that."

"Grandma Milkisen and Aunt Lena aren't going to let you go off with a strange man."

"They won't know. I'll slip out after they're asleep." She laughed. "Thunder couldn't wake either of them once they're asleep." She yawned. "We'd have so much fun, Anna. I wish you'd come." She yawned again and fell silent.

Anna stared at the faint lines of the boards of the ceiling, her mind in turmoil. Claire had everything figured out. It was just possible she could pull it off. But Anna had no doubt that Lucky would be far less a gentleman than he had led Claire to believe once she was away from the protection of family. Alone, there would be no reason for him to exercise restraint.

In the dark, the poorly formed letters of the misspelled words of his note formed in her mind. There had been a certain charm in his turn of phrase. And Claire so desperately wanted to experience such things as dances and the attentions of handsome young men. As did Anna.

She tried to close her mind against the thought but the image of Joseph as she had last seen him, dark, almost menacing, planted itself in her mind's eye. He would be with Lucky, together they would go to the dance hall. She could see him on the dance floor, his arms around a woman, smiling down at her. Anna gave over to the warmth that crept slowly over her body and her eyelids drooped languidly. She wanted to be that woman. Yes, like Claire, she wanted to dance.

CHAPTER 16
MAY, 1941

ANNA HAD NOT slept well. Scenes from the past haunted her until the early hours of the morning. Her face felt tight and drawn. She knew her appearance, even with a dusting of powder and bright lipstick, barely passed muster. Still, she had to go about her usual routine. To do otherwise would invite closer scrutiny than a haggard appearance. With that resolve, Anna gave her hair one final flick of the brush and left her room.

Rose glanced up when Anna entered the kitchen, then down at the letter in her hands. She quickly folded the pages and stuffed them into the envelope as she spoke. "Good morning, Mother."

Anna noticed Rose's cheeks glowed with heightened color. "What have you there?" She went to the stove and poured a cup of coffee.

"Just a letter." Rose slipped the envelope into her skirt pocket.

Something in Rose's voice made Anna look around at her. She started to ask who the letter was from but Rose's averted face and the stiff set of her shoulders stilled Anna's tongue. She turned her attention to the view instead.

The spring sun was just clearing the treetops, the morning air still crystalline with dew. This was her favorite time of day and she wished she were in her woods. She could almost feel the chill damp on her face and the comforting embrace of the silence. It had always been a place of solace, a refuge from the inescapable facts of her life. But now even that was denied her. There was no place, in fact, on Carroll's Hill where she could escape the memories of that long ago spring. Each place where the years had mellowed the passion and pain of the past was once again haunted. Would she ever again achieve that degree of acceptance, that state of grace? She didn't know.

Joseph's return came on the heels of so many changes in her life. Rose's marriage would forever remove the one commonality with her mother. Without Rose as the glue, how would the two women exist in the same house? And Sam. Good, patient Sam. How would Joseph's return affect her decision concerning Sam?

Anna held the cup of coffee close to her face and inhaled the rich fragrance and the warmth and felt her resolve return. All these things would play themselves out in the course of this day but only she could direct her fate. In the end, it was all up to her. If only she could have had this wisdom all those years ago. She straightened her shoulders and turned back to face Rose. "I suppose we should give some thought to dinner. We probably should invite Mr. Holt to join us."

"Yes." Rose stood and refilled her cup. "He's very nice. Not at all what I expected." She took a sip of the hot liquid. "But then I only had Nanna's reaction to go by. She doesn't much like timber men, does she?"

"No."

"Why is that, I wonder?"

Anna turned to the bread box and took out a loaf. "Because of Claire, I imagine. She can't forget what happened that summer."

"And why don't you like him?"

Anna's hand stilled in the process of spreading butter on a piece of bread. "What makes you think I don't?"

"Because his arrival has upset you. And you look as if you've hardly slept."

"You're right, I didn't sleep much." She put the bread down untasted. "I can't forget what happened to Claire either. And I remember the desolate wasteland the loggers left in their wake. I don't look forward to a repetition of that spring." She took her cup to the table and sat. "But I have nothing personal against Mr. Holt."

Rose joined her mother at the table. "I feel guilty that everyone is having to make such sacrifices for me. It isn't necessary, you know. I don't care for all this ceremony and neither does Marsh."

"Enjoy this time, darling. None of us regret what must be done. As much as I hate to admit it, your grandmother is right. This isn't just for you, it's for all of us. We're so very proud of you and we want to celebrate your happiness."

"Are you really happy about Marsh? Do you think I'm doing the right thing?"

Anna frowned. "What are you saying?"

Rose blushed. "Nothing, only everyone is making such a fuss and I don't deserve it."

Anna breathed deeply in relief. "Of course you do. You're our pleasure. Without you--well, what else is there?"

"Sam." Rose took her mother's hand. "There has always been Sam."

Anna looked down at her daughter's long slender fingers, so unlike her own small hands. "Yes, Sam's been a good friend to us all these years."

"Why have you never married him? Is it because of my father?"

"No." How could she answer such a question? She didn't dare tell Rose she hadn't married Sam out of selfishness, out of a mistaken belief that her independence was more important than the happiness of so many people, herself included. "What I felt for your father has nothing to do with my reasons for not marrying Sam."

"Then why?"

Anna tightened her fingers around Rose's hand. "That's between Sam and me."

"He loves you, you know."

"Yes, I know." Anna patted her daughter's hand and rose from the table. "Now what about dinner? Fried chicken again? Or should I have Reuben bring in a ham from the smoke house?" She took her cup of cold coffee and emptied it into the sink. "I might be able to find enough sugar snaps for one more meal. I wish the new potatoes were ready but we can make do with rice. And gravy."

Rose sighed and began clearing away the rest of the breakfast dishes. "Addie Mae hasn't baked this week but we could have biscuits. And there're a few sweet potatoes in the storeroom. We could have a casserole for a sweet."

"With some mustard greens, that should do. I'll pick them now while the dew is still on them."

Rose stacked the dishes in the sink and stared down at them a moment before turning to her mother. "Could we stretch things to include one more?"

Anna stopped in the motion of reaching a basket down from the top of the cupboard. "Are you expecting Marsh?"

Rose began to fill the sink with water. "No." She hesitated. "Walker will be passing through today." She turned off the tap and took the letter from her pocket but didn't open it. "It came on Monday. His letter." She smoothed her thumb across the lettering on the envelope. "He's on his way to Meridian. On business."

With the basket resting against her hip, Anna studied her daughter's face. "Yes, of course. But you should have told me. After all he did for us, to entertain us while we were in Mobile, I'd like to be able to offer him a little better than pot luck."

"I'm sorry. I should have said something earlier." She slipped the envelope into her pocket. "I guess I forgot, what with Mr. Holt's arrival and everything."

Anna said nothing but continued to watch her daughter as she busied herself with washing the breakfast dishes. Rose refused to meet her gaze and a frown creased Anna's forehead. Joseph Holt's arrival on Wednesday didn't explain Rose's forgetfulness of Monday. Or Tuesday. Why had she kept this to herself? And Road's End wasn't exactly on the way from Mobile to Meridian.

A chill finger of unease deepened Anna's frown as she turned to the door and the garden beyond. What was going on in her daughter's head? More importantly, what was going on in her heart?

Although her thoughts were still with Rose, Anna found herself listening for the sound of a car engine. Joseph remained just beneath the surface of her conscious thoughts and actions. She found them bubbling to the surface in any unguarded moment. Even as she worked her way down the long row of mustard greens, gathering the tender under leaves, she found herself listening, waiting for his arrival

A blush of shame washed over her as she realized there was an element of anticipation associated with the dread of their next encounter. What did she feel for him after all these years? The sense of panic of yesterday had passed. She now knew her own strength, that outwardly she could cope. But what would be left in the wake of his departure?

She stood still in the middle of the row, staring into the distance, the gentle sounds of the morning all around her as she realized she would have to know. There could be no going back. But there could be no going forward either until her own heart was settled. It was clear to her now what she must do and as she walked toward the house, she listened with purpose for the sound of the truck motor.

JOSEPH DRANK THE strong coffee Lena Milkisen placed before him and marveled at the constitution that could stand up to such a brew on a regular basis. The kitchen was redolent with the smell of ham sizzling in the skillet and the clatter of iron against iron as she fueled the old wood burning cook stove. "I haven't had a meal prepared on one of those since my logging days." He slathered butter on a hot biscuit as he spoke. "Ummm. I'd forgotten how good a country break-fast could be."

Lena waved a hand dismissively. "Go on, now. I'm sure your wife cooks up a mighty fine meal. It's just someone else's cooking now and again makes a nice change." She set a plate of fried eggs, ham, and grits before him. "You eat up now. Traipsing about in the woods takes a mite of energy."

Joseph had given up any pretense of keeping the purpose of his visit to himself. It appeared that with his first pass through Road's End the word had gone out of his arrival and people had speculated about his business on Carroll's Hill. As with his first trip here years ago, everyone knew enough of everyone else's business to draw a fairly accurate conclusion.

The hinges of the back screen door squealed and Percy entered the kitchen. He hung his cap on a peg by the door and went straight to the coffee pot. Once he had poured a cup and positioned himself across the table from Joseph, he nodded in greeting. "Aiming to talk Helen outta that old stand of timber, are you?"

"I hadn't thought about it. She hasn't said exactly what she has in mind." The look Joseph received for this response let him understand Percy wasn't deceived.

"Well, bigger fool you if you don't. There's a fella over Finley way buying up all he can. Waiting for Roosevelt to have us jump headlong into the war and the big boon from the government." He bit into a biscuit and washed it down with a big slug of coffee. "Won't be long before he or someone like him gets wind of all that virgin timber on Carroll's Hill." One of the three fried eggs on his plate disappeared in one bite. He talked around the food. "They'll be on to Helen like fleas on a coon dog." He pointed his fork at Joseph. "Best get it while you can."

"We'll see what Mrs. Carroll has in mind."

Percy grunted and focused his full attention on his breakfast. Nothing broke the quiet of the morning except the sound of utensils against china. When Percy sopped up the last bit of honey with a crumb of biscuit, he sat back in his chair and hitched his thumbs under the braces of his overalls. "I was right surprised to see Helen had called in Battle's Mill after that business the last time. Folks 'round these parts ain't over it yet." He shook his head slowly side to side.

Joseph waited for him to continue but only silence followed. "What business was that?"

"Claire."

Joseph sat back also and made another attempt with the coffee. He marveled at the fact that he held the cup so steady. "Claire?"

Lena pushed the cream pitcher across the table to him. "Our niece. Lived in the first house west of the store."

"Anna—Mrs. Moreland's cousin?" Did his voice hold the right touch of vague remembrance, he wondered.

"Yes." Lena sighed. "It was a sad day for this town. She was such a pretty girl. Spoiled, headstrong, but everyone thought a lot of her. Couldn't help but like a bubbly little thing like her."

"What happened?" Joseph felt his initial sense of dread open out like a bottomless well. This then was the innuendo behind Sam Stones comments of the previous afternoon. He knew it in his bones. When he raised his gaze to meet Percy's steely regard, he realized the old man knew he knew it.

Percy cleared his throat. "Drowned is what." He scraped back his chair and got the coffee pot from the stove.

Joseph declined a second cup but Percy refilled his own and Lena's. Joseph stared into the milky depths of his coffee. "How?"

"Tried to cross the river in a little skiff belonging to one of the colored boys. Current caught it. River was high due to all the rain that spring. It was the day they finished up logging Carroll's Hill and broke camp. The ferry took the last of 'em across the river late that day." He watched Joseph with hard narrowed eyes. "You remember that day, Mr. Holt?"

Joseph looked down at his cup. "No. I wasn't with the crew at the end. Mr. Battle had sent me on to another job."

Percy grunted.

Lena began to collect their dirty plates. "Some say she was just slipping off to that road house in Finley. Rumor was she'd been seen there before."

"It was that colored boy of Moses's. But I don't see it myself. Girl like Claire wouldn't even know how to go about getting to a place like that.

Besides, it had burnt down a good two months before." Percy shook his head again. "No sir, I don't see it."

Lena swallowed and her voice was strained when she spoke. "I near cried my eyes out over that child. She was only seventeen."

Joseph kept his gaze on the coffee cup, on the blue checkered tablecloth. He felt a tightness in his chest. "No one ever figured out why she went out on the river like that?"

"No." Lena took a sip of coffee. "I always thought–"

Percy set his coffee mug on the table with a sharp crack and stood. "No point botherin' our guest with idle speculation, Sister. I don't 'spect he much remembers the folks around here." He stared down at Joseph. "That right, Mr. Holt?"

Percy's action and comment served to stop the flow of Lena's gossip. A deep blush crimsoned her face all the way to the roots of her hair.

Joseph made no comment. Claire's death was news to him. He didn't know if that was because he had been so ill for so long after the accident that by the time he was aware of what was going on around him the tragedy had been displaced by the pressing matters of the day-to-day, or if Harry Battle had been unaware of it. Lucky had moved on by the time Joseph was able to return to work. At the time Joseph assumed it was due to the usual reasons that infected the type of men who worked in the timber business, restlessness, a golden opportunity down the road, or simply general oneryness.

"Did you know Claire, Mr. Holt?"

Lena's question caused Joseph to start from his thoughts. "Ah, yes. A little. That is, I saw her at Mr. Carroll's the first day the team arrived." He glanced from her to Percy then returned his gaze to his cup of now cold coffee. "And another time she was at the store when I came to send a telegram." He cleared his throat. "I didn't really know her, only to nod or say hello in passing. I'm real sorry to hear about her death."

"Humph." Percy turned from the table, caught his cap from the peg and left the house, the screen door slamming behind him.

Joseph stared after him. Had Claire been running away with Lucky? It had all been so long ago he could no longer say. But from what he remembered of Lucky he didn't think the wiry ladies man would have wanted to take on a seventeen-year-old girl. For Claire, unlike Anna, had been very much a child still, impulsive, willful, and reckless. No, he didn't think Lucky would have encouraged Claire to leave her secure, pampered existence to join him on the road. Not in words at least, but perhaps by his deeds.

Lucky had lavished her with attention, teased and flirted. What else had gone on between them he could only guess. He didn't doubt there had been more than chaste kisses. But by then Joseph had been so consumed with Anna that he hadn't been vigilant. The truth was he hadn't wanted to analyze Lucky's motives, his behavior, because it so closely mirrored Joseph's own.

"Well, it's all history now. I doubt we'll ever find out what really happened. And I suppose we would have gotten over it long ago if Anna hadn't up and left so soon after." Lena rose and went to the sink and began washing dishes.

Joseph remained seated, not making a sound, willing Lena to continue. She didn't.

It was obvious to Joseph that Lena loved to gossip and now that they were alone, he was tempted to prompt her. Something held him back. It was the cool reserve with which Anna had received him, the blatant manipulation of the conversation around the supper table that Sam had orchestrated. He had learned little of what had transpired in the last nineteen years. All topics had focused on Rose and her upcoming wedding, details of the young man she planned to marry and his family. The lot of them had closed ranks and determined once again that Joseph was an outsider.

He mastered the urge to pry and left the kitchen. He stood on the back porch and suppressed a groan. The left rear tire of the truck was flat. With resignation he cast about for Percy. The clank of a cowbell drew his eye and he saw the tall raw-boned man leading a line of cows from the barn toward the pasture. Joseph didn't think Percy would disrupt his routine to come to his assistance.

With a wry grin, he rolled up his shirtsleeves and jacked up the truck. It took him a good fifteen minutes to find the puncture and discover he didn't have a patch.

The screen door banged and Joseph turned to see a young colored boy skip down the steps. He came to stand beside the jacked-up truck. "Miss Lena sent me." He stared up at Joseph and grinned. One of his front teeth was missing.

Lena came onto the porch, a dishtowel in her hand. "Knee-Hi here's gonna take that on over to Sam's. He's got a boy that can patch it right up."

Joseph reached into his pocket and took out a dime and flipped it high in the air. Knee-Hi jumped and caught the coin. The grin widened and Joseph smiled in return. "Let's go."

Knee-Hi set the wheel in motion, rolling toward the road, and ran along beside it balancing it with his hand each time it threatened to wobble to a stop. Joseph followed after him at a more leisurely pace and an older version of Knee-Hi was already examining it by the time he covered the quarter mile to Toxey's General Store. He left it to them and slowly mounted the steps.

Sam Stone was measuring cornmeal into a brown paper sack for an elderly lady with wire-rimmed eyeglasses. The thick lenses magnified her pale blue irises as she turned to look at Joseph.

"Mr. Holt." Sam lifted the package from the scale and his long, slender fingers and deft movements had it quickly tied up with string. "What can I do for you?"

Joseph gestured over his shoulder with his thumb. "I've got a flat. Your boy is seeing to it."

"Ah. Percy's new roof. You must have parked around back."

Joseph removed his hat and nodded at the elderly patron. "Yes. Percy suggested it."

Sam nodded. "Guess he wasn't thinking."

Joseph watched Sam's face but saw nothing there but bland indifference. "I suspect maybe he was."

A shadow of a smile was quickly suppressed. "Why's that?"

"Oh, I don't know. Folks around here don't seem to cotton much to strangers."

"We keep to ourselves, that's true, but I'm sure Percy wouldn't wish you any trouble."

The old woman cleared her throat and Sam returned to her order. "Sure I can't interest you in some of this fresh spinach, Aunt Sadie? Knee-Hi brought it this morning. Says it's not bitter at all."

She seemed to consider for a few seconds then shook her head. "Thank you, no, Sam. I've got turnips still."

"Well, I'm putting a half dozen eggs in your basket. Helen Carroll sent them along for you yesterday. Her hens are laying more than she can use." He carefully nested the eggs in some newspaper. "Anything else I can get you?"

"No. I'll just sign the ticket."

Sam pulled a small note pad across the counter and made some notations on it. When he finished he pushed it in front of her and watched as she painstakingly read over it and signed her name in a shaky script. When she had finished, he went to the open doorway. "Knee-Hi, come take Aunt Sadie's package for her."

Knee-Hi bounded into the store. "Mornin', Miss Sadie."

"Morning, Knee-Hi. Don't you have school today?"

"No'm. It's Mr. Lincoln's birthday today."

"Is it?" Her head wavered a moment. "Well, you just help me down the steps then."

"Yes'm."

After Miss Sadie made her slow way out of the store, Sam once again turned his attention to Joseph. "Thomas will fix your tire."

Joseph was still staring out the door as Knee-Hi carefully guided the old lady across the road. "I thought Lincoln's birthday was in February."

"It is but he tells her the same thing year round." He looked through the door at the slow progress of the boy and old woman. "It seems to ease her mind."

Joseph nodded and turned in time to see Sam drop the ticket the old lady had signed into the trash barrel. "How much? For the repair."

"A quarter for the patch. You pay Thomas for the repair."

"Not much has changed around here, has it?" Joseph's gaze traveled around the laden shelves and narrow aisles of the store. When only silence followed his question, he turned to find Sam regarding him with a look close to malice.

Finally Sam spoke. "No one in Road's End wants you here, Mr. Holt, except Helen Carroll. It might be a good thing if you finished up your business and moved on."

"Does this have anything to do with Claire's death?"

Sam studied him a long moment. "You tell me."

"I knew nothing about it until this morning at breakfast. But for some reason I get the feeling folks think I should."

"Maybe you don't but there are other reasons folks don't want a repeat visit from Battle's Mill."

"Such as?"

"What this community lost as a result of your last visit can never be replaced." Sam came from behind the counter. "The whole town mourned for Claire. Especially Anna. For some reason she felt an overwhelming sense of guilt." He clenched his jaw then relaxed it. "Can you tell me why she should feel that way, Mr. Holt?"

At least Sam Stone wasn't beating around the bush. Anna was the issue here. "I think she must have cared very much for her cousin. They appeared to be close." He squared his shoulders and let his hands fall loose at his side. "But if there's something you're trying to tell me, just spill it."

"Don't make any plans to stay around Road's End. Anna's suffered enough and I won't have you dredging up old painful memories. She deserves to be happy."

"I hope she will be, Mr. Stone." Joseph dug a quarter from his pocket and flipped it onto the counter before he turned and walked out.

CHAPTER 17
MARCH, 1922

THEY COULD HEAR the music a good quarter mile before they saw cars and trucks parked along the roadside. Lights from the roadhouse filtered through the trees as they found a place to park, the truck teetering precariously on the edge of a ditch. Joseph heard male laughter as they made their way up the red clay drive, and when they were still thirty yards from the building, he smelled the sour scent of spilled beer and moonshine. Cigarettes glowed like fireflies in the night as patrons stood about on the long sloping porch that fronted the structure. The low murmur of a woman's voice reached him, followed by her throaty laughter. Joseph felt the sound deep in his belly. Lucky had been right. This was just what he needed. He took a deep breath and followed Lucky up the sagging steps and through the door.

A grizzled man with tobacco pouched in his cheek, the juice of it staining his beard, rose from a wooden barrel beside the door and barred their way. He looked them up and down then turned in the direction of a table of people playing cards. A woman in a faded and not too clean shapeless dress looked up from her hand and stared at first Lucky then Joseph. A man's hand came to rest on the pale flesh of her shoulder where the faded garment had slipped down her arm. She slapped it away before she nodded at the bearded doorman and returned her attention to her cards. He spit on the floor and returned to his seat.

Joseph and Lucky stood in the doorway and surveyed the room. Half a dozen or so scarred tables with mismatched chairs occupied the middle of the room. To one side a trio of negroes sweated as they played on a fiddle, a washboard, and a trumpet. Couples hugged their bodies together on the dance floor and moved their feet. At the far side of the room, near another door, a stack of apple crates formed the bar. Here the greatest number of patrons congregated.

A dark haired woman sat perched upon one end of the bar, her legs crossed, the weight of her body leaning back, supported by her hands. Her throaty laughter was like an undercurrent to the general hum of voices and music. She accepted a cigarette from a man standing beside her, leaning into her. She pushed him back and sat forward, brought the cigarette to her scarlet mouth and as he lit it, looked up from beneath a veil of dark curling hair directly at Joseph as he and Lucky made their way toward the bar. She shook back her hair and exhaled a stream of smoke as she smiled. It was a look Joseph knew and understood.

He ordered a shot and threw it back, enjoying the burn. When it hit his stomach, he quelled the quiver and kept it down. A good sign as to the merit of the concoction. The smell of spilled booze was stronger here, as was the scent of unwashed bodies. The woman appeared at his side, her soft breast pressing against his arm, her perfume, like everything else about her, loud and flowery. He asked for another glass and the bottle.

"Haven't seen you around here before."

Her voice was husky from too many late nights and too many cigarettes. He liked that. "No, you haven't."

"What's your name?" She entwined her arm with his and turned him toward one of the tables.

"Joseph." He pulled out a chair for her then sat down and looked at her closely for the first time. Like so many olive skinned women, it was hard to guess her age but she bore the signs of a life lived hard. He poured out two drinks. "What's yours?"

"Mara." She studied him through the haze of her cigarette smoke. "You not look like farmer."

"Should I?"

She laughed. "That's all we get around here. That and soft-bellied traveling salesmans." She leaned her elbows on the table, her eyelids drooping over dark, liquid eyes. "You no salesman."

A shrill of high, feminine laughter drew Joseph's attention and he saw Lucky running his hand over the backside of a blonde woman on the dance floor. One corner of his mouth lifted in amusement. He looked back at Mara and drained the glass. "Let's dance."

She was soft and pliant in his arms and she knew how to fit her body to a man's. And yet it wasn't the same as all those other women and other clubs over the years. Perhaps it was the strong scent of her perfume. The warmer her skin grew as they danced, the louder the fragrance. After only one dance he returned to the table and the bottle. She assumed it her right to join him and he didn't object. Perhaps the whiskey would help. He kept tipping the bottle over both their glasses and after a time, he again felt the desire to rub his belly against hers.

He didn't register the fact of Lucky slipping out the door as Mara's body connected with his in all the right places.

GRAVEL CRUNCHED UNDERFOOT as Anna and Claire hurried toward the old mill house. The trees on either side of the lane were a blacker silhouette against the night sky and the path before them stood out like a chalked blackboard in the light of the moon. When the truck came into view, Claire smothered a squeal of delight and grabbed Anna's hand as she started to run.

Anna resisted and watched as Claire ran on ahead. In the shadow of the truck, a cigarette tip glowed. It arced across the night as it was flipped aside and the shadow of a man rose and detached itself from that of the truck as Claire drew near. Anna heard the undertone of urgency in Lucky's voice as she approached and smelled the liquor. It was evident he wasn't happy to have her in the party even though he merely said "Well, get in, then."

The hard metal of the door handle dug into Anna's upper arm with each jolt. Claire sat in the middle of the seat and giggled and chattered in a high pitch of excitement. Anna felt nothing but increasing dread. She had been unable to allow Claire to make this rendezvous alone. That decision made, she had been unable to suppress a building excitement as the hour of the assignation drew near. But all anticipation left her when she realized that Lucky was the only one waiting for them at the truck.

In the clear light of reason, she didn't delude herself that all her justifications for falling in with this foolishness had been for Claire's sake. Since the first mention of it, she had been in a fever of anticipation to see Joseph, to be with him. She had been so certain he would be with his friend.

Now the full weight of their folly bore down on her. How had she ever felt they would be able to go to such a place and remain undiscovered? Someone there would surely know them. The scandal would quickly spread and they would endure a beating of the first order from her father. Claire's father wouldn't dare intervene. She thought of her cousin Liggy, then she thought of Sam. How could she defend her actions to Sam? She felt faint with shame. "We have to go back."

Claire was whispering in Lucky's ear and giggling. Neither of them appeared to hear Anna's softly spoken request. She cleared her throat. "Stop the truck."

Lucky eased off the accelerator but didn't stop. "What's the matter? You gonna be sick or something?"

"We have to go back."

The silence drew out for a few seconds then Lucky gunned the engine. "Not just yet. The night's still young."

"We can't go to this place." She clutched Claire by the arm. "People will know us, Claire. And they'll talk. It'll be known all over Road's End and lord knows where else."

Claire's voice huffed defensively. "Who in the world would we know, Anna? No one of our acquaintance would own that they'd been to a roadhouse."

Lucky chuckled. "Don't you worry your pretty little head, Miss Anna. Folks that come to Blue Betty's don't meddle in nobody else's business."

"Oh, Claire, hasn't anything I've said to you these past three days made the least impression?"

"You're just afraid there'll be trouble. Well, don't worry. If anything happens I'll say it was all my doing, that you had no part in it. That you were afraid to let me come alone."

But Anna knew Claire would be the first to cry and protest her innocence if they were caught. Everything would be laid at her door, and rightly so for Anna was the older, the more sensible one, the one who knew better. "Stop this truck!"

For a moment she thought he was going to ignore her demand but finally with a grinding of gears, he brought the truck to a halt. He looked across at her, his expression hard. Claire's lip stuck out in mulish defiance and she backed as close against Lucky as she could get.

"Please, take us back to the mill house."

Lucky continued to stare at her with an unblinking regard. "You want to go back Claire?"

"No."

They sat there a few seconds, the motor idling. "Looks like you're out numbered, Miss Anna. So if you're looking to go back, it's gonna be a goodly little walk." He shifted into first gear but didn't give the engine any gas. His expression took on that winning grin Anna had seen him bestow on Claire. "It's only a little fun, Miss Anna. No harm will come of it, you'll see."

Claire took Anna's hand and hugged it to her bosom. "Yes, Anna. Let's just go and have some fun. Lucky will look out for us. He won't let anything bad happen."

"You won't take us back, then?"

Lucky grinned broader. "Sure I will. After we've danced a dance or two." He pressed down on the accelerator and the truck began to move forward. "And you'll be glad of it, I'll warrant, before the night is through."

Anna sat back against the seat and stared out at the passing trees and fence posts as they flashed by in the surreal landscape of the night. What a mess she had gotten them into.

ANNA AND CLAIRE huddled near the table someone had shoved into a corner of the room as Lucky picked up an overturned chair. The hour was late, how late, Anna couldn't say. They hadn't left her grandmother's house until after ten o'clock and in the strange light of the moon, time and distance had become distorted. Perhaps it had only been her paralyzing fear that made the journey to this place seem to last forever. It was obvious from the state of the room and the lingering sense of excitement that a fight had broken up just prior to their arrival. Her heart hammered in her throat at the wild laughter and strangely reeling music. Bodies swayed and lurched against one another at one end of the building in an almost frenzied dance. It all held a pitch bordering on hysteria. Was this the way it always was in such a place?

"Here ya go, girls. Take a seat and I'll get us a little liquid refreshment." Lucky held out a chair for Claire and grinned down at her as she sat.

"Coca Cola." Anna sat beside her cousin. "Just Coca Colas, Lucky."

"Sure thing." He grinned and started for the bar.

Anna sat with her body in profile to the room and tried to keep her head turned from view but she couldn't. The scene fascinated her even as it frightened her with its blatant uninhibited revelry. The sweating faces of the musicians, their eyes unfocused in the throes of the building notes, their bodies swaying like puppets on the thread of the music, reminded her of the look she had once seen in Moses's face and the tension in his body early one spring morning when her father had lashed him across the back with his walking cane. It wasn't the hatred she recognized but the bare brink of control, that fleeting second in which all could be lost. She tore her eyes from the sight and watched the couples so entangled with one another that their movements, so intimate, caused a flush of that old familiar restlessness.

It was then that she recognized Mara Duardo and her heart stilled in her chest. The older woman stared straight at her but didn't appear to see. Mara's eyes, like those of the colored musicians, held a vacant, lost look.

Anna blinked and finally took a breath. In that state, she hoped the woman whose features were so indelibly etched in her own memory wouldn't recognize her. She was already in the process of turning her head away, to give Mara only a back view of her, when she realized who her dance partner was. The blood drained from her face and she couldn't look away.

As the couple turned, Joseph now faced her, his chin resting on Mara's dark hair where it spilled over her shoulder. A trickle of blood seeped from the corner of his eye and his cheekbone bore an angry red scrape. Anna gripped the edge of the table and slowly her gaze traveled down Mara's body where Joseph's hands cradled her well rounded backside. And the way they moved, like a pair of snakes entwined, caused the image of Mara and Reuben in the hayloft all those years ago to flash like heat lightning in her mind.

The sharp rap of the glass against the wooden table brought Anna's head around to stare at the dark liquid Lucky had just set before her. She looked at it as if she didn't recognize it.

"Coca Cola, just like you ordered." Lucky winked at Claire and grinned. "Drink up."

Anna took a shaky breath and turned back to the dance floor. Joseph and his partner now appeared to be nearer and, if possible, his attentions to her more blatant. Anna's gaze traveled up from his hand, low on Ava's backside, to Joseph's face and realized he was now staring straight at her. There was nothing vacant or lost in his regard. With slow deliberation, he worked his hands into Mara's hair and drew her head away from his shoulder and kissed her, long and hard.

The blood returned to Anna's face with force and she quickly turned away only to find herself alone at the table. The glass came into focus and she grasped it and took a large gulp. Like fire, the liquid traveled down her throat and when it hit her stomach, she clapped her hand across her mouth to keep it from returning. Tears welled in her eyes and after the rioting in her stomach settled, she took another drink. She felt a sense of release travel through her, the kind of release that comes after the muscles have been stressed beyond endurance. Was this what people sought when they drank liquor, she wondered, this giving over, this escape? How far could she escape if she drank the rest of the contents of the glass? Not far enough, she decided, because tomorrow morning she would still be in Road's End, no nearer to understanding herself than she was right now, and, with the added humiliation of knowing she had subjected herself to Joseph's rejection. She raised the glass but hesitated.

"What'cha drinkin'?"

Joseph's voice, so near, his voice and yet somehow different, made her hand tremble and she lowered the glass to the table. "Coca Cola." She turned to discover that he was squatting at her elbow.

He lifted the glass and it tipped precariously in his hand. He brought it to his nose and sniffed. "I see." He rose to his feet and caught the back of her chair to steady himself. "C'mon."

Anna continued to sit as she stared straight ahead.

"C'mon, I'm gettin' you outta here."

She turned away from him and remained silent.

He pulled out the chair beside her and sat heavily. "What in hell you think you're doin'? Comin' to a place like this?"

She dropped her gaze to her hands resting in her lap. "It's not your concern."

He blew out a loud breath and with his elbow resting on the table, placed his forehead in the palm of his hand. He weaved on the edge of the chair and his elbow slipped from the table. "Damn Lucky." He blinked slowly twice as he appeared to try to focus. He searched the couples on the dance floor. "Where's Claire? With him?"

A jolt of fear raced through Anna and she, too, scanned the dance floor, searching for her cousin. Finally, her shoulders sank with relief as she spied Claire's red curls weaving in and out of the crush of bodies. "Dancing." Her throat felt tight. "She wanted to dance."

"So that's why."

Anna turned to look into Joseph's face for the first time. He had slumped back in the chair. She lifted her hand to the cut just above his eye and feathered her fingers across it. With a quickness she wouldn't have attributed to him in his state of inebriation, he caught her by the wrist and brought her palm to his cheek and held it there.

"What happened to your face?"

"Davin." He grinned.

"Davin?"

"Old business. Done now." He rubbed her hand against his jaw. "I've wanted the feel of your touch since I first saw you standin' there barefoot on your front porch." His voice grew rough. "Your ankles, so small." He took her other hand and placed it on the opposite cheek. He closed his eyes. When he opened them, he smiled and ran his thumbs over her wrists. "Soft. I knew you would feel like this. Soft." He lowered her hands and stared at the delicate wrists resting in his grasp. "Like a bird, so--"

He swayed toward her then caught himself upright. A flush darkened his features. "I can't say it right." His eyelashes swept low on his cheeks. "Like it oughtta be, like in a book. Like your poems." He released her and leaned back in the chair as he grinned broadly. "I'm drunk."

Anna was drunk too, but not from the small amount of bootleg liquor she had consumed. She felt flushed and hot, unsettled by his intense scrutiny, by his clumsy words. "You need some fresh air."

He shook his head. "Dance with me, Anna."

She looked down at her hands as a tremor of anticipation ran through her. The image of Mara

Duardo's body against his returned and she looked away. "I can't." A heavy silence followed her refusal. She took a deep, shuddering breath. "I don't know how."

He rose from his chair and extended his hand. "I'll teach you."

She stared at his hand and as the seconds ticked away, she saw it tremble. Instinctively, she reached out and clasped it. He pulled her up gently and folded her into his arms where they stood.

He inhaled her scent and smiled. "Here," his hand slid along her right thigh. "Put your foot against the outside a mine. Yeah." His arm tightened around her waist as she complied. "Now, the other goes against the inside of my right. Like that." He smiled crookedly down at her as he raised her right hand in his then he buried his nose in her hair and stood still until Anna felt herself begin to relax against him. "Ummm. That's it. Just let go." He began to sway with the music.

She clutched at him, fearing that it was the alcohol that threatened his equilibrium, but gradually she eased into the swaying rhythm with him.

"Feel it, Anna. Let it settle in your backbone. Yeah, like that, now let your feet move with mine."

It amazed her how easily they fit together, how effortlessly she moved in step with him. The liquor, if anything, seemed to enhance his gracefulness. It was only when the music stopped and she tried to move back from him that he misstepped.

"So. Here is winner of Mara."

The sharp edge to the voice brought the room back into focus. Anna turned to find Mara Duardo standing beside them. The comment was addressed to Joseph but Mara stared at Anna.

Joseph looked at her but said nothing. A puzzled expression clouded his features and he weaved slightly.

Mara gave him a quick once over then returned her attention to Anna. "A friend of yours?"

"Yes." Anna was pleased that the tremor of sheer terror she felt running through her didn't reveal itself in her voice. "I've come to get him. He's had too much to drink."

Heat sparked in Mara's eyes. "Maybe he not want to go." Her stance shifted from seductive to aggressive. "And who're you to say, huh?"

"As you said, a friend."

"A friend." Mara's left eyebrow shot up in derision then something in her expression changed. "I know you?"

Anna felt the blood leave her head and thought she would faint dead away. It had been years since Mara had dared show up at Carroll's Hill, years during which Reuben had been away to war and returned a stranger. Anna had been only a child then. Would Mara know her now?

Joseph sloppily draped his arm around Anna and hugged her into his side. "Go on back to the Swede, sweetheart. He's lookin' for you."

Mara stood motionless for a moment, a moment in which the deeping lines and aging flesh of too many late nights and strange men hardened into a mask of incandescent rage. Her voice belied the look. "But you win, Lover Boy. Davin's over in corner nursing his poor ribs." She lowered her lashes seductively. "We go to my place." A deep rumble of humorless laughter welled up from her throat. "This little country girl no take care of you like Mara."

His grip slipped almost to a headlock, forcing Anna's face into his chest, angling his body to block Mara's view of her. "Go on, Mara. There's lots a guys'd be glad to buy you a drink." He tried to brush Mara aside as he started toward the door, Anna in tow, but she caught him by the arm.

"You think I just dirt on your boot, that you scrape me off like cowshit the minute a fresh, young face show up. Is that it?" Mara's voice rose with the heat of her anger and humiliation.

Anna was terrified by the attention Mara's loud accusation was drawing. One of the negroes in the band was looking their way as were a couple of dancers. "Please," she whispered near Joseph's ear, "let me go."

Joseph ignored Anna's plea and Mara's anger. He jerked his arm free of Mara's grasp and tightened his hold on Anna as he propelled her toward the door and the relative safety of the night beyond.

As soon as the door closed behind them, Anna tried to push away from him. "What on earth are you doing?"

"Trying to get you outta there before somebody recognizes you." Joseph grinned and maintained his embrace as they staggered down the steps. As she struggled against him, he stumbled and they nearly fell over the last step. He stopped and brought her against his chest, his arms around her in an embrace. "Stop fightin' me."

"Let me go," she whispered into his chest.

"Is it true?"

"Is what true?"

"What you said." He stared down into her upturned face for a long moment. "That you came for me."

Anna felt her chest tighten. She barely knew this man. In fact, she had only been in his presence on four fleeting occasions prior to tonight. What was wrong with her? What was she doing in this place, risking her reputation, her very person? There was only one answer. "Yes."

Joseph lowered his mouth toward hers and when she didn't turn away, he kissed her. He tasted of cigarettes and moonshine and a summer fever, a contagious summer fever.

When he finally broke the kiss Anna felt breathless. She laid her cheek against his chest and slowly opened her eyes. There framed in the window staring out at her stood Mara Duardo. Anna had never been subjected to a look of such hatred. No one in her short life had ever, to her knowledge, even disliked her. The raw emotion she saw in Mara's expression frightened her more than anything had in a very long time. She pulled back abruptly from Joseph. "I should go--we should--" She stepped back from the light falling from the windows. "I shouldn't be here." Anna swallowed against the panic. "Now she'll never let up until she figures out who I am."

Joseph glanced over his shoulder at the window of the building but Mara had disappeared from view. He stared down at his boots. "You're right. I gotta get you home."

They started across the small clearing near the building and had moved beyond the arc of light from its windows when Anna's muddled thoughts cleared. "Claire. She's inside with Lucky."

Joseph stopped and looked back at the building. "All right, then. You wait here. I'll fetch her." He started to move away and Anna caught him by the shirtsleeve.

"I can't wait here. Out in the open like this."

"Right." Joseph looked down the pea gravel track that led from the roadhouse to the county road. He could see the glow of a lit cigarette in the distance and hear the crunch of gravel underfoot. He pulled Anna into the woods running along the drive. They were only a few feet from the track and they waited in silence as a couple of men, talking low, passed by. When they heard the creaking of the steps beneath their heavy tread, Joseph spoke softly near her ear. "You gonna be all right? Waiting here?"

She hesitated for a mere heartbeat. "Yes." But she didn't let go of his arm.

He raised his hand to her face and let his fingertips trail along her jawline. "You sure?" His voice deepened and he moved closer, his body almost touching hers.

Anna took a deep breath and let it out on a sigh. "No."

"I'm drunk you know." He backed her against the trunk of a large pine.

"Are you?" Anna had ceased to struggle against his nearness. The image of him and Mara on the dance floor wouldn't leave her and she knew she should step free of his embrace but she didn't. Instead, she stood still as he pressed against her, the blood thrumming in her ears at the scent of him. She didn't allow herself to remember that only minutes ago he had been in a state over another woman. Perhaps even now, that desire was only a remnant of what he had felt for Mara. She didn't care. Her own desire unfurled in a wave of warmth that spread throughout her body and settled low in her groin where his body touched hers. Fear of what was about to happen heightened that desire and she felt a growing impatience to discover the secret heart of it.

He whispered near her ear. "Do you know what you're doing?" He pressed his moist lips against her throat. "Do you?"

Anna's breath caught. "No." The whispered reply was barely audible.

"I'm drunk. But not that drunk." His lips pressed against her temple, her forehead and her other temple. "But drunk enough for this." With that he kissed her full on the mouth.

Anna's knees began to tremble and she knew the only thing keeping her upright was his body penning her against the tree. With a small groan he broke the kiss and drew back a few inches. He studied her face in the scant light that seeped into the copse from the moon and the building lights.

Hesitantly, he drew close again and when she didn't resist, he captured her mouth in a torturous kiss and brought his groin hard against her as his hands curved roughly around her breasts. She made a sound deep in her throat as her fingers dug into the rough bark of the pine in an effort to resist the desire to touch him in return.

Anna struggled briefly against the last remnant of caution. This assault on her senses was nothing like the quiet passion she'd felt for Sam. This wild need roared through her like the flames of hell. Finally the restlessness of the long, endless year had been met by a matching impatience and she couldn't turn from it. So she let go. She let go of everything; her reserve, her doubts. Her body yielded and she knew the moment he realized it.

There was a hesitation, fleeting as a snatched instant of memory, then he released her and stepped back, staggering in the tangle of underbrush. The roar that tore from his throat savaged her heart. It was a shout of triumph as well as a cry of anguish. He turned to the nearest tree and punched it violently, once, twice, then he sagged against it, his back to her. Anna's knees would no longer support her. Slowly, she sank to the ground and silent tears of anger and humiliation coursed down her cheeks. She turned her face into the rough bark and welcomed the distraction as it bit into the flesh.

CHAPTER 18

MAY, 1941

ANNA WATCHED THE line of ants as they navigated the coarse bark of the pine. The solace she sought wouldn't come. Even here, in her sanctuary, the floodgate of memories couldn't be barred. Tears pricked at her eyes as the shame of that night at the roadhouse cut as bitingly as it had then.

Joseph's sudden return to her world had done this, had released the old demons of doubt and shame. She pulled a loose piece of bark free and the colonnade of ants abruptly changed course. The scrap of wood fell from her fingers as she turned and with a sigh leaned back against the tree. Recriminations were pointless and didn't help her with the dilemma she now faced.

In an effort to clear her mind, she focused her attention on the opposing sentinel. Her gaze followed the mammoth trunk until it disappeared into the canopy of branches entwined overhead. They shifted in the half-light of this dim, otherworldly place, altering reality, lulling the mind. She felt her tension ease and lowered herself to the deep bed of straw that carpeted the ground.

After a sleepless night the strain of waiting, of listening for the tell-tale approach of Joseph's truck, had worn her down. She had expected him to arrive early but the morning had slowly burned away and with it her nerves. That, coupled with Rose's strange silence and fits of furious activity, had driven Anna from the house. She feared it wasn't thoughts of Marsh and their upcoming wedding that had Rose so restless. Anna knew that feeling, that sense of expectation, of something undefined yet seemingly so necessary to her being. She had come here, to her woods, to think things through, to decide how best to advise her daughter.

There had been no one to advise Anna when she had stood at the same perilous crossroad, when her heart had been torn between the good man she knew and the empty promise of something she couldn't name. Would Walker be Rose's albatross or her salvation? And what if Rose's choice was the wrong one? How could she advise her, Anna who still suffered the guilt of her own decisions. Had she taken the other path, her life would have been different, but would it have been better, happier?

So much had gone unspoken for so long. What would happen if the truth should come out now? For the first time in years Anna questioned the choices she had made. They had seemed right all those years ago. Right for her, perhaps. But so many others had been hurt by those choices, hurt in ways that could never be healed. And she could never tell any of this to her daughter, could never find the words to defend actions that now even she couldn't justify to herself.

Rose had never known anything but unstinting love. How would she react to the knowledge of what Anna had denied her? Especially now, when she needed reassurance. Now when the turmoil between love and desire threatened her peace of mind.

Anna wanted to scream with the injustice of it all. Fate seemed to have it in for the Carroll women. Why couldn't the choices be simple for Rose? The sins of the mother, her father would have said. Well, her sins wouldn't be visited on Rose. Anna would see to that.

If Rose was having doubts about Marsh, it was better to know now and to have it all out in the open. She would see how this meeting went. Over dinner she would watch and weigh what transpired and then she would be better able to judge. Perhaps it would all come to nothing.

Rose had certainly been dazzled with the splendors of the Mardi Gras season and the high society glamour of their stay in Mobile. In a more grounded setting perhaps Walker's allure would not seem so attractive. The cold light of reality had a way of tarnishing even the brightest object.

Anna lay back on the forest floor and stared overhead at the gently swaying treetops. It was mid-morning and the warmth of the day was slowly penetrating the dense woods. Her decisions made, a somnolent ease settled over her and she gave over to the lulling sound of the trees.

Again, as she had so many times since her childhood, she entered into the illusion of a collusion between herself and this place. She listened to the secrets being bandied about overhead and her eyes drifted closed. A contented sigh rose from her lips and then the single name, the name that had been just below the surface for days, rose from that guarded secret place and whispered into the quiet. "Joseph." Her fingers unfurled in an appeal to the silent forest then slowly curled into her palm.

JOSPEH PULLED INTO the drive and sat for a moment with the motor running as he studied the house. The quiet was like a physical thing; he could feel the weight of it like a humid summer day. Finally, he killed the motor and got out of the truck. Sally Dan hopped from the back and stood at his feet, awaiting his cue. "Come on, boy."

Joseph approached the silent house, his footsteps unduly loud against the broad planks of the steps. No one answered his knock, the only sound of life the droning of a dirt dauber building a nest under the eave of the porch. He turned to leave as Rose came around the side of the house.

She hesitated when she saw him, then smiled and approached the porch. She stood at the foot of the steps, shading her eyes with one hand while the other held a basket of yellow daffodils. "Hello, there. I didn't hear the truck."

"Good morning. I'm on my way to check the timber and thought I'd leave it parked here if that's all right."

"It's awfully hot to walk such a distance. You know the way?"

"Yes, I remember the site well."

"The road's quite clear. Reuben keeps it open so he can get the crops in easily. I dare say you could drive."

Joseph came down the steps and stood facing her. He thought she looked a little pale. "I don't mind a good walk. It's been years since inspecting timber was part of my job. I miss it."

Rose smiled. "You're like Mother. I don't think she could stand to be far from her woods. It's like it's part of her." She stared off toward the distant fields. "She's there now. Do you know the spot?"

When her gaze again turned to him, he looked away. "I think I could find it."

"It's very beautiful in a scary kind of way. I'm always afraid to go there alone; it's so quiet and dim." She shivered and then laughed at herself "I suppose that's why Mother goes there. She knows no one will bother her."

"We all need a place like that once in a while."

"Yes." Rose stared down at the flowers and picked a dead leaf from the basket. "I suppose we do."

Joseph felt the change. He wasn't sure what had caused it but she mindlessly mauled one of the flowers, picking at the petals. He felt she was unaware of her actions. "Well, I'll be off then."

She nodded and started up the steps. At the top, she stopped to look back over her shoulder at him. "You'll stay for dinner? I'm afraid it'll be a little late. One o'clock or so. We have a guest coming."

"Thanks. If it's not too much trouble."

"No. No trouble at all."

He watched her until she entered the house, the hinges of the screen door making a plaintive cry as it closed after her. Something was different today, a somberness which hadn't been evident in the carefree young woman of yesterday.

Perhaps it was simply his unease projected onto Rose's behavior. The residents of Road's End hadn't been exactly welcoming. In the habit of all small communities, perhaps that distancing had made its way down the red dirt road to Carroll's Hill. That thought caused him to frown for he found he truly liked Anna's daughter. He had glimpsed a contentment and happiness in her, something her mother hadn't known at that age. He turned from the house on his way to the fields.

He let such thoughts slip from his mind as he surveyed the fields that spread out to his left into the distance. Curving rows of lush green pleased the eye and brought a sense of ease. Far to the east and south, the darker fringe of treetops defined the boundary of Reuben's domain, while on Joseph's right, the pastures and outbuildings of the homestead slowly gave way to a mixture of young pines, chestnut and maple trees. Hard behind this fringe growth stood Anna's woods. The density of the trunks rose above the landscape, dwarfing the rest of nature. A crown of dark green barely relieved the foreboding image. Rose had been right in that the place could be frightening. Joseph remembered the first time he had entered those woods, how he had felt unwelcome, like an intruder.

He had thought to go directly along the road that skirted the fields and follow the old logging trail to the site they had harvested that spring and summer but when he reached the clearing where they had first encamped, he found himself seeking the clear pool in the old creek.

Little had changed over the years except that the foliage surrounding it had matured and the spot was cooler than his memory. The water ran clearer without the herds of men and animals to disturb it but the color was blacker, no doubt due to the reduced amount of sunlight as the tree branches sought the sun. The path on the other side was still there, less defined than in the past but clearly still used. He hesitated a moment then forded the creek at a narrow spot. The water as it seeped into his boots was chill, a warning not to trespass on the person or the place, but he ignored it.

The lack of usual woodland sounds had always impressed him about this particular wood. Except for the sighing of the trees high overhead, nothing stirred. Even his heavy boots made no noise against the many layers of pine needles that the ages had laid down.

He reasoned it was the peace of the place Anna sought when she came here on her solitary walks. There was an almost church-like quality to the soaring tree trunks and a hushed expectancy, as if something powerful and mystical resided here.

He had expected to find her there but not as he did, in that same pose that was forever etched in his memory. She lay on her back in the heart of the wood, her face turned from him and her hand outstretched as if in supplication. His heart gave a great thump in his chest as it had when he first saw Rose on the porch upon his arrival at Carroll's Hill. It was as if fate had decided to torture him with images that intimately replicated the past.

Would she turn as she had then and stretch out her hand to him? But no, he realized she slept, unaware that anyone intruded upon her solitude. There would be no invitation to relive the past. How foolish of his heart to betray him in that way, to wish it so even after all these years.

Cautiously he lowered himself to a squat beside one of the ancient pines some twenty feet from her. In the dim light of the forest she looked as she had at eighteen, as innocent and soft as the petals of a rose. He wanted to lie beside her and dream her dreams but they wouldn't be the same as they had been then. The years had obliterated those naive plans of a life together. Now she dreamed of another man. She dreamed of Sam Stone.

A frown crossed her brow and he stood. She would be angry to realize he had spied on her while so unguarded. He eased away in the direction of the path until the sight of her was obscured by the tree trunks. For a brief moment he considered whistling to forewarn her of his presence but changed his mind. He would inspect the timber and return to the house for dinner. He found he no longer relished a lone encounter with her, at least not yet, for he knew in his heart his dismissal would be swift and sure. He discovered that he was not yet ready to be purged from her life.

ANNA SAW THE truck and the Cadillac parked in the drive when she came up the path. The smells of dinner greeted her as she entered the house through the back door. The space between the main house and the old kitchen had long ago been enclosed to connect the two buildings and to make room for a butler's pantry and a bathroom. Anna looked in at the kitchen and saw her mother supervising Bess. "I see our guests have arrived."

"Rose has gone for a walk with Marsh's cousin."

Anna could tell by the tone of her mother's voice and the prim set of her lips that she didn't like Walker.

"And Mr. Holt?"

"You didn't see him in the woods?"

"No."

"Well, that's where he is. He'll be along sooner or later." She lifted a heavy pot from the stove and poured the hot water and sugar snaps into a colander in the sink. Steam rose around her. "Rose invited him to dinner."

"Let me wash up and I'll come help."

Her mother made no reply and Anna escaped into the bathroom. She let the water run a long while over her hands then she splashed her face. Rose and Walker would have gone in the direction of the old well to be sure of privacy. And Joseph, he had not ventured into her wood. She brought her damp hands to her cheeks.

This wasn't disappointment she felt. She frowned at her reflection in the mirror. No, not that, merely irritation that the confrontation was yet to be endured. "Fool. Be glad that it may never happen." But her reflection stared back at her with knowing eyes. Meet they must before this day was over, and alone. A flutter of anticipation greeted that thought and Anna turned abruptly from her image in the mirror.

The table was already laid with the good china and silver and Anna noted the daffodils on the sideboard. She tried to remember when Rose had last made such an effort for Marsh and immediately chastised herself for such comparisons. Walker was company, he had entertained them in style. Rose would naturally want to offer what small splendors Carroll's Hill could muster.

Her mother entered the room with a large platter of fried chicken, followed close by Bess with dishes of sugar snaps, mustard greens and biscuits. "Everything's ready and we've made Reuben wait long enough for his dinner. Ring the bell, Anna. They can come get it if they want it."

Anna went out onto the small stoop of a back porch to ring the bell and saw Joseph approaching in the distance. He walked with a slow measured gait, his attention on the fields. At this distance he looked like the boy she had known, filled with ambition and dreams. At least he had seemed a boy then as they lay in each other arms building castles in the air. Perhaps that had been part of his attraction, that man-boy aura. He had wanted her, desired her as a man does but he had pursued her with the recklessness of youth.

Sam had seemed so damnably solid and stable in the face of that wild impetuousness that he had been easily pushed aside. How foolish the heart is, she thought as she watched Joseph. How foolish not to recognize what that difference meant. She took a deep calming breath and rang the bell.

After dinner she must make the opportunity to talk to him. As she turned to go back inside, she saw Rose and Walker approaching from the opposite direction. Her heart sank at the way Walker bent his head toward Rose as they talked and the expectant way she looked up at him.

"No good will come of it."

Startled, Anna looked up to see her mother standing on the other side of the screen door. She was staring at Rose and Walker. "Aren't you putting the cart before the horse?"

"Am I?" Helen shook her head. "It cannot be allowed. Marsh would never be so forgiving."

"And what if she has doubts, what if Marsh isn't the right choice?"

"He's the right choice."

Anna felt the old resentment building. "What makes him so? Because he'll keep her close by? Because he's known and familiar?"

"Because he doesn't just want her, he loves her." Helen turned from the doorway and disappeared into the dim interior of the house.

The reminder was so scathing Anna felt as if she had been slapped. She of all people should know the difference between love and desire. Joseph had wanted her, beyond that she couldn't say what he felt. It had been a long time since she had struggled with the need to believe he had loved her and the necessity to face the fact that he had simply wanted her, wanted what was forbidden.

CHAPTER 19

MARCH, 1922

"ANNA."

She wouldn't look at him, she told herself as she shrank back against the tree trunk.

Joseph squatted before her, his elbows propped against his knees. He ran a hand through his disheveled hair. "Lord, you know how to sober a man up fast."

Against her will, Anna looked up into his face trying to make out his features in the night as he hovered there. When he would touch her tear stained cheek, she drew back and he hesitated, stared down at his bloodied knuckles and let his hands fall limp between his knees.

"Say something."

She couldn't even if she had wanted to, the lump in her throat threatened to further humiliate and betray her.

"It's not what you're thinkin'. It's not." He caught her hand even as she tried to evade his grasp. He sighed deeply. "I could make the excuse that I'm too drunk if it was just anyone. But not you, Anna. Not you."

She couldn't listen to this, couldn't endure his rejection a second time in a matter of only minutes. She jerked her hand from his and as she rose to her feet, she turned her back to him. "Go. Go back to her."

"Anna."

He stood and caught her gently by the shoulders. She stiffened but didn't pull away. Cautiously he pulled her against him. "You shouldn't be with a man like me, Anna." He rubbed his chin across the top of her head. "That Mara, that's the kind of woman my lot knows. Someone hard, someone like us." His hand came up to trail his fingers along her neck and Anna turned her head away. His voice dropped to a whisper when he spoke. "You're too soft, too good."

Was that it? Was that really all there was behind his rejection? No. He had wanted her well enough to seek her out, to touch her when he knew his touch was unwelcome, to tempt her un-til— She pulled free of his touch. Although she wasn't worldly enough to play his game, on some instinctive level she understood what was at stake. Pride. His initially, and now hers. And he had won. She had shunned him, her father had dismissed him, and now, he would gloat at her capitulation. It wasn't that he had feigned desire or that he no longer felt it. All that and more had been revealed in his shout of triumph. Foolishly she had allowed him this moral victory over her, had proven him to be superior by his restraint. And unlike her, the desire for such a victory had been more powerful than his need of her.

She lifted her chin. "Too good?" She turned, making for the narrow drive. The underbrush caught at her skirt.

She had taken only a few steps when he caught her arm and spun her to face him. "You don't un-derstand." He wiped his hand down his face, as if that would clear his mind. "I want you because you *are* good."

She jerked against his grasp but he held tight.

"I mean--" He hesitated as if searching for the words. "You were meant to be some man's wife, a mother to his children, to have a home with all the best things." He pulled her closer until she faced him fully. "Soft things, frilly things. Electric lights and a room just for bathing." He swallowed and released her arm. "I'm not drunk enough to take all that from you." His grunt of laughter held no humor. "I'm not that drunk."

His reasoning should have softened her but now she wasn't only hurt and embarrassed, she was angry. However late in the game, she would have her pound of flesh. "And how drunk would you have to be? Out of your head? Falling down?"

"Anna." His voice was tight with restraint and exasperation.

"Well, I guess I should be grateful that you've saved me from myself. But don't worry, your admirable self-control won't be taxed again."

"Damn you!"

He caught her so quickly Anna had no time to react. Crushed against him she inhaled once, sharply, before his mouth came down on hers in a bruising kiss. Initially she resisted until he molded her body to his and spirals of pleasure weakened her limbs. Only when she was completely lost to all reason did he break the kiss.

"Is that what you want?" His mouth, pressed against her throat, so near her ear, emitted the words as a harsh growl. "Is it?"

She drew breath to speak but before the answer could form on her lips the air was rent by a piercing scream and an accompanying crash of wood against wood. Glass shattered and more voices joined the first outburst.

"Watch it!"

"Oh my god--"

"He's got a knife!"

The door of the roadhouse burst open with a jarring bang and people began to spill out onto the clearing. Nervous voices jittered in indistinguishable words. Men clutched women by the hand and hurried toward the long, narrow drive.

"Call the Sheriff before someone--" The disembodied voice broke off as a woman screamed.

"Damn fool!"

"Forget about your shoes! We gotta get outta here before--"

Another scream rent the night.

Sounds of splintering wood and excited voices continued to escalate in a jumble of crashing and banging from the building as Joseph and Anna stood frozen in each other's arms, bombarded by snatches of sentences, their eyes straining through the trees toward the commotion.

"What the hell--" Joseph put her away from him as he started toward the roadhouse.

"Fire!" The note of hysteria in the cry was chilling.

Suddenly Anna realized the extent of the danger. "Claire!" She pushed past Joseph. "Oh, my god, Claire!"

They reached the drive just as the acrid smell of smoke enveloped them and the first licking flames leapt up the curtains at the window. Anna's knees went weak with relief when she saw Claire standing at the edge of the clearing, her hand in Lucky's, her attention riveted on the growing flames. When Anna reached her, she touched Claire's shoulder and felt her body quivering.

Claire's gaze remained fixed on the burning building. She didn't respond to Anna's touch. "Isn't this something, Anna? Nothing like this ever happened in Road's End." Her voice rose an octave. "They were fighting, fighting over Mara Duardo." Her body shook visibly. "I've never had anyone fight over me."

Lucky's arm slipped around her waist and drew her nearer as he whispered something in her ear. Claire laughed deep in her throat, an excited jittery sound that sent a chill up Anna's spine.

Joseph watched the rapidly growing fire a moment longer then caught Anna's hand in his. "We've got to get outta here. The fire will bring people who know you."

Anna tugged at Claire's arm. "Claire!" Reluctantly her cousin turned with them toward the main road.

They hadn't gone ten feet when Mara Duardo stepped out of the shadows and blocked their path. Her gaze quickly traveled over the quartet before settling on Anna. She pursed her full lips and cocked an eyebrow. "So tell me, little princess, how's Reuben these days?"

Anna's blood froze in her veins. She felt the chill start at her toes and work its way up. Mara knew who she was and by association, who Claire was. Their fate was sealed.

Mara laughed, taking malicious pleasure in toying with Anna. "Is a long time. Is your brother still--" she affected a quizzical expression, "What your father called it? Whoring?" The smile took on an evil slant. "I see you take up Reuben's bad habits." Her gaze drifted to Joseph and lingered there. She shook her head. "I no think Papa approve, do you?"

Anna's body was as immobilized by Mara's taunting as her brain was. She couldn't think what to do or say. Through the haze of fear, she felt pressure on her arm as Joseph pushed her toward Lucky and Claire.

"Get them home." When Anna looked up at the sound of Joseph's voice, she saw his eyes locked with Mara's. "Now."

Anna remained rooted to the spot until she felt Lucky's firm grip on her arm. Suddenly her feet were moving as he propelled her and Claire down the dirt lane. She looked back over her shoulder to see Joseph and Mara silhouetted against the blazing building. Neither of them had moved.

ANNA STARED AT her reflection in the mirror, searching for the tell-tale signs of her inner turmoil. It was there in the high color in her face and the glitter in her eyes. Could others see it? Would anyone suspect that she was on the verge of flying to pieces?

Yes. She turned away from the mirror. Sam had seen it. He knew and, she thought, he was afraid. She was afraid, too. Afraid that she would never again be content with her life. She paced the floor of her bedroom, unable to be still with her thoughts. Joseph's words kept repeating in her head, they would not be silenced. *Is this what you want?* They had become a mantra for her over the past two days.

She knew he wanted her but what did that mean? Lucky had hustled her and Claire to the truck and the long drive home had passed in almost total silence. Even Claire's reckless enthusiasm for their adventure had been squelched by fear of discovery and punishment. Mara's barely veiled threat of exposure had left her almost catatonic.

Anna had endured the ride back to their grandmother's in a state of disbelief and with a growing sense of reprieve. Had events not conspired to save her, she would have thrown away her virtue and with it, her future. So why did she now feel so restless, so frustrated? In the late hours of the night she had begun to question the source of this compulsion toward self-destruction. Did it lie solely with the person of Joseph Holt or was it, as Mara had implied, a baser need within her?

No, it couldn't be that. She had felt similar stirrings toward Sam but she had always been able to control them. No other man had ever unhinged her so. There had to be more to it.

She returned to the mirror. Could it be that this was love? This inability to reason, to control one's desire? Although he was different, Joseph was no more a man than Sam. Was what she felt for Sam something less than the love a woman should have for a man? *Oh god, give me an answer!* She pulled at her hair and turned from her reflection. She couldn't stay cooped up in the house with her thoughts, she needed the release of physical activity.

Cautiously Anna slipped from her room and the house. She felt she might scream if she came face to face with anyone. The tension of the past days hadn't eased in her as they had with Claire. She waited in dread for Mara to reveal their secret and with each passing day, the weight of that secret grew and pressed against her heart like a stone. It would almost be a relief to have it over.

The dry sandy soil rose in little clouds around her feet as she hurried along the worn path that ran behind the chicken coop and saddle house. Within minutes, Anna was out of sight of the house and she increased her pace to a run. She didn't stop until she was well within the heart of her woods.

Breathless, she dropped to her knees then sprawled on her back on the carpet of fragrant pine needles. Her arms were flung wide and she stared without blinking at the swaying of the branches overhead. Slowly her breathing returned to normal. Minutes slipped away, she didn't know how much time passed before the whispering of the trees worked their magic. They were reassuring her, only she couldn't discern the message.

"Tell me what to do", she whispered. She pleaded for an answer, a sign that this pull, this attraction held some special meaning.

She must have slept for when she opened her eyes, she felt disoriented, slightly dizzy as she stared up into the swaying branches. She could hear her heart beating very slowly and Anna felt on the edge of some great discovery.

He would come to her here, in this place, now. If what was between them was meant to be, he would know and he would come. With all her heart, she willed it. She raised her hands toward the sky. "Come to me. Now." The softly spoken words dropped to a whisper. "Joseph."

A dry twig snapped and Anna turned her head to one side and reached out her hand. "Joseph."

JOSEPH WATCHED ANNA as she lay in the slanting beam of sunlight. It made her pale curls glitter like gold and the curve of her cheek translucent. For an instant he thought she was an illusion, willed up by his own desire, that same desire which had compelled him to come to this place. Then she moved. Her hand lifted and she turned toward him. He knew he was dreaming when he heard her whisper his name. But he wasn't asleep and the earth felt solid beneath the blanket of pine needles underfoot. And even over the strong scent of pine, he could detect that delicate fragrance she wore.

She reached out a hand to him and he lowered himself to the ground beside her. Neither of them broke the silence for a long time as they lay side by side, staring up into the treetops, their fingers entwined. Finally, she turned on her side to face him. "Why did you come?"

"I don't know." He stared into her beautiful blue eyes and wanted to kiss her but he dared not. "I couldn't stay away."

She smiled and leaned over and kissed him.

CHAPTER 20

MAY, 1941

"—AND THE LAST anyone saw of old Lamont was him hanging onto that nag for dear life as it raced along the dock trying to keep up with that riverboat."

A murmur of appreciative laughter circled the table at Walker's tale. He was at his most entertaining as conversation lagged over the noon-day meal. Anna knew everyone felt the animosity that emanated from her mother. It wasn't that Helen said or did anything that could be construed as rude. It was all in what she didn't say and how she refused to be drawn into the conversation that communicated itself so clearly to all present.

In spite of Walker's efforts, Rose's distress grew with each passing minute. She loved her grandmother and because of their closeness, would know how to read her behavior.

Anna decided she had to do something to dispel the charged atmosphere of the dining room before Rose broke down in tears.

"Shall we have dessert on the front porch? It's so warm in here."

Rose almost overturned her chair in her eagerness to grasp the opportunity to escape. "Walker and I will help Bess serve."

Helen stared down the table at Anna and she merely offered a steely return of her mother's regard. Caught up in this warring of wills, Anna was startled when Joseph touched her shoulder lightly as he stood ready to pull back her chair for her.

He took her arm as she rose to leave the room and his words were barely audible as he spoke softly near her ear. "Shall I fetch the shotgun?"

Anna frowned up into his amused expression.

"Sorry. I thought a little levity might help. Young Walker is a most unfortunate man."

"Unfortunate? What makes you say that?"

"Come on, Anna. He's in love with your daughter. It's as plain as the nose on your face."

"Is it?"

"Yes."

"How can you be so sure?" Anna had been praying she was mistaken, that she and her mother saw trouble under every bush out of fear for Rose. It didn't help that Joseph had come to the same conclusion.

"By the way he tries so hard not to look at her. He wants desperately not to give himself away. He's aware of the fact that Rose's future is all planned but he couldn't stay away from her. He has no real business in Meridian. That was just an excuse to come here."

"How can you know that?"

He chuckled softly. "You must learn to listen to the music and not just the words."

They had reached the screen door and she paused to look up at him. "And you think he's unfortunate." It was a statement rather than a question.

"He's not stupid, Anna. For all your polite manners, you could have run him through with the carving knife just as easily as your mother." At her stricken look he quickly added, "But he couldn't expect anything else. He's an intelligent man. Surely he's aware you view him as a threat to Rose's happiness."

Anna turned and looked anxiously at the young couple disappearing in the direction of the kitchen. "Was it so terribly obvious?"

"Perhaps not *terribly* obvious." He smiled reassuringly. "It'd take more than dark looks to drive him away." He watched the tall straight back of the young man as he escorted Rose down the hallway. "I feel sorry for him."

"Why?"

He stared down at her. "I know just how he feels."

Anna turned away. There was no doubting the look in Joseph's eyes. It demanded that she remember, that she acknowledge what had been between them.

Anna pulled her elbow free of Joseph's light touch and pushed open the door to step through onto the porch. "Because he makes doe eyes at her doesn't necessarily mean he's in love with her."

Joseph just managed to catch the screen door before it slammed in his face. He hesitated. "You can't simply ignore it and hope it'll go away."

She cut her eyes at him then away. This wasn't the kind of conversation she wanted to have with Joseph Holt. She was furious that he had been a witness to this crisis, for crisis it was. If only Marsh had been able to join them for dinner. But in her heart of hearts, Anna knew Rose had not invited him. He probably didn't even know of Walker's visit. And Sam, why wasn't he here? Didn't he know she needed him? Anna stared off down the drive trying to keep her thoughts to herself. Walker would be leaving soon. Then she would be able to deal with her daughter.

"It must have been hard for you, Anna. Raising a daughter alone, with no one to share the burden."

The gentleness and concern in his voice caught Anna off balance and when he again took her arm and maneuvered her toward the swing, she forgot that she couldn't risk being near him. His words invited her confidence and the desire to fall into that old pattern of sharing of that spring all those years ago was powerful. For in her reckless youth she had shared her deepest desires, her self-doubt, a lifetime of wounds, great and small, with this man. As he sat beside her, all the years she had whispered her concerns to the empty night seemed to press in on her, forcing the words up and out of her body. "She's so good. So loving and giving. Sometimes I wonder how she can be a Carroll and be as she is."

"But you're a Carroll, Anna. And knowing you, your husband must have been a good man. You have to trust Rose to make the right decision."

"But how can she? She isn't worldly. All she's ever known is Carroll's Hill. Marsh has been her whole world. How can she see through Walker's sophistication, his wealth, and his charm? I'm afraid she'll only end up hurt, terribly hurt."

"And what if this is the man for her? What if their love is mutual and he's the one who will make her happy? Would you stand in the way of that?"

"Of course I want her to be happy. But only three weeks ago she *was* happy. Genuinely happy. I know I'm not mistaken in that. And it was Marsh who made her happy. She couldn't wait to be married."

"If that's the case, you're worrying for nothing. It's probably good for her to be tested before they've pledged themselves to a life together. Then she can take that vow with certainty."

Anna clasped her hands together in her lap and wished she could believe his reassurances. But life was never that easy. She glanced up at him and gave him a smile meant to signal an end to her concerns. Perhaps men didn't suffer such anxieties. Perhaps they were always as certain in matters of the heart as they were in other things. "Well, time will tell."

"You believe that?"

"What? That things right themselves over time?"

"Yes."

She frowned and stared out toward the plum trees. "I suppose that's what I just said. And, I guess I do believe it. We go along with no particular direction in mind. Life presents choices and we choose, either wisely or not. But in the end, who's to say whether the choice was the correct one. What things, what opportunities, would have been lost or missed if we had chosen differently?" She offered another fleeting smile. "Or do we really choose?"

"My father-in-law says we choose even when we make no decision at all." He lifted a shoulder in an expression of doubt. "I prefer to think that I have more to say than that about my fate."

Anna felt his words at the core of her being and she quickly turned away. "So, your life has gone along according to your direction? No missteps, no unexpected disappointments?"

Joseph was watching Sally Dan who circled himself several times in an effort to find the exact spot to lie down in the cool earth of the flower bed. His expression turned grim. "I wish that were true. I've come to believe everyone experiences a certain number of hurts, losses. I'm no exception." He returned his attention to her. "What about you?"

She kept her face slightly averted. "Some. But on the whole, I've had a good life. Rose has made a lot of things easier. A child often does, I think."

"Your husband. You lost him early on. It must have been terrible for you."

A shiver ran through Anna. She couldn't think of the day Pete died without shuddering at the horror of it. "Yes."

His angled his body toward her so that he watched her. "You must have loved him very much. How did he die?"

Anna swallowed against the tightness in her throat. "The hurricane of 1927. It had seemed like just another spate of rainy, dreary weather. The eye of it came upon us suddenly. Pete and Rose had gone to the drug store for—" She fell silent.

"I'm sorry. I didn't mean—"

She shook her head and kept her face averted.

Joseph hesitated. "Is Rose at all like him? Like her father?"

How could she answer his question? Was Rose like her father? Yes. Hardly a day passed that she didn't see the father in the child. Not once did she look at her daughter and not see her father's little mannerisms. Did he not notice the way her brows arched whenever she was amused? Even when Rose didn't laugh outright, Anna could always tell when she found humor in something, sometimes, even her grandmother's dour moods.

She cleared her throat. "In little ways, ways that only people who know the both of them would see."

"What was he like? Your husband."

Anna toyed with the top button of her blouse. "Pete was like no other man I've ever known. Kind, gentle. Happy with life most of the time. A good father." She sighed at the memory. "He had his demons like all of us but he was, at his core, a good man. I think Rose loved him better than she did me. They were inseparable."

"Does she remember him much?"

"She thinks she does but I imagine it's mainly the stories that Liggy and I have repeated so often that form her memory of him. She was only four when he died."

"And you never thought to remarry?"

Anna almost pulled the button from her blouse at the question and abruptly rose from the swing. "I can't imagine what's taking so long with dessert." She crossed the porch to the front door and disappeared into the house. Once inside the dim interior of the hallway, she expelled a slow, soft breath of frustration. When, in God's name, would this day end? And how had she allowed the conversation to drift to Pete?

CHAPTER 21
SEPTEMBER, 1922

ANNA TURNED ONTO her side, the bulk of her stomach an anchor to the damp, twisted sheets of the bed. Her nightdress was damp and clinging with sweat, her hair stuck to her neck and back. Something had wakened her from the light sleep, the only sleep, the hot, humid night permitted. She sat up in bed. Instantly the pressure on her bladder made her ease her feet over the side and head for the bathroom.

No matter how little she drank during the day, it had been months since she had been able to get through the night without relieving herself at least once. The heat didn't help. September in Road's End had never been like this, so hot and humid. By now the leaves would be turning and the nights cool and crisp. How she longed for a soft, sweet pear from the old tree behind the saddle house. And biscuits with honey. She smiled at her cravings. This, too, would pass. Or so everyone assured her. If it didn't, she would be as big as a cow before this baby was born.

Anna used the bathroom, ran cool water over her hands and splashed her face and neck. She dried herself as she made her way back toward the bed. It was then she heard it. Her hands stilled in the motion of rubbing her neck. The towel hung limp. There it was again. A grunt of exertion followed by an answering whimper of pain. Suddenly the sound of shattering glass broke the stillness of the night and Anna rushed toward the front of the house.

Liggy was already out of her make-shift bed in the sitting room and at the front door when Anna reached it. She threw open the door and stepped out onto the stoop in only her nightdress and bare feet. "Who's there?" Liggy's voice held a warning.

It was answered by a low burst of male laughter and the sound of scuffling as the images of two or three men became apparent in the dim light of the street lamp on the corner.

"You there! Get away from here!" Liggy caught up the hem of her gown and started across the lawn at a run toward the tangle of men.

"Mind you own business, sister." The reply was harsh, challenging, and carried a heavy foreign accent.

Liggy didn't slow up. She was nearly on them when the knot of men disengaged like vultures reluctantly abandoning their prey and took off toward the intersection, only one of them lagging behind to spit in the direction of the huddled form on the street.

She crouched over what looked like a pile of discarded clothing and gently turned it over. Anna reached her just at that moment and her hand went automatically to her mouth at the sight before her.

"Bastards!" Liggy eased the man's head onto her lap. "My god, what have they done to you this time, Pete?"

The only response was a low moan.

Anna's knees buckled and she came down hard on them beside Liggy and the injured man. She couldn't speak for the sickness rising in her throat and she felt faint. Who had done this savage deed and why? The gentle, young man she knew as Pete was unrecognizable. It seemed his tormentors had attempted to obliterate his features. She began to tremble.

"Get a grip on yourself, girl. He needs help." Liggy tore a piece of cloth from the hem of her gown and pressed it tightly against a deep gash on his forehead that was bleeding heavily. "We have to get him into the house."

Anna tried to speak but her teeth chattered so she couldn't do more than make a sound in her throat.

Liggy caught her by the wrist with her free hand and applied enough pressure to cause pain. "Come on, now. Get to your feet. We have to manage somehow."

The strength of Liggy's grip penetrated Anna's near-swoon and she nodded. She swallowed against the riot in her stomach and rose to her feet. Her knees quaked but she managed to stay upright and when Liggy stood also, she followed her instructions and caught Pete under his left arm. Between them, they half-lifted, half-dragged him to Liggy's front door. There they propped him against the doorpost. Liggy bent over at the waist and supported her upper body weight with her hands against her knees. Anna cradled the swelling of her abdomen with both hands and leaned against the outer wall of the house. The only sound to break the quiet of the pre-dawn hour was their rasping as they stood for several minutes, struggling for breath in the humid, still air.

Finally, Liggy straightened her back and drew a deep breath. "Think you're ready?"

Anna nodded and together they bent over the almost senseless young man and wrestled him through the door and onto the divan Liggy had been using as her bed.

The piece of cloth had dislodged from his forehead in the struggle to get him to the house so Liggy took a table scarf from the lamp table in the center of the room. She folded it and took Anna's hand and closed her fingers around it. "Press this as hard as you can against the cut. I'll get a basin and some water. We have to clean him up to see how bad it really is."

Anna sank to her knees beside the divan and gently touched the gaping wound. The smell of blood combined with a strong odor of alcohol and she felt light headed. With an effort, she concentrated on the outline of her hand, the white of her knuckles as she applied pressure. The scarf quickly soaked through with blood and she increased the pressure. "Pete." Her lips trembled when she spoke his name. "Pete, can you hear me?"

He made no sound and fear began to weave its way through the horror and revulsion. What if he was dead? "Pete!" Her voice was sharp with fear.

His eyelids fluttered and finally he opened his eyes. He attempted a smile. Blood seeped from his mouth and his eyes rolled back and drifted closed.

Liggy appeared at her shoulder. "At least he's still alive. Here, let me get at him." She squeezed a wet cloth over the basin and began to dab at his face. "Get dressed and hurry over to Government at Rapier. Catch the streetcar to Royal. Change there and get off at the corner of Royal and Conception. Two doors down on the left on Conception is Doc Fuller's office." Liggy glanced at the window just beginning to gray with light. "He lives upstairs. Bang on the door 'til he answers. He tends to ignore all but the most persistent." She rinsed the cloth and applied it to the other side of Pete's face. Her frown deepened. "Be quick. For god's sake be quick."

"THAT BAD, HUH?"

Pete looked up at Anna, fear in every line of his face, and she realized he was watching her expression. "No, no." She tried for a smile. "You look so much better than you did three days ago. It's just that your eyebrow's a little crooked." She tilted her head to one side. "But with time, it'll do."

He shifted against the stack of pillows then grimaced with pain. "Yeah."

Anna sat on the side of the bed, careful not to jostle him, and took his hand. "No, Pete. Really." She did smile this time. "In fact, it's a little gratifying to know you're no longer prettier than a man ought to be."

The horseshoe shaped scar that began near his hairline on his forehead and cut through his right brow before ending just above his cheekbone, was still an angry red puckering held together by coarse stitches. In time it would fade along with the horrible bruising of his face and body but some of it would never leave him. She saw the little pulse at the base of his throat flutter erratically even as he tried to make light of the matter.

"You can always hide me in the attic. Only let me out for Halloween."

The doctor returned from washing his hands in time to catch Pete's words. "It's not pretty, son, but it'll get better. Just thank your lucky stars it wasn't worse. Another hair and you'd have lost an eye." His voice dropped to an accusing note. "And your kidney."

"I'm a lucky man, all right." Pete's words didn't hold anger or self-pity but rather they sounded flat, lifeless.

The doctor grunted and began putting on his coat. "It doesn't need bandaging but keep it clean, Anna. Sponge it with peroxide to keep it sterile. As for the ribs, nothing but time can help. You can take off the bandage to clean him but wrap it back tight." He picked up his bag and moved toward the door. "And for god's sake, keep him still."

Pete shifted in the bed and ground his teeth against the pain. "I can't stay here, Doc. Anna should be in this bed."

The doctor turned back to his patient, his expression hard. "Yes, she should be." With that, he left the room and the house.

Anna caught him on the front stoop. "How long, Dr. Fuller? Before he can at least get up and down."

"I'll get him out of here as soon as I can, Anna."

"It's not that. He needs someone to care for him and Liggy and I don't mind, really. It's just that he insists on getting up and— Well, you know."

He nodded. "At least they didn't break his legs."

Anna hesitated. "Why would someone do this to him, Dr. Fuller? Beat him so viciously, as if they would obliterate him? A gentle man like Pete. And why can't the police do something about it? Find the men responsible?"

Dr. Fuller studied her face. He started to speak then stopped himself.

"Tell me."

"He was where he shouldn't have been, Anna. It's not the first time he's gotten himself into a scrape. A rough lot hangs out at the Jack of Diamonds. Seamen, here today, gone tomorrow. Pete knows that."

"Then why would he go there? And what could he have possibly done to cause such viciousness? You didn't see them." Anna clasped her hands together to keep them from trembling at the memory. "It was as if they wanted to kill him."

The doctor put his arm around Anna's shoulders. "Let it go, Anna. Those men had shipped out before I'd finished stitching Pete's head. It's over and done. Just help him get on his feet and let it go." He shook his head and sighed. "There's nothing you or anyone can do for Pete. A man can't deny his true nature, no matter how hard he tries. At least not for long." He looked down into her up-turned face. "None of us can."

ANNA HEARD THE squeak of the gate and she turned her face from the weak November sun and opened her eyes. A smile softened her features when she saw Pete with the block of ice caught firmly in the large iron tongs. She swung her feet off the swing and stood, catching at the chain for a moment for balance. It seemed she would never get accustomed to the distortion of her body. With a sigh she pulled the heavy sweater more snuggly around her swollen stomach and crossed the yard to open the kitchen door for Pete. "You're a little late today."

"It's that ornery old mule of Mr. B's." Pete's voice held a note of aggrievement. "Don't know why he won't just go ahead and let me drive the truck."

"Gas prices, I suppose."

Pete was in no humor for logic. "Danged old nag stopped in the middle of Broad Street and wouldn't budge. The streetcar nearly ran us down." He dropped the block of ice into the bottom of the icebox with a loud clatter and closed the door with unnecessary force.

Anna frowned. She hadn't seen Pete in such ill humor since the early days of his recuperation after the worst of his injuries had healed and the facts of his disfigurement had become a reality. "Well, you're almost through for the day. Only the rest of Texas Street then you can take him back to the stable."

"Oughta take him to the glue factory, that's what I oughta do. He's not good for anything else, if you ask me."

Anna wasn't sure what had precipitated Pete's mood. He was normally so easygoing, unfazed by the little irritations of life. He had been driving the same old tired mule for Mr. B since Anna had first known him and had never complained.

She had begun to look forward to his deliveries. During the two and a half weeks he had spent under her care, their causal acquaintance had become a deep friendship and now when he brought their ice, he and Anna would often have a Coca Cola or a cup of coffee. Sometimes they would ride the streetcar to the Albright Drug Store for a treat at the soda fountain or would go to Bienville Square to feed the pigeons and the gold fish in the fountain. "How about some coffee?"

He shook his head. "No time. Got to get done with my deliveries."

"Then how about going to the pictures tonight. There's a new one showing at the Downtown Theater. Sophie Westover's been going on about it all morning."

Pete looked away and tucked his chin. "Can't, Anna. I uh, got some things I gotta do tonight." He glanced at her from beneath his lashes then headed for the door. "Maybe the matinee tomorrow?" He paused with the open screen in his hand but didn't look back at her. "How's that sound?"

"Sure." Anna had only suggested going to the picture show to distract Pete from his foul mood. She watched from the kitchen doorway as he disappeared down the path toward the front of the house and the street beyond then returned to the ice box and withdrew two Coca Colas. Liggy was due for a break, no matter how many heads of hair still needed to be shampooed, cut or curled. She had hired a colored girl to do the shampooing and sweeping up since Anna was no longer able to maneuver around her belly but she still worked herself into exhaustion each Saturday.

The scent of shampoo, perfumes, and the tang of citrus greeted Anna as she stepped into the shop.

"Anna. Look what Emily brought us." Liggy nodded toward the basket of satsumas sitting on the floor by the door. "Her brother grows them out at his place in Grand Bay."

Emily turned from the ministrations of the colored girl, Beth, to smile at Anna. "They're a mite tart still but I wanted to bring you a few before they were all gone. Soon as they start to ripen folks come from all over the county for 'em."

"Thanks, Emily. I haven't had an orange or grapefruit since last Christmas. Our cousin down in Florida" Anna faltered then offered up a faint smile, "always sent us some every year."

Emily's glance skittered along Anna's swollen figure then back to her own reflection in the mirror. "Well, a little fruit is good for the baby, I'm sure."

An awkward moment of silence hung in the air before Liggy spoke. "Did I hear Pete? Sure is late today."

"Yes." Anna took the broom from behind the door and began sweeping up curls of hair that lay on the floor around Liggy's and Beth's feet. "He had some trouble with the mule and it had him in a really foul humor." She paused, her hands atop the broom, her chin resting on her hands. "It wasn't like him at all. I couldn't even interest him in the new picture show. Said he had something else to do."

"Humph." Emily was looking through a Watkins Products circular as Beth shaped her hair into pin curls. "Don't suppose it had anything to do with that big old tanker that just docked down on Water Street this morning."

Her comment drew a titter of laughter from the woman sitting in Liggy's chair. When Liggy pinned her with her steady regard, the woman shifted in the chair.

"Well, it's not like he makes a secret of it, Liggy. It's no wonder he got himself all busted up. It's not natural, I say, a man behaving like that." The woman drew herself up in righteous indignation. "And he's been seen down at the Jack of Diamonds over on St. Anthony just this week. You'd think he'd learn."

"Learn what?" Anna stared at the woman's reflection in the mirror and watched as her eyes darted first to meet Anna's gaze then Liggy's.

"Don't you know?"

"Know what?"

The woman hesitated. "Well, it's not for me to say, I'm sure. I thought after what happened—" she wouldn't meet Anna's or Liggy's eyes now, "since you nursed him and all—"

Liggy sighed. "What Mary Lou is trying to tell you, Anna, is that Petey isn't right. He isn't like other men. He's—" she stopped all pretense of styling Mary Lou's hair. "He doesn't like women."

Anna frowned then laughed. "Don't be silly. Pete is our friend. Of course he likes women. He likes me. He likes you."

Liggy studied her face then sighed. "Honey, it's not that he doesn't like your company or mine. Or most women for that matter. It's that he doesn't *like* women." Her forehead creased. "You understand?"

Anna blinked and looked from one woman to the next. "No." She returned her attention to Liggy. "I don't."

Liggy crossed her arms across her chest. "He can't—well, when it comes to women, he can't—" she gestured with her hand. "Well, he can't do it. He can't get it up." She blew out her breath. "There, you see?"

"Oh." Anna sat in the shampoo chair. "Poor Pete. That must be terrible for him. No wonder he drinks and hangs out in clubs." She glanced up at Liggy. "Why can't he? Do you know?"

"Lord child, where'd you come from?" Mary Lou set her chin as she settled herself more comfortably in the chair. "There's nothing wrong with him except his head. And not the little one either."

Emily snorted with laughter and Beth placed a hand over her mouth to hide her smile.

"You mean—" Anna frowned and tried to grasp what Mary Lou was trying to tell her. "What do you mean?"

"Why just that he *likes*—"

"Mary Lou doesn't mean anything, honey." Liggy pulled the comb through Mary Lou's hair hard enough for her to give a little squeak of pain. "Pete has his problems and he's the only one can deal with them."

Anna watched Liggy finish styling Mary Lou's hair. She could see the anger in the thin set of her lips and the less than gentle application of the comb to Mary Lou's style. Whatever these women knew, Liggy wasn't about to let them tell her.

THE DAMP, CHILL wind blustered along Government Street as Anna hurried across. She turned the collar of her coat higher and clutched her purse more tightly. She regretted that she had not worn gloves or a sweater under the coat. Here near the river's edge the night was so much colder than when she had set out from the house.

Even with the cold the streets were filled with the Saturday night crowd, families eating out, going to the pictures. She had gotten off the streetcar with Liggy at the Elks Lodge. Her intention had been to see the picture at the Downtown Theater down the block but something had compelled her to forego the movie house. It was the talk of the women in the shop that afternoon that propelled her northward. Occasionally she passed a familiar face and smiled and nodded. Near the Cathedral she was stopped by Thelma Jenkins to be introduced to her husband and their two children on their way to evening mass. But slowly the streets became less peopled and with nothing but strangers as she drew nearer the rough part of town.

Mary Lou had mentioned the Jack of Diamonds on St. Anthony. Anna knew the area around De Tonti Square was where the whore houses and gambling establishments thrived. She had never ventured there even in the light of day and as she moved further from the respectable social scene of Mobile, the more uneasy she felt. She paused on a street corner, hesitant to go further.

Everything she had heard about the seamier side of Mobile society had been vague, more innuendo than fact. The memory of the roadhouse in Finley came to mind and she supposed that this couldn't be much worse. Besides, this was the city, policemen patrolled the streets day and night.

St. Anthony Street lay just ahead and she saw two men lounging under the street lamp at the corner. They watched her approach, hunched into their coats, the smoke from their cigarettes snatched away by the wind. Their laughter was dark, sinister to her ears, and she lowered her gaze to the sidewalk.

Loud piano music came from a house directly across the street. The music died abruptly and the front door suddenly crashed open. A big burly man in his undershirt filled the doorway as he tumbled a woman clad in nothing more than her slip and a ruffled dressing gown half hanging off her shoulders, down the steep steps. She screeched at him in a drunken slur and proceeded to crawl back up the steps muttering curses under her breath.

The commotion distracted the two men on the corner and Anna slipped by them and turned left. She hadn't gone but half a block when she saw a woman lounging in the doorway of a storefront with the windows boarded up. The woman watched her approach with a sullen expression made harsher still by heavy make-up and a garishly patterned dress unbuttoned low. Anna hurried along the street that became more active and better lit as she neared Lawrence Street.

A group of men argued in the middle of the street, the heat of their words escalating toward violence. Anna hadn't seen a policeman for some blocks now and a ripple of unease ran down her spine and further chilled her.

"Hey, sister, got a light?"

The man leaned out of the shadows of a doorway and Anna almost jumped out of her shoes. She stepped from the sidewalk into the street and realized when she was halfway across that the Jack of Diamonds was before her.

A burst of raucous laughter and a cloud of cigarette smoke greeted her as she opened the door. A number of heads turned in her direction as the draft of cold air entered with her. A sour odor mingled with mold and damp underlay the sharp smell of whiskey and smoke. The place was dimly lit and Anna blinked against the burning cigarette smoke as she tried to pick out the faces of the men. Someone whistled and another man made a meowing sound. Anna hovered by the door, suddenly aware just how foolish she had been in coming here.

A tired looking woman with the dark roots of her blondined hair showing passed her with a tray of drinks. Anna's hand went automatically to her own newly bobbed hairstyle. Something about the woman was familiar and Anna realized she had been an occasional customer at Liggy's. She watched as the waitress plunked drinks down on a table surrounded by a group of sailors. Their uniforms were unfamiliar and the broken English they used in the argument over the payment for the drinks suggested they were Latin.

As the argument escalated the waitress banged the tray against the edge of the table. A man with a mermaid tattooed on his forearm and a jagged scar running down his left cheek pushed away from the wall on the other side of the door and went to stand over the clamoring party. His presence quelled the more vocal of the sailors and reluctantly they began pooling money in the center of the table. The waitress scooped it up and Anna heard her mutter, "Damn Spics," as she started to pass her by.

"Naomi."

The waitress turned at the sound of her name and looked Anna up and down.

Anna stepped closer and glanced around the room. "Could you help me?"

"Do I know you?" Naomi stood, her hip cocked, the tray balanced against it.

"I work for Liggy. Cut and Curls?"

"And?"

"I'm looking for someone."

Naomi's gaze traveled down Anna's body again, a sneer settling over her features. "Ain't we all."

Anna went scarlet with shame. Her voice quavered slightly. "Pete Moreland. Do you know him?"

The waitress's features and her attitude softened. "Aw, honey, Pete can't do you no good."

"He's a friend."

Naomi hesitated then relented. She jerked her head in the direction of the far corner of the bar. "He could use a friend and not that bunch he's with either."

"Naomi!"

The bellow came from a red faced man behind the bar.

"Yeah, yeah." She called over her shoulder then gave Anna a tired smile. "Wait here and I'll get Jake to pry him loose from his new friends."

Naomi sauntered toward the bar where she plunked the tray down with force. Anna felt a tug on the hem of her coat and looked down to see a man weaving on the edge of his chair trying to look under her dress. She jerked away from his grasp and turned toward the table Naomi had indicated she would find Pete. The two chairs at the table were empty. Frantically she glanced around the room just in time to see Pete's blond head disappearing through a back door. The drunk was fumbling with the hem of her coat again. Naomi was on the far side of the room with her tray full of drinks. Anna pushed her way across the room to the door where Pete had disappeared.

By the time she reached the door she was trembling from the unwanted remarks and touches from the men in the crowded room. All she wanted was to escape. The door was solid and heavy and when she finally managed to pull it open, the blast of cold air momentarily relieved her sense of panic.

She found herself in a narrow alleyway piled high with rotting garbage and reeking of the strong smell of urine. She leaned against the door to steady herself then looked up and down in search of Pete.

A muffled sound, like a grunt, came from the far end of the alley and as she moved toward it she could just make out the silhouette of a man. As she drew nearer the sound became clearer, the groaning interspersed with whispered words. Anna's footsteps slowed as the words became more distinct, words of endearment laced with obscenities.

Abruptly she stopped as the silhouette became two, the light from the side street revealing Pete and an unknown man. They were both lost in the moment, unaware of anything outside the throes of their passion. Anna stood frozen to the spot, immobilized by the alien nature of the scene before her, revulsed and mesmerized at the same time.

The knowledge of what she was witnessing slowly registered and she stumbled backward against a trash bin. The lid clattered to the cobbled alley and she turned and fled, stumbling past the debris with the clumsiness of her swollen belly.

CHAPTER 22
MAY, 1941

"DON'T WORRY SO, Anna."

The unexpected voice startled her and she turned from watching Rose and Walker as they walked down the drive to collect the mail. Joseph stood at her side, his hands in his pockets but he wasn't at his ease.

"It's probably nothing more than a flirtation. It's the nature of the young." He jangled the change in his pocket. "Remember?"

In that instant she decided it was time to take issue with him. "Yes." How could she not remember? "That's why I'm worried. Marsh loves her."

"And Sam loved you. But you didn't marry him, did you? You found someone else." He was silent for a long moment. "Life's like that sometimes. Just because someone loves you, doesn't necessarily mean that love is returned. At least not with the same intensity."

"We aren't discussing me and Sam."

"No, but we aren't discussing Rose and Marsh either. We've been dancing around each other since I arrived." He turned to fully face her. "It's time we talked, Anna. I can't leave here until we do."

Anna couldn't look at him. Instead she stared at the button of his shirt. This was it then. She nodded. "Yes. We need to talk. But not here. Not now."

"All right. When? Where?"

"Later."

"Today, Anna."

"Yes, today." Her heart hammered in her ears. "At dusk. Things are quiet then. I'll meet you."

"In the woods."

"No!" She turned her profile to him. "Not here. At the river. By the old ferry dock." She nodded again. That was the place. No one would interrupt them there and it would serve to remind her what had been lost by her folly that spring. "You know the place."

"Yes. I'll be there."

He watched her so intently for a moment that it seemed to her his regard would leave a mark of some kind. When he finally turned and walked down the steps, she touched her forehead but found it cool, unblemished.

He didn't look back as he got into the truck and started it. Sally Dan jumped into the truck bed and just like that, Joseph was gone and Anna was committed to a course of action. She felt a tightness in her chest.

"Don't do this, Anna."

"Jesus, Mother!" Anna clasped her arms across her middle to keep from jumping from the porch. "Stop creeping up on me."

"I didn't creep. You just weren't listening. But you had better. For Rose's sake."

"And what does that mean?"

"Send him on his way. If he finds out, there'll be trouble."

Anna felt the pressure on her chest squeezing tighter. "Finds out what?"

"Do you think I'm blind as well as stupid?" Helen Carroll caught her daughter by the arm with a grip that was punishing. "If I hadn't known before, there's no denying what's right before my eyes. Just look at yourself." She released Anna's arm and shaded her eyes with a hand as Walker and Rose came into view making their way slowly up the drive. "Holt knew what was in his mind before he even came here. He's either going to buy the timber or he's not. We'll deal with it either way but get him gone from Road's End. There's still this one to worry about and that's more than enough if you ask me." With that, she turned and disappeared into the house.

Anna caught the doorpost to support herself. What was it her mother saw? Was it what Anna had wanted her to see, to believe all those years, or did Helen Carroll see the truth? Had she fooled no one? Surely Sam didn't suspect. Or did he? Did either of them see what she saw whenever she looked at her daughter? She had thought she was the only one who could recognize the father in the child. Perhaps Joseph's return had made them look more closely at what had been in front of them all these years.

CHAPTER 23
MAY, 1922

ANNA FELT THE nausea well up and she lay perfectly still on the bed, her eyes closed, willing it to abate. Perspiration broke out on her upper lip and forehead. It was the third week of the month and it was three weeks too late. She frowned at the thought and pushed it aside. It required all her concentration to keep from being sick. Slowly, the feeling subsided, the roiling in her stomach eased, and she carefully raised herself to sit on the side of the bed.

Through the window she watched the blue jay sitting on her nest. The male swooped around, crying loudly and dive bombing invisible enemies that would threaten the eggs. Anna turned away from the sight and rose. At the wash stand, she poured water into the bowl and dampened a cloth. For long minutes, she held it first against her upper lip then her throat. If only she could manage to get dressed and get away from the house before the smell of breakfast drifted along the breezeway and into her room, she would be all right.

She had dressed and was feeding the chickens when the car came roaring up the driveway. With her hand shielding her eyes against the eastern sun, Anna saw Percy Milkisen jump out of the car, the motor still running, and race across the yard to the house, bounding up the steps two at a time. She could hear the excited pitch of his voice even though she couldn't make out the words. She knew something was wrong, something was terribly wrong. She took the dishpan and threw the corn in a wide arch for the chickens and hurried toward the wire door of the pen. She was just securing the latch when her father and Percy came thundering down the back steps and looked around the grounds until their gaze fell on her.

"Anna! It's Claire! She's missing." Her father's words were an accusation and she could see his rage in his clenched fists and the vein that stood out in his neck. "Where is she?"

Anna shook her head and swallowed the fear in her throat. Claire was missing! "I don't know, Father."

"Don't know! What do you mean you don't know?"

"I haven't seen her since Sunday."

Her father had reached her and had her arm in a brutal grip as he hurried her back toward the house. "You know something. What's she gotten up to? Tell me, girl!"

Anna steeled herself against the pain and tried to school her features to reveal nothing. In her heart, she knew what Claire had done. The loggers had departed Carroll's Hill yesterday. Claire had known of their imminent departure on Sunday and she had been like a cat on a hot stove. But Anna had been too caught up in her own misery to pay proper attention to her younger cousin. What, exactly, Claire had done, she didn't know, but she could make a pretty accurate guess.

She turned from her father's relentless regard and watched Percy's features change from concern and worry to alarm at what he saw in Anna's face.

"Tell us, child. If you know anything, tell us." There was kindness reflected in Percy's eyes along with his growing uneasiness.

Anna swallowed. "I don't know." She glanced at her father then back at Percy. "She wanted to go across the river to stay with Gran for a few days but Uncle Dewey said no."

The frown on Percy's forehead deepened. "Why would she want that?"

Anna could only shake her head.

Percy studied her face a moment longer then turned to her father. "Eubie said he hadn't seen her. If he'd ferried her acrost he'd have no reason to lie about it." He caught Anna's father by the arm. "Come on, Luther. Get Reuben. We'll need all the help we can get."

Luther's hand tightened on Anna's arm until she thought she would cry out with pain. "You'd better not be lying to me, Anna." Abruptly he released her and turned on his heel toward the saddle house where the car was housed. "Ring the bell for Reuben."

Anna massaged her upper arm where her father had gripped it so mercilessly and blinked back her tears. "Can I come, Percy? Can I come with you back to town?"

Percy must have seen the fear she knew was so clearly readable on her face. "I don't mind, child. If'n your pa don't." He headed toward the house. "You could help Lena with Maree. She's beside herself with worry."

ANNA'S AUNT MAREE was resting in her bedroom, the curtains closed against the bright light of mid-afternoon, a cold compress soaked with chamomile across her forehead. Lena was in the kitchen, a great pot of soup simmering on the back of the stove and the smell of hot bread drifting through the house. Anna haunted the central hallway, walking from the front door to the back, torn between the desire to catch a glimpse of the men searching for Claire and the sense of duty to keep an ear out for her aunt's every utterance.

The search had been ongoing all day. The whole community had turned out to scour the riverbanks on either side of the swollen current. Every known acquaintance of Claire's had been sought out and questioned. Luther had taken his bullwhip to one of the Talley boys who was known to be sweet on Claire when he didn't like his response to being questioned. Eubie had ferried Reuben and their Uncle Dewey along with the car across the river made treacherous by the unusually heavy spring rains. They were on the trail of the men from Battle's Mill, hoping against hope that Claire was with them. As damning as that scenario would be for her cousin, Anna realized how much worse the alternative was.

Anna didn't doubt that Claire would be found with Lucky. She should have seen this coming. What she could have done about it she didn't know. Claire had become so headstrong, so unlike her flighty, malleable cousin of only a few short months ago. In the past ten weeks Claire had changed from the baby of the family and the darling of the community to something totally alien to her former sweet nature. She wasn't the only one. The change had started with the arrival of the loggers from Battle's Mill and it had so completely taken over their lives that neither Claire nor Anna would ever be the same again. The fabric of their lives was so torn that Anna couldn't help but envy Claire's attempt at escaping Road's End.

The bell mounted on the wharf at the ferry landing clanged urgently. Lena appeared in the kitchen doorway, her face pale and drawn. Anna glanced toward her aunt's bedroom then at Lena. "I'll go, shall I?" She already had the screen door open and didn't wait for a response.

Her feet flew over the muddy road that led down to the river. Others joined her from the houses that lined both sides of the road and she could see men heading toward the landing from either direction along the riverbank. The ferry had just docked, Reuben was tying it off on one side while Rusty Johnson, the mail carrier, tied off the other. A small crowd of a dozen or so had gathered by the time Reuben drove the car off the ferry followed by the mail truck.

Reuben sat behind the steering wheel of the Ford for a long time staring out at the murky brown current that flowed swiftly by. Finally he stepped out and looked into the faces of the gathering. His gaze settled on Anna for a fleeting moment then he spoke. "Best get your boats out, boys. Moses's skiff is missing." He stared out at the river again. "We're going to have to drag the river."

A shriek of pain and utter heartbreak rent the air and Anna whirled around at the sound to see her Aunt Maree collapse against Lena. Rusty Johnson and one of the Talley boys helped ease her to the ground where she clung to Lena and gave vent to a grief so profound it silenced even the screeching of the pair of courting peacocks that strutted in front of the post office. Anna felt the breath go out of her as if she had been punched in the stomach. The brilliant turquoise and blue of the male peacock's tail feathers in full array blurred and swam before her as she felt Reuben catch her around the waist to keep her from mirroring Maree's collapse.

IT WAS THREE days before they found Claire. The skiff she had taken from down by the colored section had been discovered two days before caught in the tangle of an uprooted tree that had lodged in the bend of the river. The whole community was exhausted with grief and lack of sleep by the time her body was recovered six miles further downstream.

Anna felt so emotionally raw that she couldn't bear the touch of sympathetic glances cast her way as she sat beside the coffin in the living room of her aunt and uncle's house. The room was filled with lilies and rosewater but neither could mask the sweet stench of Claire's decomposing body. But her aunt would not forego the ritual so all of Road's End and beyond had gathered to mourn and pay respects. Anna knew she would never step foot in this house again. She knew that she would never again be able to bear the fragrance of lilies or endure the lost look in her aunt and uncle's eyes.

Sam sat beside her, clasping her hand in his but she was barely aware of his presence. Nothing could pierce the cloud of grief and guilt that enveloped her. All she could think of was escape; escape from her grief, her guilt, from the smell of death. It occurred to Anna suddenly that Claire, who had no desire for escape, had wished only to be married, desired, fought over, was now the one who was free. She stood abruptly and ran from the room and the house. Out behind the tool shed she was ill, violently ill.

Sam found her leaning against the out-building, trembling. He tucked the rose he had plucked from the fence row behind her ear then took her into his arms. Together they gently swayed. Anna found the motion soothing, the comfort of Sam's embrace a refuge from her inner demons. With him she would be safe, absolved of all that she had wrought with her indecisiveness and selfish indulgences. All she had to do was say the words. But she could not.

CHAPTER 24
MAY, 1941

THE SUN WAS low in the afternoon sky. Anna could hear the murmur of conversation between Rose and Walker as they sat on the front porch in the swing. Through the window of her bedroom she could see her mother out in the garden weeding the corn. The chopping motion of the hoe spoke of her mood. Anna sighed and returned to her dressing table. She studied her reflection before she turned and left the room. With only the briefest hesitation, she opened the screen door and saw the guilty pulling back as Rose and Walker drew apart. Walker rose to his feet.

She motioned him to keep his seat. "I feel like a walk so I'm going into town."

"I'll be glad to take you, Mrs. Moreland."

"I won't interrupt your visit. It isn't far. I do it all the time." She noticed that Rose was keeping her eyes on her hands clasped tightly in her lap. "Besides, who knows when you'll come this way again."

Walker glanced down at Rose. "It's getting late in the day. I really should be going." He looked back at Anna and smiled. "I insist on giving you a ride. I wouldn't want you to be caught on the road after dark."

"I should make it there well before dark and Sam will drive me home. Don't shorten your visit out of concern for me, Walker."

"No, no, it'll be my pleasure."

Anna hesitated. "All right. I'll just go out to the garden and tell Mother."

The heat of the day was abating and the clanking of cowbells could be heard as the small herd Reuben kept made their way toward the feedlot. Helen looked up at Anna's approach. "He still here, is he?"

"Yes." Anna watched as her mother went back to her attack on the weeds trying to invade the garden and inhaled the damp scent of freshly turned earth. "But he'll be gone soon. He's giving me a ride into town."

Helen grunted. "Another mistake."

Anna straightened her shoulders. "I didn't ask for your advice."

"Never have." Helen had reached the end of the row and she stopped and leaned on the hoe as she leveled Anna with her steady regard. "More's the pity."

"You don't understand, Mother. You never have."

"You think that, do you?" Helen returned her attention to the garden as she looked off down the long straight row of corn. "You think I don't know what took you from here?" She glanced at Anna but her gaze drifted back to the corn. "It wasn't your father sending you away. You were gone long before you ever left that spring. Just as gone as Liggy. And for the same reason, more or less."

Anna stared at her mother's profile. Never had she suspected such insight from her. Living under the same roof all these years they had nonetheless been as strangers to each other. Even in her childhood Anna had felt more connected to her Aunt Maree and Lena.

"But Rose isn't like you. She wants to be settled. Needs to be settled." Helen started hoeing the next row. "Remember that, Anna."

"I can't interfere, Mother."

Her mother stopped and looked directly at her. "Can't or won't?"

"It's for Rose to decide. It's her life, after all."

"Life? What does Rose know about life?" Her mother once again brought the hoe down with force. "Don't you want to save her?"

If only she could save her, thought Anna, save her the pain of doubting, of having to choose, right or wrong. "Only Marsh or Walker can save her now."

"No man can save a woman."

"Then she must save herself."

Anna watched her mother in silence for a while as she vented her anger and concern on the hapless weeds of the garden before she turned toward the house. What other concerns made her mother so adamant against Walker? Or was her anger at something else altogether?

The weight of the past wrapped around Anna like a shroud and the weight of it had the power to pull her carefully constructed life apart. A small panic gripped her and she swallowed against it. Whatever her mother's concerns it didn't matter now. Everything would be resolved before this day was over. Everything.

Walker was standing beside the car when she came around the corner of the house. Rose was nowhere to be seen. He opened the door for Anna then went around and got into the driver's seat.

"Nice car." Anna ran her hand along the leather of the seat. "Is it new?"

Walker started the engine and put the car into gear. He grinned as he cast a sideways glance at Anna. "Just delivered Monday."

"Is that when you decided you needed to go to Meridian on business?"

He eased out on the clutch and they started down the driveway. "That obvious, huh?"

Anna smiled. "Yes."

"Well, I guess if you know that then you know there's no real business in Meridian." They turned onto the road and the car picked up speed.

"I guessed as much."

Walker didn't speak again for a good half mile. "I love her." His voice cracked with emotion and he didn't take his eyes off the road.

"I guessed that much as well."

They rode in silence a while longer. "You're not angry?"

"Not angry. Sad."

"Why? Because it's a hopeless cause?"

"Only Rose knows the answer to that question." Anna weighed her words carefully. "Is it love, Walker? What you feel?"

His knuckles went white as he tightened his grip on the steering wheel. "I can't sleep, I can't stop thinking about her. I want her more than anything in my life."

"You want her."

He glanced around at the sadness in her voice. "What?"

"You wanted this car, you wanted to take a little side trip on your way to Meridian." She looked him in the eye. "You want my daughter."

"No." He slowed for a deep rut in the roadway. "It goes far beyond wanting. I--" For a moment he didn't speak as the automobile lurched in and out of the rut. "It's just that I can't imagine tomorrow without the hope of seeing her, of hearing her voice." The car began to build speed again and he shifted gears. "My life isn't my own any longer. I can't move forward and I can't stand still." He banged the palm of his hand against the steering wheel. "I've never been more confused or miserable in my life. You tell me, if this isn't love, then what is?"

Anna watched the swiftly passing foliage of the trees as they sped toward Road's End. "I'm the last person to ask that."

"All I want is her happiness."

"And what do you think that would be?"

His smile was rueful and held no real humor. "It would seem that that would be Marsh."

"Would it?"

He didn't answer immediately. "I know he loves her." He inhaled and slowly let out a deep breath. Finally he looked at Anna. "The thing is, I think she cares for me."

"Did she say that?"

"Well, yes, sort of."

Anna made no response to his statement. She couldn't bring herself to pry further. She had already seen as much as Walker had admitted in Rose's behavior. His affirmation of what she already knew only added to her unease. In her heart she knew it would be unfair to try to influence Rose's decision. It had to be her choice and hers alone.

"I told her, you know."

"Did you?"

"It was probably wrong of me but I couldn't help it." He gave Anna a look of such pleading. "I couldn't just let her marry him without telling her how I felt."

He wanted assurance from her. Anna saw it in his expression, in the hopeful lift of his brows. "She's loved Marsh for a long time. She hardly knows you."

"She knows me." There was a note of defiance in his voice.

Did she, Anna wondered as the church spire came into view. Did anyone really know another person? Perhaps. Certainly her mother had just proven an insight that Anna could never have guessed. "Give her time, Walker."

"There is no time."

Anna heard the despair in his voice and had no answer for it. Only Rose could relieve his suffering, or not.

"Would you drop me off at the church?"

ANNA TRAILED HER fingers along the arms of the pews as she walked up the aisle. About half way to the alter she sat, the worn wood of the seat cool and unyielding beneath her. It was not solace or inspiration she sought by coming here, only privacy as she waited for the appointed hour. She would see Sam soon enough but not before her meeting with Joseph.

The windows, each of which was crowned by a gold crucifix at the apex, created a shadowy cool sanctum with their designs in darkly stained glass. They represented the stations of the cross and had been the gift of a long dead ancestor. Rather pagan for a Baptist church, Anna thought, but certainly costly in their time.

In the past the Carrolls had always been dutiful of their position in the community, taking the lead in civic and religious matters with equal fervor.

They would be disappointed by the current state of affairs.

Since the death of her father there had been no Carroll to fill the void. Reuben had long ago absolved himself of responsibility for anything but the crops in the field. Her mother attended Sunday services but nothing more. Perhaps that distant relative had foreseen such an eventuality and his benevolence had been guided by his ego, his need to remind the good folks of Road's End of his existence, the merit of his soul.

This was the first time Anna had entered the church since Claire's funeral. It had been just as long since she had prayed. Would the god of her father, of her magnanimous ancestor, answer her now?

What would she pray for if she could? For Rose's happiness? For Sam's forgiveness? She didn't think God would intervene on her behalf at this late hour. She had long ago embraced free will and that would be the road she must travel now.

Rose would be happy in the end. There would be sadness and perhaps guilt over the young man she must send away but Anna knew both Marsh and Walker loved her. Whoever she decided on would cherish her and make her happy in time.

But Sam, what would Sam do?

CHAPTER 25
APRIL, 1922

ANNA STOOD IN the doorway of the post office and watched Claire skipping across the road toward her house. She heard the small noises of Old Ben as he prepared to lock up. There had been no letter again today. Joseph had been gone over a week and still no letter. She had stayed in town since Wednesday night prayer meeting so she could intercept his letter before Rusty Johnson could deliver it to her house. Tomorrow she would have to return home with her parents after church.

Anna felt the heat in her face and throat and knew she was flushed. Old Ben had given her a knowing look as he shook his head in response to her query about a letter. His asking after Sam had not been lost on her. And yet caution was beyond her. She had been in a fever of restlessness that made her hands tremble and the collar of her blouse threaten to choke her since Joseph's departure on the thirteenth day of April. She had known him exactly five weeks and two days and yet she had believed him so completely. What if there was no letter, now or ever? Anna shied away from such thoughts. She wouldn't let them take root.

Eddie Talley came out of the store and intercepted Claire in the middle of the road. Even from this distance Anna could tell that Claire didn't mind. It was as if Claire couldn't get enough male attention these days. Only two months ago Claire kept poor Eddie in misery by refusing to speak to him for days on end.

The sun beat down on the couple making Claire's hair a fiery halo. Anna didn't think she could endure Eddie's silliness just now. She eased down the steps and along the side of the post office until she was out of their line of vision.

A slight breeze lifted the fine hair that had escaped the combs in her upswept hair and they tickled her neck as seductively as Joseph's breath had done when he whispered near her ear. Anna turned her face toward the breeze and the river and her restless feet carried her in that direction.

The planks of the ferry landing were silver with age and exposure to the elements. They held the heat of the sun and Anna felt it rise through the soles of her shoes as she stood gazing at the distant shore. It shimmered in the late morning heat, a wavery illusion that seemed more distant and inaccessible than it had ever been.

Anna felt the sun beating down on her bare head and thought the collar of her blouse would choke her. Her heart raced and her breath came in short frantic bursts. The ferry was on the other side of the river and she desperately scanned that distant shore in search of it. Her hands gripped the splintered, weathered railing as she leaned her upper body out over the brown, sluggish swirl of water in a sudden urgent need to locate the ferry, to somehow will it to return to the landing. She felt an overwhelming need to escape the confines of Road's End, to cross the river and find herself. If she didn't do so, she knew she would die.

But the ferry did not come and Anna's grip on the railing began to tire and weaken. It didn't come and she wouldn't go. Slowly she uncurled her fingers from the battered wood rail and turned her face from the unattainable. She felt drained, stunned by the realization and her feet carried her idly, slowly away from the river.

Her path was an aimless ramble, chosen without thought as she walked along the county road to the churchyard. Large oaks overhung the area to the far side of the building where long wooden tables served the community for social gatherings and family reunions in the form of dinner-on-the-ground. She sat on one of the wooden benches and loosened the top button of her blouse.

It was only the last week in April but it felt like mid-June. Bees buzzed in the Indian hawthorne and the low bellow of a cow reached her from somewhere in Percy's field.

Anna lazily fanned herself with her handkerchief and felt the heat rising as the morning burned away toward noon. An occasional light breeze stirred the hair at the nape of her neck as her thoughts wandered aimlessly. The heat grew heavier as did her eyelids and she laid her head on her arms on the table.

The sound of Lena calling Percy to his dinner roused Anna. She opened her eyes and blinked as she lifted her head from the table. How much time had passed she wasn't sure but she had obviously dozed off. Her neck felt stiff and she slowly stretched and yawned. Her Aunt Maree would be putting dinner on the table shortly and she would be missed if she wasn't there but Anna couldn't muster the energy to move.

The sound of a door closing loudly drew her attention and she watched as Sam locked the store and turned toward home. He passed in front of the church on the other side of the road. He didn't see Anna sitting there in the deep shade of the oaks and she followed his progress with her eyes. When he reached the gentle curve in the road that would take him from view, she stood and began to follow. When she rounded the curve his house came into view, standing there at the fork in the road. There was no sign of Sam and the house lay in silence as she approached.

At the foot of the steps she stopped and looked up into the shade of the porch and the open doorway. Not even lazy Mama Cat was in evidence.

Anna felt flushed and jittery inside. She unbuttoned another button on her blouse then ran a hand through her hair. The porch railing felt cool and smooth beneath her palm as she slowly mounted the steps. When she reached the porch she placed that hand on her forehead, then her cheek, then her throat.

She stood in the open doorway, holding onto the facing on either side as if to hold herself back. The grandfather clock tick-tocked from the hallway and underscored the total silence of the rest of the house.

Anna stepped over the threshold and was engulfed with the scent of lemon polish. The furniture gleamed softly in the dim interior and the carpet underfoot cushioned her steps as she walked the length of the hall to the kitchen at the rear of the house. This was where she had expected to find Sam but it was empty and silent, an enameled pan of washed greens sitting on the table, a clean plate, cup, knife, and fork resting on the drain board. There was no fire in the cook stove.

The faint sound of metal clinking against metal came from her right and she turned in that direction. Down a narrow hallway she came to Sam's bedroom. The room was in deep shadow, the drapes drawn to keep out the light and the noon heat. Lined up with the open bedroom door was the door to the bathroom. Sam stood there in his undershirt, the braces for his trousers hanging from the waist of them, a straight razor in his hand. A window on the far wall of the bathroom backlit him with bright light as he watched his reflection in the mirror and shaved.

He was unaware of Anna's presence and she watched as he drew the sharp edge of the blade down his cheek then swished it in the wash basin to clean it. As he brought the blade up again Anna felt desire to the soles of her feet. She could hear and feel her heart thumping in her chest.

Sam must have sensed her presence for he turned and slowly lowered the blade. "Anna." He laid the razor on the washstand and took up the towel, his eyes never leaving her face.

She took two steps into the bedroom unable to speak.

Sam wiped at the soap on his face and came toward her. "Anna." There was a question in his voice.

Anna felt on the verge of tears. She stepped closer to him and placed a hand on his smooth warm cheek. "You've shaved."

His brows lifted in amusement and he placed his hand on top of hers. "Yes."

"In the middle of the day."

He was watching her closely. Her behavior had him puzzled, she could see it in his expression as he tried to figure out what she was doing there.

"I've never seen your bedroom before." She heard the quaver in her voice.

Sam gently took her by the upper arms and drew her closer. "What do you want, Anna?"

The color had risen in his cheeks and Anna ran the backs of her fingers along his chin. "Oh, Sam." She gazed up at him, willing him to understand what she did not.

He folded her into his body and kissed her long and leisurely. Her arms went around his neck and she clung to him even after he broke the kiss. "You shouldn't be here." His words came out rough but he didn't let her go. "I'm only a man, Anna." He held her face against his chest as his long fingers massaged the nape of her neck and up into her hair. His breathing was ragged. "You should go."

She inhaled the scent of sun in his undershirt and the maleness of his flesh and ran her fingers along the muscles of his shoulders and upper arms. "Sam."

His name whispering from her lips seemed to be his undoing. He held her slightly away and stared down into her upturned face, his eyelids heavy with desire, his face flushed. Very tenderly he laid the back of his knuckles against the pale flesh in the open throat of her blouse. When she sighed and closed her eyes, he slowly unbuttoned the next button and then the next.

CHAPTER 26
MAY, 1941

ANNA DREW A quick sharp breath and blinked away the images of the past. The church had grown dimmer as she sat there lost in the tangle of her thoughts. She stood and left the way she had come. The warmth of the early summer twilight embraced her as she stepped through the door and made her way along the edge of the road toward the old ferry landing. She welcomed that warmth and her pace picked up as the river came into view. It seemed she had been lost in a long chill winter for all those years and she hurried toward the end of it, ready to immerse herself in life again.

Joseph paced the warped and aged boards of the landing, the glow of his cigarette like a firefly in the growing shadows. He didn't see her approaching and she slowed to observe him and gather her wits. With a calming breath she stepped onto the dried and splintered planks and felt them yield dangerously underfoot. He turned at the first sound of her footsteps and flicked the cigarette into the river.

"Anna." He said nothing further until she was right in front of him. "I thought you had changed your mind."

"No, Joseph. I needed to see you."

"Yes." He carried a candy tin caught between his upper arm and his body. With his free hand he ran his fingers lightly down her arm until he reached her hand and took it in his. He held it in a loose grip as he stared down at her "I should have come before this. Long before."

"Why have you come now?"

"Your mother's letter."

"No. That's not the reason. You could have sent someone, written your refusal." She studied him in return. "Why didn't you?"

"Mr. Battle--" He stopped and slipped his hand from hers and took her by the elbow as he turned her toward the covered bench near the end of the wharf. "I wanted to see you, had to see you. I was glad for the excuse. All these years I've wondered what made you leave home like that, so suddenly, without any word, without any explanation. But now I think I know."

"How did you find out I had gone?"

"Your mother."

Anna sat on the bench and drew her hands together in her lap. She stared out at the dark body of water silently flowing by. "Mother?"

"It was August. Late in the month." He sat beside her and took her hand again, an urgency to his voice. "I couldn't come any sooner. You have to believe me on that, Anna."

She stared at him but made no reply.

"No one would spare me a civil word. She was adamant that it was too late, that I had waited too late. I couldn't convince her to tell me where you were. Your father was away. The store was closed up tight as a drum. The whole town had a deserted, dry look, as if the summer had sucked out all the life." He increased the pressure on her hand until she withdrew it and looked away.

"Why did you even bother at all?"

"Because I love you, Anna."

A semblance of a smile passed fleetingly across her features. "Three months without a word. Not a single letter."

He pressed the candy tin into her hands. "Open it."

She stared down at the container, running her finger along the lettering on the lid. "What's in it?"

"Open it, Anna, then I'll explain."

The lid came off easily and the letters fell out onto her lap. She picked one of them up and fingered it. The edges were frayed from much handling and even in the scant light she could tell that the writing had faded with age. She looked through all of them. They were sealed but bore no stamps. They were addressed to her. She gripped them with a sudden fierceness and felt the sting of tears. Quickly she averted her face.

Joseph moved closer and brought her head against his shoulder as he placed a kiss on the top of her head. "Darling, Anna. How I have ached to touch you, to have you look at me and see the man who loved you all those years ago."

Anna allowed herself to relax against him for a brief moment, to relish the old familiarity and tenderness of that spring.

Gently he lifted her head and lowered his lips toward hers. The kiss was sweet and tender and it made her heart ache for their lost youth, their lost dreams. Slowly she pulled away from him and stood, the letters still in her hand. "This explains nothing."

He sat silently, the only sound shushing of the current as the seconds drew out. "I wrote you nearly every day after I left. The site was remote, no way to get to a post office or even a store. I planned to mail them as soon as I could slip away from camp."

"But you didn't."

"There was an accident. A bad accident. For weeks I was out of my head with fever from the infection in the wound. After I began to mend, I was as weak as a kitten." He cleared his throat. "Mr. Battle took me in. His wife and Sarah nursed me until I got back on my feet." He stood and laid the palm of his hand on her cheek. "She promised to mail them." His paused. "She promised."

Anna caught the hand against her cheek, held it there for a moment then removed it. "But she didn't."

"No."

"Because she loved you."

"Yes."

"And she does still."

"Just as Sam still loves you."

Anna looked toward the town, the lights of the houses revealing the nocturnal activities of the citizens of Road's End. "Yes."

CHAPTER 27
APRIL, 1922

"COME UP, THERE! Come up!" Joseph pulled with all his weight on the lead of the oxen team, slipping and sliding until he was almost sitting in the mud. A steady light drizzle ran mud and sweat into his eyes. His body steamed with heat and a bottled up rage that threatened to choke him. Clay County was exactly what its name implied. With the exception of pine forests and a sprinkling of scrub hardwoods, the hills and gullies consisted of nothing but slick, red clay and a few hardscrabble farms. The fully loaded log truck was stuck up to its axle and Joseph didn't see how they were going to get it out of the mire in this lifetime.

His resentment toward the truck, its driver, the work crew, and Harry Battle grew with each day that passed since his exile from Carroll's Hill and Anna. The missing of her was like a steady ache in the joints. It affected his whole body and consumed his mind. If the truth were known, that was the reason the truck was stuck. Joseph's desire to quickly finish this piddling little job had caused him to forego the precautions the inclement weather of this spring demanded. For ten days they had been floundering in this quagmire and the end was in sight. With three or four more runs, the job would be finished.

The lead ox slipped to its knees and the whole shebang sank back into the mud.

"God *damnit* all to hell!" Joseph roared as he dropped the lead rope and slowly made his way back to the cab of the truck, the slick ooze sucking at his boots with each step.

Half a dozen men, so covered in mud it appeared they had risen fully formed from the clay at their feet, stood around the axle on either side of the truck. They had long poles that they had tried to wedge under the wheels to give the truck some traction. None of them said a word as Joseph knelt and inspected the tires just behind the cab of the truck where most of the weight of the load rested. Some of them had worked with him before but most hadn't and since his arrival at the camp he had been like an angry hornet looking for a target. He had made their days long and hard, harder than necessary in most everyone's opinion.

Joseph sat back on his heels and thought. Finally he stood and took one of the poles from the nearest man. "Neil, get all those loppings and bring them over here." He ran his shirt sleeve across his eyes but it did nothing to clear them of mud or rain. "We'll need some for the other side, too."

Neil and a couple of the men began hauling the small pine branches over to the truck. Joseph got down on his knees and began jamming them on both sides of the wheel, front and back. One of the men did the same on the opposite tire.

Joseph jerked his thumb in the direction of the tangle of mangled underbrush and discarded tree limbs. "Get some of those saplings in here. A goodly number."

As the men gathered the two to three inch thick felled trees Joseph caught his breath while he studied the situation. If they were lucky, damn lucky, this just might work.

When everything was to his liking he took up one of the long poles. "Okay boys, when Amos guns the motor I want one man on a long pole prying the wheel from behind and if it moves so much as an inch I want one of those saplings stuck under it so it can't roll back." He looked around at the weary group. "Got that?"

Heads nodded and two of the men started around the truck to join Neil on the other side.

"You," Joseph nodded at one the men he didn't know, "you're up front."

Amos craned his head out the window of the cab to see if everybody was set. Joseph slapped the side of the door. "Ready?"

The gears ground and Amos revved the engine a little. "As I'll ever be."

Joseph jammed the long pole into the mud as hard as he dared for fear of puncturing the tire. With a deep breath he set his feet, his knees flexed, the end of the pole resting on his shoulder. "Now!"

It all seemed to happen in a heartbeat. Gas fumes clouded the air as the engine strained. Joseph felt the movement in the pole and he used every ounce of strength he had in this one great effort. One, then two saplings went under the wheels when suddenly the pole in his hands snapped, the bed of the truck began to tip and before the startled cries of the crew or the warning rumble could register, Joseph felt the fire in his chest and the breath go out of him as he hit the ground.

He couldn't breath, he couldn't move, something on his chest was slowly smothering him. Loud voices, excited voices echoed in his head but he couldn't make out the words. And the pain, the pain consumed him, drowned out everything, the lack of air, the voices, until all he could think of was the pain. He became the pain and the only way to end it was to cease to exist, so he stopped struggling for air, stopped listening to the voices; he simply stopped.

JOSEPH NEEDED TO pee but he couldn't see and he didn't know where he was. It was hot here, wherever here was. This much he knew. His chest felt heavy like a bad cold only worse and every time he moved so much as his little toe it hurt all over. But he had to pee. It seemed to take an eternity to raise his arm to his chest. He needed to get this heavy weight off so he could stand up.

With his teeth clenched against the pain he fumbled with the sheet or blanket but it was wrapped so tightly that he couldn't move it. His arm fell to his side and he felt the sweat trickle down his brow and sting his eyes. For a long time he lay there panting for breath.

He thought he must have dozed off but now he was awake and he needed to go so bad that he had to do something. He tried to take a deep breath to steel himself but found that more painful than his earlier movements. He tasted blood and realized he had bitten his lip.

Suddenly the room was flooded with blinding light and he groaned, his eyes tightly shut, lightning bolts of pain ripping through his head. A hand pressed against his forehead, cool and smooth and a low murmur of sympathy, not quite words, just that gentle sound like a mother soothing a baby. His eyelids fluttered taking in a kaleidoscope of images, strawberry hair, a dusting of freckles, brown eyes. He knew that image.

"Lower the shades, Mama. The light hurts his eyes."

And that voice, he knew that, too. The light dimmed and he was able to open his eyes. "Sarah?"

The croaked name brought a smile to her lips and she placed that deliciously cool hand to his forehead again. "Awake at last." The smile faded from her features. "We were so worried, Joseph. I didn't think you'd ever wake up."

He watched her lips move as she spoke and he blinked. The sound didn't quite match the movement. He swallowed, his throat as dry as the cotton batting of an old quilt. "Where am I?"

"Why, you're home, Joseph."

At the sound of a door opening and closing he looked away from the worried expression on Sarah's face. His gaze swept the room and its contents lurched and bent in a strange way. Nausea swept through him and he closed his eyes and swallowed hard. A man's voice rumbled in his head, a deep gravelly sound like stones rubbing against stones but he couldn't make out the words. Hands probed the back of his head and he gritted his teeth against the pain. The light seared his eye as the lid was lifted then released. The probing moved to his upper abdomen and it felt like a cattle prod had pierced his chest. The room echoed with the sound of a bellow of pain.

IT WAS GOOD to sleep under a real roof again in a soft feather bed. Joseph had been on the road with a crew for so long that he'd almost forgotten how good a hot bath could be. He lay propped up against a mountain of pillows so weak from the exertion of the bath that his hands trembled.

"Here, let me." Sarah sat on the edge of the bed, took the cup from his shaking hands and held it to his mouth.

The coffee was good, hot and strong just the way he liked it. She wiped his chin and held the cup ready again. Joseph shook his head. "Thanks. Maybe later."

She placed the cup on the nightstand and adjusted the sheet higher on his chest. "Dr. Pritchett says the infection is all gone. No more fevers. Isn't that good news?" She smiled down at him.

Joseph nodded. "Yes. Good news."

The smile faded and she studied him, a solemn expression on her face. "I was so worried, Joseph. Dr. Pritchett didn't think you were going to make it. All those weeks--" Her lower lip trembled and she caught it between her teeth. "The limb piercing your lung clear through like that and the infection--" She blinked and straightened the bedding once again. "But I knew you'd be all right. You had to be, that's all. You just had to be." She blushed and wouldn't look at him as she tidied the water pitcher and glass on the nightstand.

Joseph watched her as he had so many times over the past days and weeks. He frowned. Yes, it had been weeks that she had hovered above him in his fever dreams as she bathed his forehead with cool water, pressed her soft hands against his flushed cheek, kissed his parched lips. Or had she? Had it all been a dream, one long continuous dream of pain and fire and bone chilling cold? No, that had been true enough as had her ever vigilant presence. It was there in the pallor of her face, in the dark smudges beneath her eyes. "You're tired. You should rest."

She looked at him then. "Oh, no, I'm not tired. Truly." She laughed. "But poor old Toby is almost done in. I couldn't say for sure which of you had been in the bath when he came downstairs, he was that wet."

Joseph grinned. "I was so glad to be out of this bed I guess I didn't go slow enough. I was floundering 'round like a baby."

Sarah tenderly touched a spot on his chin. "You cut yourself shaving."

"I'm out of practice, spoilt to having you do it."

"I like spoiling you." She blushed again and abruptly rose from the edge of the bed. "Well, now all we have to do is feed you proper so you can get your strength back and you'll be good as new."

Joseph caught her hand in the act of smoothing his hair back from his forehead. "You said weeks."

"Weeks?" Her brow furrowed in confusion.

"That I'd been sick for weeks."

"Oh my, yes." Sarah seemed to be counting in her head. "Yes. Three weeks tomorrow since they brought you home. They were afraid to move you from Alex City right after the accident."

Joseph felt a flutter of anxiety. He tightened his grip on her hand. "What day is it?"

She smiled. "Saturday."

"The date. What's the date?"

"The nineteenth, I think."

He released her hand and relaxed against the pillow. "May nineteenth." His gaze drifted toward the window and he frowned.

"No, Joseph. It's the nineteenth of June."

His head jerked around so that he stared at her. "June!"

She laughed, a nervous sound that died on her lips. "Yes, June." The smile tried to reassert itself but something in his behavior caused it to flutter then disappear. "You've been very sick, Joseph. The infection and your lung collapsed and something about your spleen. I—we all feared you might die." She fussed with the bed linens. "Dr. Pritchett came every day and Papa had to get old Toby from the yard to come help move you and—all." She nodded toward the cot in the corner of the room where Toby had slept every night. "Papa didn't want you alone because you were so out of your head with the fever."

Joseph's mind raced. June. How could he have been so unaware of the passage of time. Anna would think he had forgotten her. He tried to sit up and swing his feet over the side of the bed.

"Joseph!" Sarah hurried around to the other side of the bed where he was attempting to stand. "Get back in bed! You're too weak." She glanced toward the open doorway. "Mama!"

Joseph tried to push her aside but he was so weak that his legs wouldn't support his weight. He sank back into the comfort of the feather mattress, his limbs trembling, sweat beading on his brow. "I have to go."

"Where?"

He turned his head so he didn't have to look at her. He didn't want to see what was so clearly there in her face.

When he didn't answer her question she began to straighten the bed linens around him. "There's no need to go anywhere, Joseph. You're where you belong. Here where I can take care of you." Her voice had a higher pitch to it, almost a frightened sound. "You're too ill to be out of bed."

Her words grated in his mind like the turning of a lock. The image of Anna lying on the forest floor, her golden hair spread around her head in a halo, the distant light igniting a blue flame in her eyes, filled his mind. He had to get to her, get word to her what had happened. "My things." He turned to Sarah. "My suitcase, where is it?"

She stood there watching him, her hands clasped tightly together. "In the wardrobe."

"Could you—would you bring it to me?"

She hesitated as his heart pounded in his chest. For a moment he thought she would refuse.

"All right." She rubbed her hands together as if to warm them, to return the flow of blood and life to them, then she turned to the wardrobe.

The suitcase was scarred and battered, the brass of the clasp discolored and scratched. She placed it on the bed beside him and opened it with a loud click of the lock.

He stared into the jumble of contents, the plaid of a shirt, socks a dirty grey, the top of one boot just visible. Sarah crossed the room to sit in a chair beneath the window. She sat on the very edge of it, her hands in her lap, her eyes on Joseph. He raised himself higher against the mound of pillows piled against the headboard of the bed and looked across the room at her. "Could I get a pencil and some paper?" When she didn't move he continued. "I'd like to write a letter."

"Of course." She stood and left the room, stopping at the open doorway to glance back at him before she disappeared down the hall.

Carefully he positioned himself and the suitcase so he could paw through the contents. Just under the torn fabric of the lining he felt what he was searching for and pulled the envelopes free. There were four of them and they felt slightly damp and smelled of mold. He smoothed them against his thigh and ran his thumb over the name and address. Suddenly he looked up to see Sarah standing in the doorway watching him, the paper tablet and a pen in her hand.

Heat suffused his throat and face and he wouldn't meet her eyes. "Letters."

Sarah said nothing, only came to stand beside him and hold out the paper and pen.

"I never got a chance to mail them." He saw the pen tremble in her hand and he took it and the tablet. "I was wondering," he glanced up at her then away, "if you would post them."

She hesitated for the space of heartbeat. "Yes." She held out her hand for them. "Of course."

He slowly placed them in her hand and at last looked her full in the face. "There's no stamps."

Sarah was staring at the envelopes in her hand. "I'll see to that." Her gaze slid away from the letters and she stared at the foot of the bed. "I'll take care of them."

Joseph took one of her hands in his and rubbed his thumb slowly back and forth across her knuckles. "Today, Sarah?"

She wouldn't look at him and he gave her hand a tug. "Today?"

She nodded. "Yes." She looked down at him then. "Don't worry, I'll go right away." She withdrew her hand from his and left the room without looking back.

Joseph felt a tightness in his chest. Sarah, so sweet and kind, so gentle. She would do as he asked, he was sure of it. Why then did he feel so anxious? He felt anxious because he had been laid up in this bed for nearly two months without being aware of the passage of time. Two months in which Sam Stone sat down to Sunday dinners under Luther Carroll's roof with Luther Carroll's blessing.

CHAPTER 28
MAY, 1941

They stood there on the rickety wharf in the encroaching night, each staring into memory, reliving the truths and lies that constituted their history, their path to this place and this moment.

"He doesn't know, does he?"

Anna turned her back to Joseph and retrieved the candy tin she had left on the weathered and splintered wooden bench. She placed the letters inside and closed the lid. "Know what?"

"About Rose."

"What's to know?"

"Anna."

She saw the knowledge in his eyes. "How did you guess?"

Joseph didn't answer immediately. He felt in his shirt pocket for the pack of Lucky Strikes then changed his mind. "Her hands, I think. That expression she gets when something amuses her, the way her brows lift." He grunted. "And a little math."

Crickets sang along the riverbank and a whip-poor-will called out. "A little math."

"I left here for the Clay County job at the beginning of April, you left in June. Rose told me Marsh proposed on her eighteenth birthday. January sixteenth. You were pregnant when you left here. And we both know I'm not her father."

He stood behind her and lightly brushed the hair from her neck. Anna felt his breath against her bare skin and waited for the kiss that didn't come.

"Why didn't you tell Sam? Marry him? Why did you let him believe I was her father?" He spoke softly near her ear. He couldn't conceal the hope in his voice, the need to believe that she had acted out of her love for him.

Anna closed her eyes and let the sounds of the night soothe her. "I wanted my freedom." She sighed. "I selfishly wanted what men have without thought or effort, the ability to go or stay, to pick and choose. To simply walk away." She opened her eyes and uttered a humorless laugh. "I thought that if I held myself apart, didn't let Sam in, I could have that freedom." She felt him withdraw and experienced a sad relief. "And that was the biggest lie of all."

Joseph remained silent for a long time. Both of them stared out at the river. "How is it that he never suspected? He could easily have made the same connections I did."

"I imagine it's because he didn't want to know."

"But I get the impression he truly cares for Rose."

Anna lowered her head. "It isn't because of Rose that he wouldn't see." She turned to look at Joseph. "He would have to see me for what I truly am and he couldn't bring himself to do that. So he lies to himself, as we all do when the truth is unbearable."

The purple twilight settled more deeply around them. "And your mother?"

Anna shrugged. "Who can know another's demons, why they feel a need for self-deception. Didn't you deceive yourself when you asked Sarah to mail your letters? Couldn't you look at her and know her heart? Didn't you know, even then, that you and I would never be?"

Joseph made no reply.

"When will you go?"

"Tomorrow morning."

She touched him gently on the cheek then handed him the tin filled with unopened letters.

He took them and stared at the container. Finally, he looked at her. She felt the intensity of his regard as if it were a touch of his hand. "Be happy, Anna."

"It's in the hands of Fate now, isn't it Joseph? What will be, will be."

He smiled sadly. "Perhaps." He placed a feather light kiss on her cheek and turned to go. At the end of the wharf he stopped and looked back. "I'll buy the timber. Tell your mother. She'll get a contract and a check in the mail in a few days."

"That's not necessary."

"Yes. It is. It's necessary for me."

JOSEPH THREW THE Whitman's Sampler tin through the window of the truck then made his way up the back steps of the Milkisen's house. The kitchen was thankfully empty and he could hear the voice of President Roosevelt speaking from the radio in the front room. Quietly he eased down the hallway to his bedroom. At the mirror he stared at his ashen reflection then drew his satchel from the wardrobe. It took him only a few minutes to cram his few belongings into it. Back in the kitchen, he took a sheet of paper from his clipboard and scribbled a note for Lena Milkisen and left a five dollar bill with it on the table.

The night was cooling down and the wind through the open window of the truck blew through his hair. Sally Dan sat on the passenger seat, his head out the window, his tongue lolling from his mouth. Joseph didn't even slow down as he passed through Road's End but when he reached the high point of the bridge he suddenly braked and brought the truck to a screeching stop.

He sat with the motor idling as he stared through the windshield into the blackness beyond the reach of his headlights. Finally he turned the key and the motor died. He took the Whitman's Sampler tin and got out of the truck. For a long time he leaned against the parapet of the bridge and stared into the black nothingness far below. Sally Dan sat beside him, constantly glancing from the man to the truck.

Joseph looked down at the dog as he restlessly repositioned himself on the hard concrete of the bridge, uncertainty evident by his behavior.

"Enough." Joseph held the tin against his chest and closed his eyes. "Enough."

With a flick of his wrist the tin went sailing into the night. The distant plop was indistinguishable from the sound of a fish jumping. Sally Dan was instantly alert, his ears pricked forward in the direction of the sound. Joseph whistled softly through his teeth. "Come on, boy. Let's go home."

Sally Dan hopped into the truck and as they started down the far side of the bridge, he moved closer to Joseph and whined. Joseph reached across and scratched his ears. "Melissa will be glad to see you. And me."

They would be at supper now, his family, having something the children liked but rarely had. Sarah would have indulged them while he was away. That was Sarah.

He reached into his shirt pocket and withdrew the pack of cigarettes and fumbled to extract one. Next he searched his pockets for matches and could find none. With a grunt he took the cigarette that dangled from his mouth and threw it out the window. His fingers went to the old scar low on his ribcage and felt along the length of it. He pulled the pack of cigarettes from his pocket and threw them out the window as he set his heart and mind firmly against the memories of that long ago spring and summer.

THE SOUND OF Joseph's footsteps against the wharf slowly died away to be replaced by the sounds of the night. Anna sat on the bench for a long time until she began to feel the damp of the river. She watched it lazily flowing by and no longer thought of it as her jailer. She stood and walked up the embankment toward the town and beyond. When she rounded the curve Sam's house came into view, the windows lit in the kitchen and bedroom. She stood in the middle of the road and watched as the night came down hard and she experienced a longing that she hadn't known in a very long time.

The house lay in silence as Anna mounted the steps. The scent of honeysuckle that grew along the fence row hung heavily in the air. Light from the kitchen fell into the hallway as Anna stood looking through the screen door. With her hand on the door knob, she hesitated. There would be no going back to the old comfortable life she had known all these years once she stepped across the threshold. She closed her eyes and listened to the slow, steady tick-tock of the grandfather clock standing in the hallway. Finally she drew a deep breath, opened her eyes, and entered Sam's house.

The lack of sound told her that Sam would not be in the kitchen but she went there first following in the footsteps of memory. As she stared into the room she realized not much had changed since she was a little girl sitting at the white enameled table eating cookies fresh from Sam's mother's oven. Their lives had been in limbo for a long time. Too long.

She followed the hallway to the bedroom, Sam's room. It would be fitting that he should be there, allowing her to take the path she should have chosen all those years ago. But would he want that now? Or would he turn his back on her once she told him what he must hear.

It was the same yet not the same as that fateful spring day. Then it had been early afternoon instead of evening. The light that had backlit him on that day had been the sun instead of the harsh glare of a bare electric light bulb overhead. But he stood there as he had then, the straight razor smoothly following the contour of his jaw, and she felt the pull of desire.

Anna watched him across the darkened bedroom where he stood before the bathroom mirror and was suddenly unsure of herself. The full weight of what she would loose before this night was over brought tears to her eyes. And the realization that the loss was of her own doing made it all the more painful.

He must have sensed her presence for he turned and simply stared at her in return. "Well." He laid the razor on the wash stand and wiped his face free of lather. "I thought I might see you tonight."

"You shaved."

He smiled sadly. "Yes."

"Why?"

After a heartbeat of a pause he crossed the bedroom until he stood before her. "Wishful thinking perhaps."

"Can we never go back, Sam?"

"No. Not back, Anna. Only forward."

Yes, she thought, there could be no other course for them. She placed a palm against his cheek and felt the muscle in his jaw clench then relax. "I would like that."

He covered her hand with his, pressed it there tightly for a moment then drew it away. "Why are you here, Anna?"

She withdrew her hand from his and turned slightly so that she didn't look into his eyes. "I came into town earlier."

"I know."

She glanced up quickly then away. "You never miss anything, do you, Sam? You know me so well."

"Do I? I'm not so sure anymore." He had turned his face away from her. All she could see was his profile. "You didn't answer my question."

"I don't love him, Sam. I don't think I ever did."

Her words were followed by a long silence then she felt him tremble beneath her touch. "I see."

She wrapped her arms around his waist and pressed her cheek against his chest. "Do you?"

He relented and brought his arms around her, his long fingers massaging the nape of her neck.

"I've been a fool, Sam. I want to come home."

Sam grew very still. "Where is home, Anna?"

425

She tightened her grip around his waist. "Here with you. In Road's End."

He held her slightly away from him and searched her face for the truth of her words. "Are you sure?"

"For the first time in my life I'm sure."

The power of his kiss rocked her to her toes and she felt the response of his body as he crushed her against him. He lifted her in his arms and carried her across the room to the bed. "This time I won't let you go."

Anna felt limp with desire, desire for his touch, for his kiss, for the life she had denied herself for so long.

He kissed her face and neck as he stretched out on the bed beside her, planting each kiss lower still as he worked at the buttons of her dress.

"Sam."

He covered her mouth with a long lingering kiss. "God, Anna, do you know what that does to me? To hear you say my name like that, like you did that day you came to me? I've dreamed that afternoon a million times, dreamed it so often that I almost thought that was all it had ever been, a dream."

She traced her thumb along the line of his eyebrows, down the ridge of his nose and along his lips. "Sam."

He stood then to unfasten his trousers. She watched him undressing and felt the fluttering in the pit of her stomach. He sat on the edge of the bed and traced the lace at the top of her slip where it revealed the swelling of her breast. As he did so he watched her reaction to his touch and the color deepened in his cheeks.

He trailed his hand along the silky length of her slip to the hem and slid the smooth fabric up her thigh. She gasped softly and felt her body tremble and knew she would never tell him. To do so would extinguish the heat in his eyes, would turn his heart into a black rock of hatred. All those years she had lived the lie and she would live it still.

Anna watched his face, flushed with desire for her, his touch as urgent as it had been that long ago spring day, and as necessary. She had suffered the price for her independence. Her selfishness, that cold black place she had recognized in her soul as a young woman, had cost her this, this moment and a thousand more like it. In that instant she knew she wouldn't deny her true nature. Her selfishness would not give way. Some things were more important than the truth. Sam's love was one of those things and she would cling to it through the rest of their years until death laid final claim to that truth.

She sat up in the bed and pushed the straps of her slip off her shoulders and allowed the silky fabric to fall to her waist. "Sam."

THE END

95762458R00259

Made in the USA
Lexington, KY
13 August 2018